THE COLD TAP

THE COLD TAP

Tom Beckerlegge

ISBN-13: 9781502925749

HOT WATER

So now the end is near. Shadows gather in the corners of the bathroom, massing at the outer limits of the lamp's macabre glow. When the light goes out, that will be it for me. I lie stretched out in the bathtub, half-submerged and fully dressed, a damp damsel tied to a set of underwater railway tracks. The air is thick with steam and strangled panic. Frank Sinatra is playing at deafening volume on the living room stereo, drowning out my cries for help. A final, calculated indignity. It has all been planned so *well*.

I am too exhausted to try and escape again. My hands have been tightly manacled around the cold tap above my head, so that every attempt to manoeuvre myself into a standing position only succeeds in flooding my mouth and nostrils with bathwater. My wrists are bloodied and raw where I have tried to work them free. I am completely alone, with no prospect of rescue. Even Curtis is absent from his usual spot by the side of the tub, and there is a limit to the kind of help he can offer anyway.

My nemesis has long since left the room, content to leave me with my deadly predicament. A snaking extension cord runs the length of the bathroom, from a plug socket in the outside corridor all the way to the lamp carefully positioned on the lip of the shelf directly above the tub. The lamp is propped up on two ice cubes, whose proud, frozen edges are softening under the caress of the heat emanating from the bathwater – Clytemnestra's last kiss upon Agamemnon's brow. When the ice cubes finally bow to the inevitable and melt away the lamp will topple forward and fall, like a blazing guillotine, into the bathwater. I will be deep-fried.

The fear of impending electrocution is only compounded by the fact that I have only myself to blame. I should have worked things out sooner. I confess to having been distracted, flattered by a mystery handcrafted so exquisitely for me. The pace of events has denied me the space and time to think – in the past week alone I have been chased, knocked out, half-drowned, and seriously scalded my testicles. Enough to put Archimedes himself off, had he ever been foolish enough to venture into the murky world of private detection.

As the orchestra in the living room swells, Sinatra builds to a bloated, red-faced climax. His audience bursts into applause, and there follows a few seconds of delicious silence before the song starts again. By my reckoning 'My Way' has been playing on repeat for the best part of an hour. Perhaps dying won't be so bad after all. Judging by the perilous glistening of the ice cubes, I don't have that much longer to wait. My thoughts turn to other people: Gill and Ray, Keiko, my parents. And Diana. Even now – after everything – I cannot bring myself to blame her.

There is a loud crack above my head; I cry out as something plops into the water beside me. Expecting instant death, the realization that I am still alive comes as a faintly hysterical surprise. Then an ice cube bobs treacherously past my eyeline. I look up to see the lamp teetering on the remaining cube before that too shoots out from beneath it, and the light comes plummeting down through the steam.

The bathroom plunges into darkness.

SENECA'S HEADACHE

Seneca the Younger was having trouble concentrating. The Stoic philosopher and dramatist had taken rooms above a bathhouse, only to discover that the din from below was "strong enough to make me hate my very powers of hearing."[1] In a letter to his friend Lucilius, Seneca indignantly outlined the various offending noises. There were the laboured pants and grunts of the weightlifters, the slap and knead of the masseurs' hands upon human skin, tuneless singing, and the general splashing of the patron he acidly characterized as "the enthusiast". From time to time a pickpocket would be caught with his hand in another's toga, only adding to the hullabaloo. "Imagine!" Seneca trilled peevishly, "the hair-plucker with his penetrating, shrill voice... the cakeseller with his varied cries, the sausageman, the confectioner, and all the vendors of food hawking their wares, each with his own distinctive intonation!"[2]

Whilst the philosopher gingerly massaged his temples, downstairs the world continued with its heedless racket. For the ancient Romans, the bathhouse was more than a mere amenity. It was a tribute to their conquest not just of foreign lands, but nature itself. They had wrestled wild streams into submission, enslaved brooks and rills and frog-marched them across aqueducts through the countryside. Upon reaching their towns and cities, the water was channelled through a complex series of pipes and heated in hypocausts until it poured from the taps like steaming nectar. Emperors built ornate public baths, giant cathedrals dedicated to epicurean delights. As Seneca knew to his chagrin, Romans went to bathhouses not only to wash

---

1 "Moral letters to Lucilius/Letter 56." *Wikisource.* <http://en.wikisource.org/w/index.php?title=Moral_letters_to_Lucilius/Letter_56&oldid=4163322> Accessed 7 September 2014.
2 *Ibid.*

but also to exercise and to socialize, to eat and drink, to plot and gossip. Each bathhouse was a small forum, a neighbourhood Senate, a miniature empire of its own.

...

I was in the bathroom when it started, so it wasn't *entirely* my fault. It was late, clouds of steam drifting sleepily around the light bulb above my head. I was reading *A Streetcar Named Desire* in the bath, holding the book aloft with practiced care to avoid dipping its pages into the water. White tiles sweated in the unforgiving light. Books were piled up on the linoleum floor, running the length of the wall like a musty mountain range. High up on the shelf next to the sink, a set of ring-binder folders filled with notes was arranged in a neat row. Coloured biros poked out from a box of cotton buds. The room was wrapped in a studious hush, disturbed only by the soft rasp of paper as I turned the page, and the occasional pregnant splat of a water droplet from the tap.

Then, without warning, my sister's raised voice exploded through the wall from the living room.

"You fucking *bastard*!"

Gill didn't swear very often, and the unfamiliar edges of the words in her mouth gave them added violence as she spat them out. I winced as the swearwords thudded in the wall above my head, grateful that I was safely out of range. A man's voice murmured an indistinct reply; presumably Gill's boyfriend Richard. Even through the wall I could appreciate the soft, sonorous swoop of the actor's voice as he tried to reason with her. But whatever he said only seemed to enrage my sister even more.

"Get out!" Gill yelled. "Go on, piss off!"

Footsteps stormed away down the corridor, and then the front door slammed so violently that the entire flat winced. As my bathwater shivered, I picked up a plastic wax applicator and slipped it between the pages of my book to mark the place. When I had first moved into Gill's flat the bathroom had been an exotic apothecary, stocked with all kinds of peels and masks and polishes. But gradually the special formula shampoos and conditioners had been removed and the moisturizers taken away. Now abandoned deodorant cans spluttered and gasped for breath in the bin, and old pots of face cream sat in cold storage inside the mirrored cabinet. All that remained was a handful of basic cleaning products – toothpaste and toothbrush, shower gel and soap – and my books, their spines arching and curving in the damp heat like contented cats. I called them the Ulpian Library, after the thousands of Roman scrolls that had been housed within the cavernous Baths of Diocletian during the 4th century AD. My collection was an eclectic mixture of novels and plays, art books and works of history, all based around a single, fitting theme: bathing.

In the bruised aftermath of Richard's exit I listened out for smashing glass or choked sobs, ready to leave my bath if necessary to comfort Gill. But the flat remained resolutely tight-lipped. Knowing my sister as I did, this was not necessarily a good sign.

. . .

It wasn't just the raucousness of the Roman baths that bothered Seneca. On a trip to the coastal town of Liternum he visited the villa that had once belonged to the legendary general Scipio Africanus. Inside the rustic bathing house, through its narrow slit windows, Seneca glimpsed a lost vitality. Nowadays, he sighed, in another letter to his friend Lucilius, "people regard baths as fit only for moths if they have not been so arranged that they receive the sun all day long through the widest of windows, if men cannot bathe and get a coat of tan at the same time."[3] But then this was the residence of the Terror of Carthage, not some popinjay's palace – Scipio bathed "to wash off sweat, not ointment".

Seneca was concerned that his generation had been seduced and emasculated by the luxuries of the bathhouse. Men drenched themselves in thick clouds of perfume, unlike Scipio's peers – the soldiers and the politicians who had built the Roman Empire – who "smelled of the camp, the farm, and heroism". "Now that spick-and-span bathing establishments have been devised," Seneca concluded sadly, "men are really fouler than of yore."[4]

3 Wikisource contributors, "Moral letters to Lucilius/Letter 86," *Wikisource*, <http://en.wikisource.org/w/index.php?title=Moral_letters_to_Lucilius/Letter_86&oldid=4163379> (accessed October 2, 2014).
4 *Ibid.*

The philosopher was right to spy hidden dangers through the scented steam. In AD 65, Seneca was accused of participating in the Pisonian conspiracy against his former pupil, the Emperor Nero. Ordered to kill himself, Seneca dutifully slit arteries in his arms and legs, but his circulation had been enfeebled by old age, making the subsequent blood loss agonizingly slow. In the hope of ending the pain, Seneca took poison and had himself carried to a hot bath where, according to the historian Tacitus, the steam suffocated him.

· · ·

Minutes drifted silently by. I left *A Streetcar Named Desire* resting on the rim of the bath and sank back into the water. Swaddled in a warm, liquid cloak, my eyes were drifting dangerously shut when suddenly there came a thunderous knocking upon the bathroom door, the Visigoths at the gates of Rome. Reluctantly I climbed out of the bath, pulled a dressing gown over my damp skin and unbolted the door. Gill was standing in the corridor outside, her arms folded.

"How did you know?" she demanded.

"How did I know what?"

"Don't play games with me, Edgar. It turns out that my lousy, lying *shit* of a boyfriend" – she shouted the swearword, presumably in the hope that Richard remained somehow within earshot – "has been lying to me all along, and the only person who knew was you."

My lips twitched as I fought back a smile. "Really? He's still doing drugs? I was right?"

"Yes, Edgar, you were," Gill said icily. "Dead right. 100% accurate. Spot. On. Despite the fact that Richard had sworn to me he'd stopped doing cocaine, and despite the fact you've never even bothered to lay eyes upon him, let alone sit down and discuss his addiction issues with him. So how the hell did you know?"

"I think you'd better come inside," I said, moving to one side. "Step into my office."

THE STRUGGLE FOR THE BATHROOM

Gill entered the bathroom warily, glancing around for booby traps, the possibility of an oubliette hidden beneath the bathmat. She rarely came in here these days, preferring the speed and convenience of her en suite shower. It was hard not to feel guilty about the way I had annexed this corner of her flat – on the other hand, I reassured myself, it wasn't as though Gill had time for leisurely soaks in the bath. Her work saw to that.

She was dressed for the office, in a sober grey trouser suit and sensible heels. Apparently her firm was part of some kind of legal Magic Circle, but I saw no signs of conjuring or enchantment in her work. There were no puffs of smoke, no doves fluttering out of top hats – just endless hours at the office, stress headaches, and the constant angry buzzing of her phone as it swarmed with emails.

I had learnt from bitter experience that silence was by far the safest policy when my sister was angry. So I said nothing as Gill picked up *A Streetcar Named Desire* from the edge of the bath, her lips pursing as she noted the wax applicator sticking up from the pages.

"Good read?" she asked briskly.

I nodded.

"Well, at least you're keeping busy, I suppose."

It did seem a *little* unfair that I was getting the blame for what had happened with Richard, especially when I had tried to warn Gill that the actor was using again. She had dismissed my suspicions, preferring to believe Richard's tearful pledge that he had performed his final white line. I couldn't entirely blame her for that. After all, surely being an actor – no matter how second-rate – gave Richard an unfair advantage when it came to lying: it was his life's work to pretend and to feign.

For all her boyfriend's failings, I was sorry for Gill that they had split up. Ever since our parents' divorce – our charming, useless father's multiple affairs finally bobbing to the surface like sewage – my sister had been the one family member I could rely upon. When I had needed help and had nowhere to go, it had been Gill who opened her door and allowed me to stay in her flat rent-free. As she had said at the time, what else are sisters for?

. . .

A Streetcar Named Desire opens with Blanche DuBois' arrival at her sister Stella's apartment in Elysian Fields, a crowded and cosmopolitan neighbour-hood of New Orleans. With her pearl earrings and white gloves, and a single valise stuffed with her possessions, Blanche is an empress in exile, a fugitive tsar's daughter. Fleeing from a dead husband, a lost inheritance, and a shat-tered reputation, she shields herself with lies. Completely out of place amidst the whistle and holler of Elysian Fields, Blanche seeks refuge in the bathroom, soaking in the tub to calm her nerves. Her hiccups of laughter carry through to the rest of the apartment, to the seething dismay of Stella's husband Stanley.

One night Blanche and Stella return to the apartment and find the men still playing poker. The atmosphere is thick with tension: the sharp jostle of ice cubes in the glass, sausage fingers tugging at sweaty collars, the calling and folding of hands, the resigned toss of chips into the centre of the table. Lurid silk bowling shirts blare out like mating calls, or ambulance sirens. Whilst Stanley drunkenly rages at the interruption, Blanche spies salvation in the form of his ungainly friend Mitch. That she pins her romantic hopes on him is a sign of her desperation – Mitch is a lumbering piñata, mocked by the other men for his devotion to his mother; a spare part from the spare parts department.

Worse, Blanche's hopes of marriage make her vulnerable to Stanley. Armed with the knowledge of her chequered past, he warns his best friend away from her. And when Mitch does finally reject Blanche, he stumbles across the most painful words imaginable for the constant bather – telling her that she is too dirty to meet his mother.

. . .

Gill perched on the edge of the bath, staring at me expectantly.

"Go on, then," she said tartly. "I'm waiting. Tell me how you knew about Richard. Amaze me with your brilliant powers of deduction."

"I don't know about brilliant," I said cautiously. "It was pretty simple in the end. I pieced it together the night you came back from the opening of his play."

"You were still up?" said Gill. "I thought you'd gone to bed."

"I was in here."

She rolled her eyes. "I should have known."

"You wouldn't have heard me – you were both pretty drunk. I heard you talking in the corridor. You said you were going to bed but Richard wanted to stay up. Something about his voice... I don't know, he sounded a bit furtive, so I thought I'd better keep an eye on him."

"Little brother," groaned Gill, "*please* tell me you weren't spying on my boyfriend."

"Of course not!" I replied indignantly. "I just checked how many times he went to the toilet."

"You did *what?*"

"Five times in an hour, Gill! Do you call that normal?"

"Says you, weirdo! What did you do, hide in the cistern?"

"I didn't leave the bath!" I protested. "I didn't have to. When someone uses the sink in the toilet the water runs cold in here. All I had to do was keep the bath taps running."

"So Richard went to the toilet a lot. Big deal! Maybe he's got a weak bladder."

"He *went* to the toilet five times, but he only *used* it twice. There were only two flushes."

"Hang on a minute." The lawyer in Gill had been roused to action. Even after everything that happened, she still didn't want me to be right. "The toilet's on the other side of the flat. You couldn't have heard the flush in here, especially with the taps running."

"No, but I could hear the pipes as the cistern fills up. You want to stay here while I go prove it?"

"I'll take your word for it," said Gill. "Freak. Did it not occur to you that it might have been *me* using the toilet?"

I shook my head. "You usually spend a minute or so washing your hands. Richard isn't quite so thorough – a quick rinse and he's gone. It was him, every time. So a self-confessed drug user was locking himself in the toilet but not using it. There seemed to be only one logical explanation."

Gill shook her head. "Unbelievable."

"Thank you."

"It wasn't a compliment!" She sprang to her feet and jabbed me in the chest with her finger. "All this time you've been sitting here like a big fat spider in a web, keeping tabs on my boyfriend, timing me in the bathroom, not to mention running the taps for hours on end!"

"Yes, but I don't think that's the real issue—"

"You wouldn't, would you? You don't pay the bloody bills around here!"

In her anger Gill had gone on the attack, reaching for her most trusted and effective weapons. Though her job made her tired and tetchy, I had to admit my unusual lifestyle did not help diplomatic relations. In recent months there had been pointed comments about water bills and access to the bathroom, complaints about wet footprints on the hall carpet. War was brewing.

. . .

A Streetcar Named Desire opened on Broadway at the Ethel Barrymore Theatre on 3 December 1947. The fall of the curtain was greeted by shocked silence, before the audience erupted into an ovation that lasted for half an hour. But not everyone was impressed. In a vinegar-soaked review in the *Partisan Review*, critic Mary McCarthy suggested that Tennessee Williams should have rewritten the play as a lightly comic production, "The Struggle For the Bathroom". Yet this struggle lies at the very heart of *A Streetcar Named Desire*, a struggle for Blanche's sanity and her soul.

From the first description of Stella's apartment Williams presents two worlds abutting with uncomfortable proximity. The kitchen – where the men gather to drink, play poker and tell lewd jokes – and the bedroom – where Stella accepts Stanley's frantic coital apologies – are placed directly in front of the audience. This is the real world: inescapable and implacable. It is the bathroom that remains out of sight, the last remnant of Blanche's beautiful dreams. On some level Stanley recognizes this, mocking his sister-in-law's frequent ablutions and trying to drag her out into the apartment.

The two worlds are set for a brutal collision that finally occurs during the preparations for Blanche's birthday celebrations. As Blanche soaks in the tub, her singing audible from off-stage, Stanley sets about dismantling her reputation. He tells Stella about her sister's stay at the Hotel Flamingo, where Blanche's multiple liaisons with men led to her ejection. For all her protestations that she is a virgin, Blanche's bed has been almost as busy as her bathtub, shared by soldiers and schoolboys, tradesmen and passers-by. But her disgrace isn't enough to satisfy Stanley. His pride demands her complete obliteration.

At the end of the party scene Stanley barges past Blanche into the bathroom, invading her private sanctum – a grim foreshadowing of the rape that takes place the night after Stella has given birth. Under Stanley's assault the fragile barriers Blanche has erected between reality and fantasy are brutally demolished, a paper lantern ripped from the light. Forced to choose between worlds, she rejects the real world and opts for the comfort of her fantasies, even as she is led away to a mental institution.

. . .

Gill tightened her ponytail in the mirror, turning her head left and right to check that she was satisfied with the result.

"I haven't got time for this," she said. "I'll see you later."

"Are you going to work?"

"It's half-past seven on a Tuesday morning, Edgar," she replied tightly. "Of course I'm going to work. That's what people do. Everyone else, at least."

I wondered if Gill had slept since the fight with Richard. Judging by the dark smudges beneath her eyes, I doubted it.

"To top it all off, I think Richard broke the lock on the front door on his way out," she told me. "Can you get someone round to fix it today?"

I grimaced. "You know I'd like to help," I said hesitantly, "but I'm still in a lot of pain, and I don't know whether... today, I mean..."

"OK. Fine."

"Maybe tomorrow, I could—"

"You can't go on like this, Ed, you know?" Gill said suddenly, almost blurting out the words. "Spending every day wallowing alone in here. Is this how you want to spend the rest of your life?"

"I don't know, Gill," I retorted. "I didn't want to be ill for the rest of my life, but that happened, didn't it?"

The lines around my sister's eyes softened. She really did look tired.

"Look, I'm not saying it's been easy for you," Gill said quietly. "You got this horrible disease from nowhere, and then it turned out that you were allergic to the dapsone, so you couldn't take the one drug that could help you. Now you're trapped in medical limbo, Mum and Dad are no use since they split up and I'm in the office all the time. I can see why you'd want to hide away in your own little dream world, with your bath and your books. But this is *my* flat, that I work all hours to pay for, and you're not going to sit around doing nothing any more. I'm tired of being the only adult in our family. Either get a job and start paying rent, Ed, or get out."

She hurried out of the bathroom, seemingly fearing a pang of compassion or a softening of her stance. Our time living together has turned Gill into a confusion of Stella and Stanley, unsure whether to hug me or hit me. This wasn't the first time that she had threatened to kick me out, but this was the first time she had meant it. Things were looking bleak.

The front door banged shut as Gill left the flat. I gingerly took off my dressing gown, catching an unwanted glimpse of myself in the mirror as I did so. My skinny frame was a patchwork of blisters, red and sore in the light. Slowly I lowered my blotched body back into the water, closing my eyes in relief at its soothing caress. Unmooring my mind from the cares and anxieties of the real world, I let it drift blissfully free.

GREETINGS FROM HELSINKI

The king rode north beneath grimacing skies, his mind consumed with thoughts of vengeance. Henry Bolingbroke, Henry IV, was a monarch under siege. Six years earlier, in 1399, he had wrestled the crown from his cousin Richard II and restored the House of Lancaster to the throne, yet his realm remained under constant threat from enemies both within and without its borders. The Scots, the French and the Welsh had all taken arms against the vulnerable new king, whilst Richard's death in captivity at Pontefract Castle hadn't prevented a host of imposters from rising up and laying claim to the throne. There had been several assassination attempts, including a plot to smear Henry's saddle with poison.

The latest challenge had been laid down by the Yorkshire Rising, a loose confederation of nobles led by the Earl of Northumberland and Archbishop Richard le Scrope. Henry had hurried north to find a handful of the leaders already in custody – including the mutinous archbishop. Previously the king had shown mercy in his dealings with the rebels, but this time his wrath was implacable. On 8 June 1405, he ordered Archbishop Scrope's execution and immediately left York for Northumberland's castles.

As the royal party galloped on, pennants fluttering in the rising wind, the heavens opened and rain came down like thundering hooves. The ferocity of the summer storm forced the riders to abandon their journey and seek shelter at the nearby manor of Green Hammerton, nine miles from York.

That night, the household was jarred awake by the king's screams. Henry's skin was burning, his face and hands covered in angry boils. Convinced he had been the subject of another assassination attempt, the king writhed in pain as his servants frantically tried numb the pain with wine.

The next day Henry was moved to Ripon, where he spent a week in convalescence. But his health would never fully recover. The youthful king who had seduced mainland Europe with his prowess at the joust became enfeebled. His hair fell out, his skin continued to cause him pain, and he fell victim to a series of life-threatening illnesses before his death in 1413. Though Henry's maladies remained an enigma to his doctors, for his subjects the strange happenings at Green Hammerton were easy to explain. The timing of the attack left no room for doubt: Henry had contracted leprosy as divine punishment for Scrope's execution – and thus the murder of an archbishop, a holy man of God.

. . .

The water had grown cold and stale. My buttocks squeaked across the bottom of the bath as I struggled into a sitting position and fumbled for the plug around my feet. My fingers settled upon the chain and I pulled it free. The plughole gargled and gulped, and I let the bath drain completely before replacing the plug and turning on the taps.

Filling Gill's bath was a precise operation that fell somewhere between mixing a cocktail and making a bomb. This was due entirely to the hot tap; a mischievous, elemental being given to playful squirts of scalding heat amid long stretches of tepid water. To protect myself I ran both taps on low, swirling the mixture together whilst keeping more sensitive body parts out of the potential blast zone.

As the water trickled into the bath I warily examined the rashes on my body. *Dermatitis Herpetiformis* – to give the villain of the piece a formal introduction – is a chronic skin disease characterized by outbreaks of irritated rashes and blisters. It torments its victims like a school bully, leaving them in peace for weeks on end before leaping out from the shadows of the biology block and administering Chinese burns to the tender extremities of their bodies. The severity of my strain had been exacerbated by the fact I was allergic to dapsone, the necessary antibiotic. With no other medical options available, all I could do was soak my angry skin in water until the symptoms died down.

Thankfully this had been a mild attack. The furious red and purple blotches on my elbows had dimmed to an irate pink; the poisonous itching on my knees was now a mild prickle. Running my hands across my lower back and buttocks, I could feel that the pimples had reduced in size. There had been times in the previous two years when I had been marooned in the bathtub for days, unable to do anything but splash about in the shallows, the awkward offspring of a mermaid and a manatee.

The hot tap let out a sudden splutter, coughing up a glob of boiling water into the bath. As I hastily reduced the flow I heard the front door to the flat open and footsteps move down the hall. Either Gill had forgotten something, or she had come back to apologize for snapping at me.

There was a knock at the bathroom door. Good old Gill.

"Hello?" I called out.

To my surprise the handle turned and the door began to open. In my alarm at my sister's earlier ultimatum, I had forgotten to lock it.

"Gill, I'm in the bath!" I squawked. "Leave a note!"

It wasn't Gill.

The man standing in the doorway filled with space with uncanny precision. He was shaped like a rectangle: tall and broad-shouldered, with a jutting head that appeared to have been hammered into his torso at the expense of a neck. His blond hair was cropped short, and a stud gleamed in his left ear. He was dressed in grey tracksuit bottoms, with a small white T-shirt making a valiant effort to cover the man's upper body, leaving the light-blue letters of the word 'Suomi' stretched across his bulging pectorals.

"Hey!" I cried, pushing my sodden fringe out of my eyes. "What are you doing?"

The man stomped over to the bath, casually swatting me down when I attempted to stand. Caught square on the chin, my legs buckled beneath me and I crashed backwards into the bath. As black inkblots swirled before my eyes the man reached over me, turned off the cold tap and jammed the hot tap on to full power. A jet of scalding water shot out over my feet. I yelped with pain and tried to scramble out of the way, only for my attacker to grab my neck with a giant hand and pin me to the bottom of the tub. My flailing legs could just about avoid the liquid lava pouring down from Mount Vesuvius, but no matter how hard I struggled I couldn't free myself from the man's grip.

The temperature of the bath began to rise.

. . .

Is there a more pitiful creature in the whole of mythology than the Minotaur? Half-man, half-bull; a biological abomination and mindless vassal of rage; offspring of an inventor's conceit and a god's petty vengeance. Enraged by a perceived slight by King Minos of Crete, Poseidon responded by hexing the king's wife Pasiphae into lusting after a bull. The queen enlisted the help of the inventor Daedalus, who constructed a cow's shell for her to crawl inside and satisfy her desire. The result of this coupling was Asterion the Minotaur, so brutish and shameful a creature that Minos felt compelled to bury it out of sight. The ingenious Daedalus was once more pressed into action, constructing a fiendish labyrinth to house Asterion. There the beast dwelt, alone in a maddening world of wrong turns and dead-ends, feasting on terrified Athenian sacrifices delivered to Crete as tribute.

Though the Minotaur had been hidden from view, Minos's humiliation continued to gnaw away at him. Aware the king blamed him for assisting Pasiphae in the first place, Daedalus was forced to flee Crete. The wrathful Minos gave chase, eventually tracking the errant inventor down in Sicily, at the court of King Cocalus. Although Cocalus welcomed Minos with open arms, he had no intention of parting with Daedalus, who – as was his habit – was already proving his weight in gold. According to the ancient Greek historian Diodorus Siculus, the deceitful king of Sicily attacked Minos whilst he was bathing and killed him. Another version of the tale had Minos overwhelmed in the hot water by Cocalus's daughters, who had also been taken with Daedalus's charms, albeit for significantly different reasons…

. . .

The bath was nearly half-full with boiling water, and it felt as though my organs were being cooked from the inside. But for all my writhing and spluttering pleas, my attacker maintained his merciless grip. His crystal blue eyes betrayed not a single flicker of emotion. He could have been rocking a baby to sleep, or toasting a crumpet. The hot water didn't appear to be hurting his hand but I could feel my skin burning and there was a second, equally pressing problem – my face was sinking below the water line, my breaths taking in more fluid than oxygen. It seemed to be 50/50 whether I burned to death or drowned. Was it possible to do both at the same time?

Finally the blond monster yanked my head out of the water by the hair, allowing me a precious gasp of air. Water streamed from my nose in a sorry protest.

"You keep fucking nose out, yes?" he demanded, dragging my face next to his. "You keep fucking nose out!"

"Let go!" I cried. "You're hurting me!"

"You keep fucking nose out?"

"What?"

In a single move he hooked my legs up in the air with his other arm, like a wrestler preparing to pin his opponent, and I felt myself sliding along the tub towards the front of the bath. Too late I realized the full horror of his design. I tried to kick out, but what little strength I had had been already sapped by our struggle. The man guided my body underneath the taps, careful to leave my upturned genitals directly beneath the scorching waterfall.

"AAAAAAAH!"

White-hot pain coursed through my groin, fusing nerve endings and threatening to knock me unconscious. A tide of bile surged up my throat.

"You keeping fucking nose out?"

"I KEEP FUCKING NOSE OUT!" I screamed. "Anything! Turn it off!"

With a disapproving cluck of the tongue the man staunched the burning tap and pushed me back up the tub, dunking my head back beneath the surface. But this time he left his hands free of my throat, and as I bobbed back up for air I saw through tears of pain his hulking form stomp out of the bathroom. I clawed my way out of the tub and collapsed on to the wet linoleum, retching with each fresh lungful of air. My entire body was shuddering with shock; my skin had turned shellfish red, and it was impossible to tell what was rash or burn. I heard the flat's treacherous front door click shut, and then I gratefully blacked out.

THE BALLERINA'S FEET

The plug had been pulled from my bath, turning the gently lapping waters into a churning whirlpool, wicked fingers threatening to drag me under. I was wading through sewers, faeces lapping around my knees, the echoing shouts of my pursuers only spurring me deeper into the filthy mire. I was standing in a swimming pool of rotten milk, smiling seductively beneath bright lights whilst fighting back the urge to vomit. I was a fish thrashing in a net, desperately trying to escape the murderous arc of a falling axe...

"Edgar! Are you all right?"

I opened my eyes, fighting back a wave of nausea as the world swam into focus. I was sprawled in a puddle on the bathroom floor, surrounded by the ruined towers of the Ulpian Library. Though my body had stopped trembling, my skin was red-raw and my groin throbbed painfully. A young woman's face loomed over me, her eyes wide with concern. She was crouching down beside me on the floor, a single lock of red hair escaping from behind her ear to brush against my cheek.

"Has he gone?" I croaked.

She frowned. "Has who gone?"

"A man broke in. He did this to me. I don't know why."

"Damn!" The young woman swore in a whisper, clenching her fist. "Damn him to hell! How did he know?"

I stared at her, uncomprehending.

"Edgar, I'm so sorry," she said. She touched my cheek, her palm a blissful cold compress against my burning skin. I caught a faint hint of her deodorant, an unexpectedly boyish scent that reminded me of P.E. lessons and school changing rooms. "This is all my fault."

"I don't understand," I said groggily. "How do you know my name? Who are you?"

"I'm Diana."

Something about her tone told me I was expected to know this already.

"Diana Mayweather?" she added. "An old friend of Gill's?"

I smiled weakly.

"Oh." Her face fell a fraction. She was used to being remembered. "Sorry for barging in. The front door was open, and when I heard someone groaning I thought I'd better check they were OK."

My head had cleared a little as Diana talked, allowing me to properly take her in. She was tall, with slender, almost gawky limbs – the sweeping arch of a swan's wing rather than a cat's graceful curves. Her skin was pale in the bludgeoning glow of the bathroom light, with a defiant dusting of freckles; her tumbling red hair tied loosely back. Her beauty was undeniable, somehow careless and artful at the same time. It was the kind of beauty that caused damage wherever it went.

"Gill's not here," I told Diana. "She's at work."

"I know. I came to see you."

"Me?"

She nodded, biting her lip. "I need your help."

Diana looked away, and when her gaze met mine again her eyes were damp with tears. At that moment I felt a twitch against my thigh: my penis, which currently resembled a fricasseed sea slug, had for some unaccountable reason chosen that moment to stir. Somehow I had forgotten that I was naked.

I smiled awkwardly. "You couldn't pass me a towel, could you?"

. . .

One spring evening in Jerusalem, David, King of the Israelites, paced through the lengthening shadows along the roof of his palace. As he marked out a sentry's path, across the city rooftops he spotted a beautiful woman bathing. When David inquired about the woman's identity, he learned that her name was Bathsheba, the noble daughter of Eliam and the wife of Uriah the Hittite, a soldier who was away besieging the Ammonite city of Rabbah.

The Bible – perhaps out of a sense of decorum, perhaps a sense of shame – describes what followed in a single terse sentence: David summoned the bathing beauty and the pair of them slept together. In just a single sentence Bathsheba had handed over her virtue, tossed away her fidelity. Her reputation remains tarnished in perpetuity – at best a shameless slattern, at worst a voracious social climber who purposefully exposed herself in order to hook a king.

Yet there were some who felt that there was more to this story than just a single sentence. In *Bathsheba at Her Bath*, the Dutch painter Rembrandt showed Bathsheba sitting on the edge of the bath, sorrow drenched on her face as she clasps David's summons. The painting powerfully drives home a crucial point – *to refuse her king's request would mean Bathsheba's death*. In effect, she has been forced to choose between infidelity and death.

David himself is absent from the painting, reducing him to the status of a voyeur, just another member of the audience. Rembrandt eloquently helps us see the king's letter for what it truly is: part royal command and part pinch of the backside; a twist of the arm and a grope of the breast.

…

Having dried off and struggled into my dressing gown, I ushered Diana out of the bathroom and into the living room. Sunlight was pouring in through the windows, alighting on spare, gleaming surfaces. Whilst Diana took a seat at the dining table I headed for the open-plan kitchen, my bare feet padding damply across the lacquered floorboards, and flicked the kettle on. Diana said nothing as the water boiled, staring out of the window at the city sweating and shimmering in the heat. She sat bolt upright, her posture simultaneously graceful and severe. When I brought over a mug of coffee she murmured a thank-you, cupping her hands around the warm drink without looking down at it or attempting a sip. I took a seat on the black leather sofa opposite her, ignoring the squeals of protest from the handful of stubborn pimples still clinging to my backside.

"So then," I began, blowing on my coffee. "What can I do for you?"

Wordlessly Diana pulled a postcard from her tasselled tan bag and handed it to me. The front of the card was a picture of a ballet dancer. Her back was to the artist and her head was bowed, her hands adjusting the zip above the blue sash around her waist.

"It's by Degas," Diana told me, helpfully.

The Dance Studio, pastel drawing (1878). To be precise.

There was a message on the postcard's reverse, in elegantly sculpted handwriting:

My dear Diana,

I am troubled by your silence – did you not like the flowers I sent you? I hope that your time in the land of skyscrapers and the Big Mac has not ruined your love of beautiful things. Meet me this Friday at La Baignoire Pleine (8.30) and reassure me that my Giselle is not too jaded to dance again. I have a position I would like to discuss with you...

Sincerest compliments,
Oscar

I could sense Diana studying me as I read, but I wasn't sure how I was supposed to react. The message seemed polite enough. And what could it possibly have to do with me?

"So you've been in America?" I asked, playing for time.

"Well, the Chicago Academy isn't in Nepal," Diana replied breezily, "although given the attitude of some of the choreographers out there, I might have been better off trying to do a *pas de bourrée* up the side of a mountain" – she broke off – "and I've *just* realized that I'm talking as though you know what I do, when there's no earthly reason why you should. I'm sorry."

Diana let slip a little laugh of embarrassment. She was used to being remembered.

"No need to apologize," I told her. "So you're a dancer?"

She nodded. "Ballet. If you need proof, just take a look at my feet."

I did as I was told. Half-expecting Diana to be sporting pink ballet slippers with ribbons winding up her legs, I was a little disappointed to see that she was wearing a pair of worn flip-flops. This was a brave move, given that her feet looked like mouldy turnips. The nail on the big toe of her right foot was black and dead, while the left foot was covered in corns and plasters. Her gnarled, sclerotic feet bore the scars of every arch and tiptoe, every spring and jarred landing. It was as though all of Diana's physical imperfections had sunk to the bottom of her body, leaving everything above her ankles in a state of unsullied perfection – a cathedral built over the ruins of a charnel house.

"Not a pretty sight, are they?" she laughed gracefully. "I always think that if I couldn't dance any more I could return to the States and find gainful employment at a travelling freak show. Roll up, roll up, dare you take a peek at The World's Ugliest Feet?"

I smiled. "Did you like it in America?"

"Very much so."

"So why did you leave?"

Diana emitted a lengthy sigh. "A new artistic director took over and we had some problems seeing eye-to-eye blah blah blah, so I decided to come back to Britain and see if I could get a job with a *ballet de corps* here. Preferably the Walker Ballet, naturally, but I wasn't fussy. I've been an unemployed ballet dancer before and it's no fun, let me tell you. So when Lilia Kutznetsova had to drop out of the benefit gala last month I was happy to dance in her place. I thought it might put me in the shop window, so to speak."

"Did it go well?"

"The dancing went fine, it was the rest of the gala that was ghastly." She wrinkled her nose. "Filled with businessmen and socialites who don't know the difference between first and second position, yet think that because something's considered expensive it confers some kind of class upon them. Usually I'd avoid them like the plague *but* I was getting desperate so I held my nose and I danced the solo from *Giselle* for them and everything seemed to be going fine. And then I met Oscar Salazar."

She paused to take a sip from her coffee. I waited patiently, trying not to think about the wave of itching that was now sweeping across my back like bushfire.

"Oscar's some kind of ludicrously wealthy dealer or broker," Diana explained. "You can smell the money hanging off him like aftershave. He was charming enough, asked me whether I was having a nice time, how my career was going. Then he told me he'd come to the gala specifically to meet me."

I gritted my teeth, fighting back the urge to dig my nails into my back. Just one scratch, one sharp edge. Just to ease the pain. "Did you believe him?"

She shrugged carelessly. "I had no reason not to. I know it sounds a bit big-headed, but as a dancer you get used to that sort of thing – older men sending you flowers, asking you to dinner, the opera. Propositions of one sort or another. And it was obvious that Oscar liked me, I just didn't realize how much. He asked me out later that night. I told him I had a boyfriend I was very much in love with, and said thanks but no thanks."

"But that didn't stop him."

Diana shook her head. "If anything it encouraged him. More messages. More cards. More flowers. My flat looks like a greenhouse at Kew Gardens. And then, yesterday, this postcard arrived."

I inspected *The Dance Studio* once more, noting that the dancer's hair was the same shade of red as Diana's. Oscar Salazar was clearly a man who paid attention to detail.

"Can't you just ignore him?" I asked. "He'll get bored soon enough, and if the worst he's doing is sending you cards and flowers…"

"Didn't you read the postcard? I *have* to meet him. He has a position to discuss. A *position*." A note of desperation crept into Diana's voice. "Oscar Salazar isn't just any old businessman. He's patron of the Walker Ballet, which just happens to be most prestigious company in the country. He's practically bankrolling it! Why do you think he was invited to the gala?"

"Ah. I see. So if you turn him down…"

"…I'd better learn a new skill because I'm finished as far as ballet is concerned. After the fuss in Chicago I can't go back to America, and one bad word from Oscar would end my career in Britain. At this rate maybe I might actually end up in Nepal. I'll do anything to keep dancing, Edgar. I've sacrificed too much to throw it away. That's why I came here – to seek your help."

It was no use. Slipping a hand behind my back, I scratched through the thick fabric of my dressing gown, barely managing to keep an ecstatic smile of relief from my face.

"Why me?" I asked.

"Who else could I go to? As far as I know sending flowers and asking someone to dinner isn't illegal, so there's no point going to the police. I doubt anyone in the media would be interested, and anyway if I went public I could kiss my career goodbye. I need someone with brains who can think of a way out for me. That's why I phoned Gill this morning."

"Gill told you to ask me?"

"As if!" said Diana, throwing back her head with laughter. "She's mad at you like you wouldn't believe. But when she was telling me about Richard and how you'd worked everything out, I was reminded what you were like when you were younger – always the clever one, walking around with your nose in a book. Like some kind of Sherlock Holmes!"

I tried not to make a face.

...

Sherlock Holmes's greatest mystery is that of his own popularity – The Case of The Overrated Sleuth. The 'great detective' is a boast and a bore, an insufferable smartarse and tedious drug addict who drones on about footprint casts and the different classifications of cigar ash. He is an abacus, a lab technician posing as a classical thinker. He professes modesty but his vanity frequently reveals itself – both in his coquettish references to Dr Watson's records of his exploits and his frequent redress to disguise. Holmes plays dress-up with the eagerness of a toddler, or worse, an actor.

Why should the reader like Holmes, when no one else – save the plodding Watson – does? Holmes shuns company, having made the princely total of one friend at university. He is distrusted by the police and ignored by his brother. He will never find love: Holmes is a misogynist who doesn't trust women. Little wonder Irene Adler made a run for it.

Take *The Crooked Man* as a case in point. Holmes arrives unannounced at Dr Watson's home in the middle of the night, proclaiming that the weary doctor must be relieved to see him, before reeling off some trademark deductions based around splashes of dirt and scuffmarks – less a detective than a pernickety mother-in-law. Having made Watson wait whilst he smokes, Holmes finally deigns to reveal the purpose for his visit, talking at length about a case he has been working on before badgering the doctor to ditch work the next day and accompany him to Aldershot instead.

The case itself – the mystery of an army wife accosted by a deformed tramp, and whose husband is subsequently murdered – is resolved with a minimum amount of fuss, and arguably Holmes could have left his old friend in peace. The most interesting aspect of *The Crooked Man* is the fact that it owes its structure to a much older tale, a tale from the Bible: the tale of King David and Bathsheba.

. . .

Apparently no mean detective herself, Diana spied the slight curl of my lip.

"I've said the wrong thing, haven't I?" she said. "I didn't mean to offend you."

"It's fine," I said hastily. "It's just, I'm not really a private detective. I'm a writer – or at least, I hope to be."

It was true. Since falling ill I had spent the last two years immersed in a study of bathing and the bath, hunting down every obscure reference I could find, following a trail of damp footprints though footnotes and appendices in histories and textbooks. I had filled my ring-binder folders with voluminous notes of the connections and coincidences I had found, along with detailed plans for an epic novel. Part-fiction, part-history, it would be a lengthy meditation on the bath in all its different aspects. I was too close to writing it to get distracted now.

Stung by my hesitation, Diana reached into her tasselled bag and pulled out her purse.

"I can pay you," she said. "A hundred pounds a day."

Opening her purse, she pulled out a thick wad of £20 notes and handed it to me. "That's for one week. An advance."

I stopped in mid-scratch, astonished. Seven hundred pounds? At a stroke, I had found a way to pay Gill *and* stave off my ejection from the flat.

"OK," I said, with feigned reluctance. I didn't want to look *too* desperate. "I'll see what I can do."

Diana broke into a grateful smile. The sun emerged from behind a cloud and planted a warm kiss on my cheek.

"Thank you," she said. "But promise me you'll take care. Oscar's already showed what he can do to you this morning. Don't take him lightly."

I looked up in surprise. "You think *Oscar* was the reason that guy attacked me?"

"Have you made any other enemies recently?" Diana asked pointedly. "When I spoke to Gill I asked for your address. If Oscar was tapping my phone, he could have sent round one of his goons before I got here."

"He'd tap your phone?" I said. "He has *goons*?"

"Goons, henchmen, lackeys, I don't know, Edgar! This is a rich and powerful man who's not used to people saying no to him. I wouldn't put anything past him."

"If that's the case, you'd better warn your boyfriend too."

"Yuri?" Diana gave me a sharp glance. "What about him?"

"If Oscar's happy to get me before I've even spoken to you, don't you think he might try and get your boyfriend out of the picture?"

"But Yuri Ivanov's an internationally renowned dancer! Oscar wouldn't dare!"

"I'd have a word with him all the same. Where is he?"

"New York," replied Diana, taking a dangling strand of hair and wrapping it around her finger. "He's principal dancer for the Met – they've just finished a production of *Swan Lake*. You wouldn't believe how much I miss him."

"Well, when you do speak to him…"

Diana nodded, putting down her coffee and gathering up her bag. As I showed her out she paused in the front door, decorating the hall with another stray waft of deodorant. Was that Lynx she was wearing?

"You really think Yuri might be in danger?" she asked, fingering the ruptured lock on the door.

"I'm sure he'll be fine," I replied.

Diana smiled at me gratefully and waved goodbye. I waited until she had disappeared down the stairs before closing the door, a thoughtful expression on my face. There was a lot I didn't understand about what had taken place that morning, but one thing was bothering me more than anything else – if Diana wanted my help so badly, then why was she lying to me?

STORM WARNINGS

Ordinarily I would have returned to my bath for a celebratory dip, but as Diana's flip-flops pattered away down the stairs I found myself hurrying into my bedroom and pulling on clothes. The searing pain in my groin had subsided to a dull ache, but the rashes on my knees and elbows still cried out in protest as I pulled on a pair of trousers and buttoned up a shirt. I picked up my front door keys on the way out, but judging by the battered state of the lock I wasn't going to need them to get back in. No wonder people seemed to be coming and going at will.

I was halfway out of the door when I turned and dashed back into the bathroom. Snatching up the plastic yellow duck from the side of the bath, I stuffed it into my pocket. Curtis was a sarcastic Christmas present from Gill, who seemed a little disappointed when I laughed out loud and gave him pride of place beside the tub. She dismissed Curtis as a plaything, a child's toy. Which just goes to show how much she knows.

. . .

On 10 January 1992, a container ship bound for Tacoma, Washington, was ambushed by a storm in the North Pacific Ocean, where the 45th parallel intersected with the International Date Line. The churning waves knocked one of the ship's containers overboard, scattering thousands of tiny objects into the ocean. They were plastic bath toys – a multicoloured menagerie of red beavers, green frogs, blue turtles and yellow ducks known as Friendly Floatees. The ship ploughed on through the storm, leaving toys in its wake like a nursery school oil spill.

Ten months later, in November 1992, beachcombers scouring the shores of Alaska began turning up some unusual finds: brightly coloured animal toys. Somehow the Friendly Floatees had survived the storm's fury and navigated the Pacific Ocean all the way to America. The appearance of these plastic pilgrims was noted by an oceanographer called Curtis Ebbesmeyer, who used commercial flotsam to monitor ocean currents. (Two years earlier, he had tracked 80,000 pairs of trainers after they had been washed overboard off the American coast.) With the help of a computer model that simulated ocean currents, Ebbesmeyer set about predicting the course the remaining Friendly Floatees would take: round the Subpolar Gyre – a huge ocean current rotating counter-clockwise around the North Pacific Ocean – and up into the Bering Strait. There they would come to a frozen standstill amid the ice floes. Eventually, Ebbesmeyer calculated, the ice would thaw and the toys would battle their way free into the North Atlantic.

It took eleven years for the oceanographer's prediction to come true. In 2003, weather-beaten bath toys were spotted off the east coast of America and Scotland, having traversed halfway across the globe. Perhaps there are intrepid Friendly Floatees still on the ocean today, bobbing towards a distant shoreline. Part of me hopes that, somewhere in the South Atlantic Sea or in the Arctic Ocean, they have found some deserted craggy landmass to colonize – their own Tierra del Fuego, their own private utopia where it is always bath time.

. . .

Gill's flat was situated in the middle of a gated complex in north London, a smart, expensive block of flats populated almost exclusively by young professionals. The heat assailed me as soon as I stepped on to the outside landing, and for a second I thought about diving back into the flat. These days I only went outside when I had to, scuttling like a hermit crab from rocky pool to rocky pool. It took the sight of Diana's willowy progress through the square below to harden my resolve, and send me hurrying towards the stairs.

I was aware that private detectives weren't necessarily supposed to follow their own clients, but I was certain that Diana had lied to me and I wanted to know why. She claimed that she had no idea where her boyfriend Yuri was, but at the same time she was conspicuously wearing male deodorant. My bet was, she had come directly from his room. But why hide the fact?

By the time I had entered the square Diana had reached the exit, just as a couple were passing through the electric gate. The man stopped to hold it open for Diana, who smiled at him in thanks and said something I couldn't quite catch. The couple laughed and Diana had passed through the gate. When she had passed out of sight the smile vanished from the girlfriend's face, and she gave her boyfriend an aggrieved shove.

As I followed her out of the complex and down the main road towards the tube station, I realized that this kind of reaction to Diana was typical. The mere sight of her appeared to divide opinion firmly down gender lines. Teenage girls screwed up their faces; older women looked on with a complex combination of pity and envy. Men smiled and couldn't resist a second glimpse: some with furtive embarrassment, as though they were stealing a purse; others brayed and honked and nudged their friends; others just stared dully. None of them looked at her feet.

Amazingly, Diana appeared utterly oblivious to any of this. She floated down the street, neatly stepping over piles of rubbish and skirting around the damp patch of pavement outside the fish shop. Not once did she turn around. Perhaps it was no surprise that she didn't feel my gaze upon her back. *Everyone* looked at her. No wonder she was used to being remembered.

I followed Diana into the tube station and down the escalators, hanging back on the southbound platform until the last second before dashing on to the train in the carriage adjoining hers. I watched her through the window in the adjoining door as she stared dreamily up at the adverts above the seats, some unexpected memory bringing a smile to her face. Even though my carriage was empty, my skin chafed in the hot, second-hand air, and I scratched my elbow as I spied on Diana.

The tube train hurtled through the darkness towards the heart of the city. As the carriage gradually filled with passengers, my view of Diana became obscured by newspapers and backpacks, and I nearly missed her when she slipped off the train at Green Park. I had to elbow past a bemused elderly couple to escape the carriage, catching a trailing arm in the doors as they slammed shut. By this stage it felt as though Diana was the only person in the entire station *not* looking at me, but she remained oblivious, lost in a reverie. I threaded my way through the crowds on the escalator and followed her outside.

Diana led me down Picadilly through the tourist throng, deaf to the sudden eruption of camera clicks that greeted her passage. When she breezed up the driveway to the entrance of a five-star hotel, the doorman scurried over to open the door for her. The lobby was cool and quiet, voices murmuring over the gentle hum of the air-conditioning. A Japanese girl in an electric blue minidress and knee-high boots sat at one of the tables, toying with the straw in her orange juice as she talked into her mobile. She pouted slightly, brushing her long fringe out of her eyes. At the next table, a businessman pretended to read his paper whilst mentally measuring her inside leg.

At first I thought they were the only people inside the lobby, but then I noticed a man nursing a coffee at a table in the corner, almost entirely obscured behind a large fern. He had a long, shadowy face with a prominent nose – darkly handsome, for all its equine echoes. As Diana approached he glanced up from his coffee, and there was the briefest flicker of apprehension before a smile broke out across his face. Bounding to his feet, he enveloped her in an embrace. I noted the man's frame, muscular yet wiry: a dancer's physique.

"What are you doing here, beautiful?" he asked in heavily accented English, planting a kiss on Diana's forehead. "I thought I wasn't going to see you until tonight."

"I know, Yuri, but I couldn't wait. I had to see you."

It appeared Yuri Ivanov wasn't in New York, after all. Diana stared up into his eyes and the two of them melted into a passionate kiss. I looked away with an embarrassed cough, only to discover that I was also being watched. The Japanese girl had put down her phone and was now staring at me with open amusement. She finished off her orange juice with a slurp and uncrossed her legs, her boots making a soft leather sigh. Either someone had set off the hotel fire alarm, or a warning bell had gone off in my head. She rose from her table and walked towards me, moving with a languid assurance on a teetering pair of heels. The warning bell had become a klaxon, but I was rooted to the spot. As the girl leant in towards me I caught a tantalizing scent of jasmine. I wondered if she had mistaken me for a blind date or a soft touch, and then a hand touched my side and a pair of lips brushed against my cheek.

"I'll be waiting for you," she whispered.

. . .

A nation reveals itself in the way that it bathes. The English communal shower is a stilted affair caught between pleasure and propriety, whilst the Russian *banya* is drenched in gloomy mythology; the Turkish *hammam* hides its secrets in shadowy side-rooms. Yet no nation can lay claim to a more sophisticated and sensual relationship with bathing than the Japanese. Better than anyone else, they understand the difference between the mechanical necessity of washing, and the philosophical act of bathing.

This aquatic love affair has its roots in geography and religion. Japan is an island nation, the very country immersed in water, while its mountainous landscape is punctuated by some 20,000 hot springs known as *onsen*. The introduction of Buddhism into Japan in the 6th century brought with it an emphasis on the need for cleanliness, and temple baths were duly opened up to the people, allowing them to experience the luxury of bathing. During the 8th century, the Emperor Shomu spent a small fortune constructing Buddhist temples and monasteries, whilst his consort the Empress Komyo was said to have demonstrated her pious devotion by pledging to wash 1,000 beggars at the Horyuji Temple in Nara. Similarly, the Shinto faith placed great importance on bathing as a form of ritual purification. Perhaps the most dramatic example of this can be seen in the hardy practitioners of *misogi*, who plunge into freezing mountain waterfalls to cleanse themselves.

Bathing in modern Japan is separated into two major forms: private (*furo*) and public (*sento*). The crucial aspect of either process is that participants wash *before* they enter the bath, taking care to remove the last traces of soap and shampoo from their bodies. To enter a bath unwashed would be considered the height of bad manners, especially in the *sento*. Public baths offer an opportunity to relax and socialize with others, the hot water eroding social barriers and turning bathers into *Hadaka no tsukiai* – "naked relations".

. . .

"Yuri!"

I opened my eyes to find that the Japanese girl had vanished. A blonde woman carrying a travel bag was standing in the middle of the lobby, her face frozen with contempt as she stared at Yuri and Diana. The woman was beautiful, in a merciless kind of way, with bobbed hair and high, slashing cheekbones.

"Lilia!" said Yuri, hastily disentangling himself from Diana. "I thought you were in Kiev!"

As I stared at the blonde woman, some words of Diana's came dripping back into my mind: *So when Lilia Kutznetsova had to drop out of the benefit gala last month I was happy to dance in her place…* It was starting to look like dancing wasn't the only thing Diana had been doing in Lilia's place.

"I thought *you* were in New York," Lilia replied icily. "It seems we were both mistaken."

"I-I got a call from the Walker," stammered Yuri. "They wanted to meet me."

"So I can see," said Lilia, staring directly at Diana. "I was about to fly to Kiev when I got a call from Valery telling me to go to London instead. He thought you might be up to no good. And he was right."

As the temperature inside the lobby plummeted I tried to withdraw behind a pillar, knocking into a tea trolley with a guilty rattle of crockery. Lilia shot me an angry glare, her eyes narrowing.

"Valery?" said Yuri. "But how could he… I don't understand!"

"Of course you don't understand," Lilia retorted, turning her attention back to the other couple. "You understand nothing but dancing and whoring. And as for you," she said, turning to Diana, "I thought I had made myself clear in Chicago."

"Perhaps I didn't understand. Perhaps you should tell me again." Diana's voice was cool and composed, completely free from embarrassment. Yuri looked almost desperate in comparison.

"Please, Lilia, darling," he tried. "Listen to me—"

"Hah!" Lilia's haughty cry echoed around the lobby. "Don't even try. Your words mean nothing. First you lie to me. Now you lie to *Valery*? Are you crazy? You're risking everything, and for what? This cheap slut?"

A concierge materialized at Lilia's elbow, politely requesting that she lower her voice. She shook him off and marched towards Diana, forcing Yuri to hastily interject himself between the two women. Lilia said something in Russian to Diana, who tossed her hair back and laughed magnificently.

Howling with fury, Lilia swooped on the redhead, nails outstretched. Yuri wrestled her away, sending the pair of them crashing into his table and knocking his coffee cup to the floor. The concierge raced over to stop them, only to receive a backhanded slap in the face from Lilia as she tried to claw Yuri's face.

The scuffle was drawing an audience, and I realized it was time to go. I slipped out through the front entrance, leaving Yuri and the concierge still grappling with the enraged Lilia whilst Diana glared defiantly on. I headed back to Green Park deep in thought. Halfway down the steps to the underground, I realized that I had acquired some extra luggage during my trip. Curtis was still happily stationed in my left trouser pocket, but there was now an unfamiliar object in my right. I pulled it out and stared at it, bewildered.

In the palm of my hand was a small pink bar wrapped in transparent plastic. A small pink bar of soap.

THE WISDOM OF THE SCYTHIANS

I kept my eyes closed on the tube journey home, my mind's ocean disturbed by complex tides and currents. The bar of soap was weighing heavily upon me. Seen in its natural habitat, squatting in the milky pond of a soap dish, it was an utterly inconsequential object. But taken out of context – carried around in a handbag, then slipped into an unsuspecting pocket in the middle of a distracting kiss – it had acquired a new and urgent significance. Was it a pointed instruction? A coded plea for help? Or an obscure warning?

The short journey into the city had left me sweaty, dirty and itchy. I stood for the last four stops, unable to bear the clawing of the seat fabric upon my backside. Yet as I emerged from the underground I decided against an immediate return to the flat. Desperate as I was to plunge back into my bath, the scene in the hotel lobby had raised several questions and I needed more information. I needed a confidante, someone to talk things over with. More than anything, I needed someone who would be at home in the middle of the day.

There was only one person I knew who fitted that particular description. Luckily Ray's flat was only a twenty-minute walk from the tube station. As the road curved up a hill the sharp incline robbed the air from my lungs, sweat trickling down my back. A jogger pounded past, startling me with a blare of music from her headphones and her sharp pant of exertion. It was a relief when I reached the crest of the hill and spied my destination at the end of a quiet side road. I pressed the doorbell for the ground floor flat and waited. At least I knew that Ray would be in. Ray was *always* in.

. . .

The roots of the word 'cannabis' can be traced back to the Scythians, a nomadic barbarian tribe who occupied a vast swathe of Iron Age Eurasia, their lands stretching from modern Iran to the Ukraine and southern Russia. History has not been kind to the Scythians, their name becoming a byword for acts of generic cruelty like blood drinking and baby eating. But dirtiness could not be counted among their many sins. The Scythians bathed regularly, favouring a vapour bath in which they filled their tents with steam in order to sweat out their impurities. This process demanded one special ingredient, as the Greek historian Herodotus described in his *Histories*:

> "The Scythians… take some… hemp-seed, and, creeping under the felt coverings, throw it upon the red-hot stones; immediately it smokes, and gives out such a vapour as no Grecian vapour-bath can exceed; the Scyths, delighted, shout for joy, and this vapour serves them instead of a water-bath; for they never by any chance wash their bodies with water."[5]

Given the notoriously enervating side effects of most hemp-related activities, it's impressive that the Scythians summoned the energy to extend their empire as far as Egypt. If they had opted for cocaine instead of hemp, they might well have galloped through Europe and gone on to discover America, all the while forcing their voices above the thundering hooves of their steeds to boast incessantly of their great deeds to one another.

. . .

I watched as a woman pushing a buggy bumped into an old friend on the pavement outside Ray's house. They chatted briefly before heading off for a coffee. A bus pulled up at the stop at the end of the road, disgorging passengers, and then a second one followed quickly in its wake. An elderly man shuffled past the driveway, his back seemingly sagging lower with every painstaking step.

And then the door opened.

5 Henry Cary, *Herodotus* (Bohn's Classical Library, 1885), IV:75

With his unruly hair and heavy-lidded eyes, Ray resembled an animal awoken midway through hibernation. He looked up into the sky, shielding his eyes from the sun's glare.

"What time is it?" he asked.

"I have absolutely no idea."

Ray nodded and disappeared back inside his flat, leaving me to close the door behind him. Swallowed up into the gloom, it took my eyes a couple of seconds to adjust before I could find my way to the front room, where a pair of thick curtains repelled the fierce sun outside. There was a gentle hush in the air, a soft sweet fug, the echo of rustling cigarette papers. The room was studiously tidy, and largely empty save for the large computer processor and two screens on a work desk, and a laptop open on the coffee table. Beside the laptop there was an object that I initially mistook for an oversized toy gun, before correctly identifying it as a handheld vacuum cleaner.

A foreign language TV programme was running on the laptop, flooding the room with unexpected syllables. The accent was strangely familiar, and every now and again I caught an English world. I scratched my elbow thoughtfully.

"Are they speaking Welsh?"

Ray nodded. "It's *Pobol y Cwm*. Ever seen it?"

"It's a Welsh soap opera, Ray. Of course I haven't seen it." I looked at the screen. "Jesus, there aren't even subtitles."

He shrugged as he sat down, in one generously shambolic movement. "You pick it up after a while," he said. "Eventually."

I had first met Ray about five years ago, when we shared a room whilst interviewing for a Cambridge college. Neither of us got an offer but to my surprise Ray continued to email me throughout university, and when I moved into Gill's I discovered that he was renting a flat close by. He was my closest friend; perhaps my only friend. More than anyone else, he seemed to understand how I could spend so much of my time surrounded by the same four walls. If anything Ray saw even less of the outside world than I did. In between joints he designed websites, a profession for which he appeared to have a happy knack, and which paid him obscenely well.

Reaching down behind the arm of the sofa, Ray brought up a wooden box and began neatly laying out cigarette papers and filter tips, tobacco and a plastic packet stuffed with marijuana. Suddenly he had come alive, his fingers dancing across the delicate papers as he deftly sprinkled them with pungent buds. I paced up and down the room as he rolled, telling him about my eventful last few hours – the shocking assault in my bath, Diana's entrance, the confrontation at the hotel. Although Ray nodded occasionally to prove that he was listening, I knew for a fact that most of the information I told him would slip through the blim burns in his cerebral cortex. Still, talking aloud helped me order my thoughts.

Once his joint had been rolled into a scrupulously thin cylinder, Ray lit it and inhaled deeply. Then he picked up his laptop and began to type.

"What are you doing?" I asked.

"You said this girl was doing some kind of charity benefit, yeah? What was the dance again?"

"Something from *Giselle*, she said."

"Right…" Ray tapped on the keyboard. "And that's a ballet, right?"

"Yes, Ray."

"OK…" He took a thoughtful toot. "And this girl's name…?"

"Jesus Christ, Ray, it's Diana. Diana Mayweather. Do you want me to write it down for you?"

"Calm down. I've found a video of her."

I stopped scratching. "What? How?"

"The magic of the 21st century, my friend – mobile phone cameras, video sharing sites… electricity…"

He turned the laptop around and, sure enough, there was a video of Diana dancing across the stage. She was dressed in medieval clothes, with a white skirt and bodice, her red hair trussed up in a bun. To see Diana merely walk into Gill's lounge was to appreciate the graceful potential of movement, but this was something else entirely – a lyrical expression of years of training, of pointe and bend and leap, of endless stretches at the barre, the constant terse correction of the slightest misstep or quiver of muscle.

"This is her?" Ray let out a low whistle. "Nice."

"I didn't realize you were a ballet fan."

"For her I'll make an exception."

Diana exploded into a series of spins, whirling faster and faster, her skirt billowing out around her waist as the crowd erupted into cheers. Then, suddenly, it was over, and she swept to the floor in a graceful bow. There was prolonged applause, and a bouquet of roses was flung on to the stage. Diana picked them up and blew a kiss to the crowd, before the video cut away and suddenly we were watching dignitaries glad-handing each other after the performance.

"So there we have our damsel in distress," Ray said theatrically. "Now for the dastardly bad guy. Who did you say was the guy who was after her?"

"Oscar Salazar."

"Got you." He balanced his joint on the lip of an ashtray and began to type, his fingers blurring across the keyboard. Ray's hands were a photo negative of Diana's feet – blessed with a nimble dexterity of which the rest of his lumbering body parts could only dream.

He whistled softly.

"What is it?" I asked.

"You've got to see this."

He showed me the laptop screen again, which was now displaying a wall of photographs of Oscar Salazar. If I had been expecting Diana's suitor to be some kind of wizened, greasy-palmed Rumpelstiltskin, I was to be disappointed. Oscar was a tall, olive-skinned man with gleaming white teeth and jet-black hair, heading towards middle age with a confidence born of success in the boardroom and on the tennis court. Many of the pictures appeared to have been taken on board a luxury yacht, the sea breeze ruffling Oscar's hair as he stared out over the ocean. His life looked like a series of Duran Duran videos.

But it was the women who demanded my attention.

In every photo, a different star graced Salazar's arm – an actress at the premiere, a singer at the awards, a model at the grand prix. Yet somehow they were all the same: tall, slender, impossibly beautiful, and hair in glorious shades of red; deep, husky hues of ginger, copper, auburn and saffron. A Red-Headed League; a Red Sea; a Red Army, haughtily parading their firepower in front of the world's camera lenses.

"OK," said Ray, blowing smoke rings into the air. "He's definitely got a type. And you're sure Diana's not interested?"

"She's already got a boyfriend. She doesn't need another." I gave him a sideways glance. "Why, you think she should reconsider?"

Ray shrugged. "He's rich, he's powerful, he's good looking. *I'm* thinking about sleeping with him."

"You'd have to dye your hair first."

"I'd imagine there'd be shaving involved too."

He stubbed out his joint, looking at me inquisitively. It was only then that I realized I was furiously scratching my elbow.

"You all right?" asked Ray.

"Yeah. Fine." I gave him what I hoped was a winning smile. "But do you mind if I use your bath?"

. . .

When the Spanish conquistadors landed in Mesoamerica in the 15th and 16th centuries, they were baffled by the small, igloo-like stone huts they found in every village. Eventually they learned that the structures were steam baths known as temazcals. Centres for hygiene, healthcare and treatment, temazcals played a vital role in Mesoamerican life. Inside the stone huts volcanic stones were heated to extreme temperatures before being doused with water, filling the hut with billowing steam that was believed to help in the treatment of an astonishing array of illness, from coughs and back pain to broken bones and leprosy. The baths even had their own goddess, Temazcalteci – literally, 'the grandmother of the steam bath'.

The Spanish simply could not comprehend this. In the Europe of the later Middle Ages, bathing was considered not just unnecessary but actively unhealthy, a significant factor in the spread of immorality and diseases such as syphilis. What was worse, Aztec men and the women shared the steam baths, presenting – to Spanish minds, at least – all manner of licentious opportunity in the sweaty, fervid darkness. In 1546, Emperor Charles V set down an order forbidding healthy Aztecs from using the steam baths. This was more than just an act of moral Puritanism, it was an attempt to sever the link between the Aztecs and Temazcalteci. By removing the temazcals from Aztec life, the conquerors were – symbolically speaking – trying to rip out the wombs of Mesoamerica.

The Spanish were able to bring the area under heel with astonishing speed. But this was due less to the invaders' military organization than the invisible weapons they carried into battle: European diseases such as small-pox, chickenpox, and measles. Lacking the immune systems to ward off these alien diseases, the local population was devastated by epidemics. A fundamental contradiction lay at the heart of the European conquests: they strode into villages, dirty and sweaty, enveloped in musk and body odour, cloaked in disease, and set about trying to 'clean up' the local population...

...

I felt better almost as soon as I closed the bathroom door behind me. Usually I wouldn't have imposed on someone's hospitality in this way, but the *Dermatitis Herpetiformis* was stubbornly refusing to die down and I knew I could rely on Ray's bath to be clean. True to form, the bathroom was as spotless as the front room: the tiles a pearly American smile, shower gel and shampoo bottles aligned with military precision. The only drawback was the lack of a lock on the door, but then again I wasn't expecting company.

I ran a shallow, emergency bath, climbing in before it was barely an inch deep and turning the taps on full. As the tide rose I retrieved the bar of pink soap from my trouser pocket and removed it from the plastic wrapper. I ran my finger thoughtfully over the small heart that had been carved into one side, inhaling the tangy perfume. Seized by a sudden brainwave, I sliced open the bar with a razor blade I found in the bathroom cabinet, but there were no secrets hidden within its core. Whatever message the Japanese girl was trying to give me had been lost in translation.

It wasn't all bad news, though. The soap produced a luxurious lather that covered me like a silk skin, quieting my rebellious rashes. I was hit by a sudden, unsettling thought: was it possible that I been selected precisely because of my condition? Perhaps the Japanese girl was the glamorous front of a shadowy government agency engaged in germ warfare. Was I a hapless guinea pig testing out an antidote? Was Imperial Leather a codename?

I lay back in the bath, allowing the distant chatter of Welsh voices in the living room to wash over me. All thoughts of ballet dancers and businessmen began to slip blissfully from my mind. Nothing seemed to matter any more. I lay back and let the steam rising up from the water overwhelm me.

There was a knock at the bathroom door and a voice asked, in an atrocious Welsh accent:

"Nice bath there, boyo?"

"Lovely. Thanks."

"Found something on the net, boyo. Thought you should see."

"I'll be out in a minute."

But the door was already opening. Ray stumbled into the bathroom, his head turned away and a hand clasped over his eyes. In his other hand he held out his mobile phone.

"Really, Ray?" I sighed. "It couldn't wait?"

He thrust the phone towards me insistently.

"Look!"

Wiping my hands on a towel, I reached up and took his phone. It was showing an article from the website of a Russian-language newspaper, with a glossy holiday photo in the middle of the page.

"I Googled the other dancer," Ray explained. "The Russian bloke Diana likes."

Sure enough, the man in the photo was Yuri Ivanov. He was standing on a Caribbean beach, in a white shirt and pale chinos. Lilia Kutznetsova was beside him, in a white dress that cut off at the knee, a triumphant grin upon her face. In between them stood a short, bull-headed man with a beard, his arms draped around the couple's shoulders. Yuri was holding a champagne flute, and Lilia clasped a bouquet of flowers. Suddenly I twigged. This wasn't any old holiday snap. This was a wedding photo.

I glanced up at Ray, who was playing peek-a-boo with his reflection in the mirror above the sink and giggling.

"When was this photo taken?"

"Mm?" He broke off from the mirror. "Oh, about four weeks ago."

No wonder Lilia had been so angry. She'd only been married a month, and already her husband was cheating on her.

URIAH THE HITTITE IS DEAD

"All I'm saying is, you might have mentioned it."

I leant forward as I spoke, unwilling to raise my voice above a whisper. The atmosphere in the half-deserted theatre café was heavy with frowns, lips poised in the shape of a shush. A spoon clinked at the table next to us as a middle-aged woman with an aggressively large handbag stirred her tea. The café walls were covered in moody black-and-white portraits of dancers – lithe, muscular figures springing from the shadows, their limbs dramatized in taut poses like punctuation marks. Through the windows, banners trumpeting an upcoming production of *Coppelia* rippled in the soft breeze above the street.

Diana shrugged. She was sitting on the opposite side of the table, dressed in a shapeless blue sweater that hung off one shoulder, matching grey vest top and shorts, and a pair of black tights. Her hair was tied back, her feet stowed away in a pair of scuffed ballet shoes. Beads of perspiration glistened on her forehead and her cheeks were flushed from exertion, her pale skin turning a shade somewhere in-between a self-conscious blush and a defiant glow.

"I don't see what difference it makes," Diana said. "Oscar's the problem, not Yuri. Now if you found *he* was married, that would be a different story."

She flipped up the top on her water bottle and took a deep swig. A stray droplet escaped down her neck, glistening as it travelled down her pulsing throat before disappearing inside her vest top. Diana put down the bottle and wiped the back of her hand across her mouth. Every movement she made seemed to be a performance, or a promise, of sorts.

"The problem *is*," I told Diana patiently, "is that you told me you didn't know where Yuri was, then you walked straight out of the door and went to meet him. You lied to me. How can I be sure you're telling the truth about the other things you said – about Oscar, for example?"

"Like, does he even exist?" added Ray, meaningfully.

I rubbed my temple. "I think we can be *fairly* sure Oscar exists, Ray. Remember all those photos we saw of him?"

Perhaps bringing Ray had been a mistake. His eyelids were drooping even lower than usual, as he struggled with the aftermath of five joints, a large Hawaiian pizza with extra ham, a packet of bourbon creams, and twelve episodes of *Pobol y Cwm*. By the time I had climbed out of his bath and he had finished smoking the pair of us were too fatigued to speak, and I had awoken that morning on his sofa. I went to the kitchen to phone Diana, closing the door to drown out the roar of Ray's handheld hoover as it sucked up biscuit crumbs and stray flakes of tobacco from the living room carpet. I was surprised when he volunteered to come with me – Ray didn't leave his flat without good reason. Perhaps he liked the *Giselle* video even more than he let on. Diana hadn't appeared overly impressed to meet him, but then again she didn't seem exactly delighted with me either.

"I still don't see why you were following me," she said defensively, as the woman at the neighbouring table took a loud slurp from her tea. "I never said you could do that."

"You wanted me to help you," I replied, as gently as possible. "I can't do that if I don't know the whole story. Yuri's wife Lilia, the dancer you replaced at the charity gala – she's a principal dancer with the Chicago Ballet. That's why you had to leave America. It wasn't anything to do with artistic differences at all, was it?"

Diana let out a long sigh, and then nodded her head in defeat. "Lilia Kuznetsova is one of the most famous prima ballerinas in the world. I'm just another face in the *corps*. As soon as she found out about me and Yuri I was finished in Chicago. It didn't matter who was right or who was wrong."

She produced a scrunched-up tissue from somewhere inside her sleeve and blew her nose. Over Diana's shoulder, the lady with the giant handbag started talking on her mobile, asking for the latest tennis scores from Eastbourne in the manner of an Obergrüppenfuhrer demanding news of Allied advances.

"It was probably you, though, wasn't it?" Ray said thoughtfully. "In the wrong, I mean. Given that Yuri married Lilia and not you."

I made a mental note not to let Ray out of his flat again.

"It might seem that way – if you didn't know anything about the situation," Diana said frostily. "Yuri may have married Lilia but he doesn't love her. The truth is, Yuri's not very good with money and he got himself in a bit of a hole in America. Lilia was able to help him with that. Her price was marriage, but I'm the one Yuri loves. He was with me two nights after they got back from Bermuda, for heaven's sake! Telling me how miserable he is, how Lilia has this violent temper, how she hits him. They'll be finished by the end of the year, take my word for it. And then we'll be together properly."

She blew her nose again.

"Summer cold?" I inquired.

Diana shook her head. "Hay fever. It's all the flowers Oscar bought me. My flat's like a pollen time-bomb."

"Maybe you could throw them away?" suggested Ray.

"They're too beautiful," she replied sadly. "I can't bring myself to do it. I think he knew that when he sent them."

I hurriedly leapt in before Ray could say anything else. "At least you've been able to dance today!" I tried brightly. "It must be a good sign if the Walker are letting you use their studio."

Diana toyed with her tissue, looking slightly discomforted for the first time "Well, apparently Oscar put a word in for me, and I needed the rehearsal space, so…"

"You know, Diana," I said, sucking in through my teeth, "if Oscar knows that you're keeping his flowers, and accepting his help, there's a chance he might think he's getting…"

"Mixed messages?" tried Ray.

"Exactly," I said. "Mixed messages."

Diana laughed incredulously. "I've told Oscar I've got a boyfriend and I'm not in the slightest bit interested in him. How confusing is that?"

"I know, but—"

"Edgar, I know all this probably sounds crazy, and I'm sorry I didn't tell you everything yesterday. But you have to understand that Oscar is threatening the only two things I care about in the world. When I first saw Yuri dancing Siegfried at the Met it was… indescribable. I felt breathless and helpless and giddy all at the same time. The only time I've ever experienced the same intense feeling has been dancing on stage. People love to say how *passionate* they are about their hobbies – about cooking, or reading, even watching bloody football matches. But ballet is more to me than a passion. It's a fire, an inferno that burns right here" – she pressed a hand over her heart – "so strong that I can feel it, so strong it almost hurts me. And if I don't feed the flame it will burn out, and all that will be left inside me will be soot and ash. Can you understand that, Edgar? Have you ever wanted anything that much?"

I think I had an idea.

. . .

Jayne Mansfield's journey from a Texas acting class to a Hollywood movie-set was a calculated series of photo opportunities, public wardrobe malfunctions and pageants, a campaign as finely calibrated as an underwired bra. She was the Babe Ruth of the beauty contest, the Sultan of Swimwear. Ladies and Gentlemen, Please Be Upstanding for this Non-Exhaustive List of her Pageant Titles…

Miss Photoflash, Miss Fourth of July, Princess of the Freeways, Miss Magnesium Lamp, Miss Third Platoon, Gas Station Queen, Miss Blue Bonnet Belle, Miss Direct Mail, Queen of Refrigeration Week, Miss 100% Pure Maple Syrup, Miss Negligee, Queen Cotton, Miss Standard Foods, Miss Tomato, Cherry Blossom Queen, Miss Lobster, Miss Electric Switch, Queen of Palm Springs Desert Rodeo, Queen of the Chihuahua Show, Miss Fire Alarm, Miss Orchid, Miss Fire Prevention Week, Miss One for the Road…

On and on the list winds, like a road trip, or a beat poem… Miss Nylon Sweater, with her chest a landscape of eye-popping contours… Miss Geiger Counter, sending needles into a clicking frenzy… The Hot Dog Ambassador, handling wieners for the boys. Jayne Mansfield hovered over magazine stands like a UFO, casting her unmistakable shadow across the centerfolds. Her IQ was thought to be in the 160s, up there with the chess players and theoretical physicists, but as the actress herself pointed out, the public were more interested in her figure measurements – which were published amid feverish speculation, as though they were the combination to the vaults of Fort Knox.

And didn't she just love it?… Miss Behaviour, hijacking a promotional event for the Jane Russell flick *Underwater*, her overworked swimsuit exposing her breasts to breathtaken journalists… Miss Chief, her nude spread in the February 1955 edition of *Playboy* single-handedly increasing the magazine's circulation… Miss America, teetering and jiggling her way through Hollywood films like *The Girl Can't Help It*, following the Yellow Brick Road all the way to her 40-room mansion in Beverley Hills.

Which is not to say that Mansfield didn't have her limits. She did turn down one beauty title – Miss Roquefort Cheese. Yet there remains a faint lingering odour about her career, a sense that for all her success not everything was quite how it should have been. Perhaps it was Mansfield's death in an horrific automobile accident; or maybe it was her fragile smile, which hinted that she needed thicker armour than a draping of pageant sashes. Somewhere along the line, had the girl who couldn't help it made a terrible Miss Take?

…

Diana sat back in her chair and took another long, deliberate sip of water.

"Have you talked to Yuri about Oscar?" I asked her.

Diana's face darkened. "I didn't need to. The bastard told Yuri himself."

"What?"

"Two nights before I came to see you Yuri went to dinner with Oscar. Everyone knows that Yuri's contract with the Met is up soon, and the Walker won't be the only company trying to persuade him to sign with them. Only it turned out that Oscar wasn't there to talk about ballet. Instead he got Yuri drunk on champagne and took him to a club he owns."

"That doesn't sound *so* bad," said Ray.

"The kind of club where women take their clothes off."

"Ah."

"Believe me, I know what those kind of places are like, especially around men like Oscar. The girls drape themselves over them, whispering all sorts of promises and invitations into their ears. But Yuri wouldn't touch them." Diana smiled proudly. "He loves me too much."

She caught Ray and I exchanging a dubious look.

"And you needn't think I'm some silly woman who'll believe anything her boyfriend tells her," Diana said sharply. "Oscar told me himself, would you believe. He wanted me to know the effort he was going to in order to break us up." She snorted. "As if resorting to such… *lies* and *deceit* are going to make me fall in love with him. He's crazy."

"They say love can make people do strange things," I offered weakly.

"How strange, exactly?" Diana leant across the table, dropping her voice. "I know it sounds paranoid, but when Yuri and I were together in Chicago I was sure that someone was following us. And now we're back in London, I've seen the same car a couple of times."

"Car? What kind of car?"

"A black people carrier." Diana smiled ruefully. "I know, I know, there's a few of them about in London – I'm not *completely* paranoid. But I am convinced someone's watching me. Oscar's already stooped pretty low and I'm worried he's not done yet…"

As she trailed off into meaningful silence her tasselled bag let out a loud electronic chirrup, startling Ray. Diana fished out her mobile phone and checked the caller ID.

"I have to get this," she said. "Excuse me."

She rose from the table and went over to an empty corner of the café, her voice dropping to a conspiratorial whisper. I nudged Ray in the ribs.

"What do you think?"

"I'd kill for some breakfast."

"About Diana!"

"Oh. Yeah, she's hot. Not sure how much I trust her, though." He rubbed his eyes. "How's Gill doing?"

"Hmm?"

"Your sister."

"Thank you, Ray, I know who she is," I said testily. "She's pretty pissed off, if you must know. She split up with Richard."

"Good. He sounded like a tosser."

"No arguments there."

Apparently satisfied, Ray wandered over to the canteen in search of food, leaving me alone at the table. Diana was still deep in conversation on the phone. Her back was turned to me, and I couldn't help following the line of her exposed shoulder, a pale ridge dappled with freckles and still glinting with droplets of moisture. Something about my guilty glance felt strangely familiar, a distant echo from my teenage years.

"Lovely thing, isn't she?" a voice boomed in my ear. I looked up to find that the woman from the next table was standing at my shoulder, following my gaze. She must have been in her fifties, small with a comfortably rotund figure and grey streaks in her black hair.

"The name's Margery," she told me, without preamble. "Margery Connors."

"Edgar Mallender."

"Charmed."

"You know Diana?"

"I make it my business to know all the interesting dancers. I first saw her in the Walker's production of *The Nutcracker*... ooh, must have been five years ago. I'd dragged my boy along with me – he complained all the way to the theatre, but as soon as he saw Diana he soon shut up."

"She's a really good dancer."

"That's not quite what I mean, young man, but I appreciate your delicacy. Diana's not the most precise of dancers, and her pointe work lacks finesse, but she's more than competent. That won't help her here though, I'm afraid."

"What do you mean?"

"Your friend has a reputation that precedes her."

"With men, you mean?"

Margery nodded gravely. "She'll fuck anything that moves, my dear."

"Oh. Right."

"I mean, there were rumours when she started out in London, but there always are in ballet, especially when the girl is as pretty as young Diana there. But then she left London for America, and the rumours kept on coming... Don't get me wrong, she's a lovely girl. Lovely. But she rubs the other girls the wrong way, especially the Eastern Europeans. They're so serious, they don't appreciate a frisky British filly."

"I wouldn't know."

Margery gave me a perplexed look.

"You haven't had the pleasure yet?"

"No, I didn't mean—"

"Give it time, dear boy. I'll wager you won't be waiting long."

Margery winked and patted me on the hand, before bustling out of the café. I was so startled that it took me a few seconds to acknowledge that Diana had appeared in her stead. Her lip was trembling, and her eyes glimmered with tears.

"What is it?" I ask. "What's wrong?"

"It's Yuri! He's been hit!"

. . .

If King David believed that his liaison with Bathsheba would have no consequences, then the news that she had fallen pregnant soon set him straight. At once David ordered the return of her husband, Uriah the Hittite, from the Israelite siege of Rabbah. Had the king's slumbering conscience awoken – did he intend to confess his transgression to Uriah, and seek the soldier's forgiveness?

Not *exactly*.

In fact, David's hope in recalling Uriah to Jerusalem was that the Hittite would sleep with Bathsheba, thus forestalling any suggestions of impropriety when his wife's baby made its presence known. But to the king's chagrin, Uriah chose to stay at the palace rather than his house, arguing that whilst his comrades-in-arms remained in camp it was unseemly that he alone should enjoy marital comforts. The entire exchange served as a pointed reminder that the Israelites were still at war with the Ammonites. Why was Joab in command, not David? Why had the king – himself a war hero, the slayer of mighty Goliath – chosen to linger in Jerusalem with the women and the children?

Faced with such implacable principles, David adopted a time-honoured tactic: he invited Uriah to a feast and got him drunk. Yet still the high-minded Hittite refused to go home! (By this stage the cynical onlooker could be forgiven for wondering whether the lady in question was really as beautiful as the Bible suggests. Was Bathsheba's allure dimmed by a pimply backside or a thick moustache upon her upper lip, or perhaps a pair of lumpen, knobbly feet?)

In despair, David sent Uriah back to the front bearing an order to his commander to place the Hittite in the fiercest of the battle by the city walls and abandon him. Finally the king's cunning was rewarded, and a messenger returned to Jerusalem with the news that he had been longing to hear: Uriah had been killed. The plan had worked, albeit at the cost of other innocent soldiers who had been sucked into Uriah's suicide mission. With the Hittite's death, David was free to take Bathsheba as his wife – and indeed, bask in the acclaim he received for taking care of a widow.

But if David's subjects were fooled, then God was not. The son Bathsheba eventually bore died as punishment to both father *and* mother. With regard to the matter of blame in this grubby tale of treachery and infidelity, the Lord chose not to differentiate.

. . .

"I'm going to kill him."

Diana threw her phone and her water bottle into her tan bag and slung it over her shoulder. She untied her hair, shaking it out until the strands fell like molten fire down over her face.

"Wait!" I grabbed her arm, catching her before she could storm away. "Kill who? What's happened?"

"That was one of Yuri's friends on the phone. There was a hit-and-run outside the hotel last night. Yuri was crossing the street." Diana gulped back a sob. "He didn't see the car coming."

"Jesus! Is he OK?"

"I don't know. The hospital aren't allowing visitors. Apparently he's got broken bones, head injuries... it's really serious. I'm going to make Oscar pay for this."

"Hang on a minute. You think Oscar was behind this?"

"Hello, Edgar?" Diana said sarcastically, waving a hand in front of my face. "First Lilia gets tipped off that we're together and now Yuri gets hit by a car! Are you not sensing a pattern here?"

"All I'm saying is, you don't know that for certain."

"I know all I need to know," she replied stubbornly. "I'm going to meet Yuri's friend. I'll see you tomorrow night."

"Tomorrow night?" I called after her retreating figure, as she threaded her way out through the empty tables.

"At La Baignoire Pleine. With Oscar."

"You're still going?"

"Damn right I'm going," replied Diana, over her shoulder. "And you're coming with me."

SLEEPING WITH THE ENEMY

It wasn't the menu that told you that La Baignoire Pleine was a high-class establishment. It was the space. There were only about ten tables in the entire restaurant, and it wasn't a small room. Vast boulevards ran between each table, wide expanses of ocean. The message was clear: every person who walked through the door was special. Even me.

Diana had dressed for a funeral, in a simple black dress without make-up or jewellery. She wanted Oscar to know that she hadn't made an effort. Yet as little as she had tried, her beauty betrayed her. As I escorted Diana through the restaurant I noticed the glances I received from the male diners: a pinch of jealousy, a squeeze of respect, a dollop of utter bafflement. I had done my best to look respectable, bathing thoroughly before squeezing into an old suit. My hair was combed and my fingernails were clean. Yet I felt like a fraud as I followed the waiter through the restaurant, towards a booth near the open-plan kitchen where Oscar Salazar awaited us.

The photos I had seen on the internet didn't quite do him justice. Dressed in a midnight-black shirt and pale chinos, Oscar was certainly no less handsome in the flesh. But he also possessed a feline grace that revealed itself in the smallest of gestures, the arch of an eyebrow or the checking of a watch. If he was surprised or disappointed by my appearance, Oscar was too smooth to let it show. Another actor, I thought to myself darkly. He stood up and took Diana's hand, kissing her on both cheeks, unaffected by her icily polite reception. Then he took my hand and shook it warmly, treating me to a brilliant smile.

"A pleasure to meet you, Edgar," he said. "I confess I am jealous of you. What I would give to be able to accompany such a beautiful woman to dinner."

Diana rolled her eyes.

"I was half-expecting Yuri to be here," continued Oscar. "Where is our Russian friend?"

"Recovering in hospital," said Diana. "*Someone* ran him over."

"What?" Oscar's eyes widened with surprise. "How horrible! Please, pass on to him my best wishes."

Diana was clenching the grip of her handbag so tightly that her knuckles had blanched. Fearing she was about to take a swing, I ushered her into her seat and we sat down. Oscar made an imperceptible gesture and suddenly a waiter was by his side, filling our glasses with red wine.

"Such a terrible affair," murmured Oscar. "I pray that Yuri's injuries are not serious. The maestro must dance again. Are you familiar with the ballet, Edgar?"

I shook my head.

"For me it is the pinnacle of all the arts. The music, the drama, the physicality, the fragility…" His dark brown eyes flicked towards Diana. "There are times when it takes my breath away."

"Dancers always appreciate an attentive audience," said Diana, evenly meeting his gaze.

"Attentive? Seeing you dance the *Giselle* solo I was positively spellbound," he told her. "I've been keeping my eye on you ever since. How is your search for work going?"

"I'm getting by," she said guardedly.

"Rest assured I will do everything I can to help you," smiled Oscar. "But times are hard, and the arts are more sensitive than business – they tend to flinch first when the heat is on. On the plus side, there are no question marks over your ability. I was talking with the Walker's artistic director about you the other night and he confirmed it."

"But there are question marks."

Oscar winced slightly. "Forgive me, it is not easy to talk about private matters. But you know there are concerns regarding your life off-stage, don't you?"

"Yuri, you mean."

"When his contract with the Met expires – and injuries permitting – I am convinced that he will join us here at the Walker. The fact is that Yuri is a married man. We cannot be seen to be encouraging any illicit affairs, especially as we hope to persuade Lilia to join him in London. To see the pair of them on stage together… it would make the Walker the preeminent ballet company in the world. Audiences would come from across the globe."

"So we have a problem," Diana said frostily. "No doubt you've got a solution."

"A solution? No. A suggestion? Perhaps. Perhaps if you could show that your personal life was more settled, then the Walker would be willing to hire you."

"Settled with you, you mean?"

Oscar shrugged. "It is your personal life, Diana, your heart. Your choice. I can only offer you advice. What you choose to do with it… The premiere of *Coppelia* is next week – why don't you accompany me and we'll discuss it further?"

He settled back in his chair and took a measured sip of wine, his gaze never once leaving her face. Half-expecting a cutting rebuff, I was taken aback by Diana's silence. She glanced over towards the kitchen, a pensive expression on her face.

She wasn't thinking about it, was she?

Diana bit her lip.

...

If I had to choose a famous woman to share my bath with me, I know exactly who'd I'd pick. Who else could it be but Julia Roberts? No one else occupies the intimate space of the bathtub so naturally, with such gauche loveliness. In the cinematic world, men bathe either out of necessity or for comic effect, women to display their sexuality or their vulnerability – preferably both. The poster for Roberts's 1991 thriller *Sleeping With The Enemy* is a classic example. She glances up from the bath at some out-of-shot disturbance, long-necked and gamine, an exotic, startled animal.

Pretty Woman is a different prospect altogether. A romantic drama in which a businessman pays a prostitute to have sex with him, the fact that audiences were willing to overlook the film's complicated sexual politics was largely down to Roberts's performance – a winning mixture of gawky charm and vulnerability. The film had been developed from a script entitled *$3,000*, which was a far darker and more bitter affair than the sugary confection that eventually made it into the multiplexes. Audiences were willing to accept Julia Roberts's character giving head for money, but they didn't want to see her lips around a crack pipe.

In the film's most memorable scene, businessman Edward Lewis (Richard Gere) is distracted from a work call by the sound of Vivian's (Roberts's) off-key singing. He enters his penthouse bathroom to find her in a giant tub filled with bubbles. She is listening to 'Kiss' by Prince on a walkman with her eyes closed, lost in luxury. It's impossible to begrudge Vivian her moment, especially as she's had to rent out her vagina like a hotel room to get it.

Unaware that she has company, Vivian is startled when she realizes Edward is watching her. He has decided that he isn't ready to send Vivian back out on the street just yet, and asks if he can hire her for a week. In the blink of an eye the bathroom becomes the boardroom, as Edward and Vivian haggle over how much he will have to pay to continue having sexual intercourse with her. Eventually settling upon $3,000 dollars, Vivian celebrates by submerging herself in the bath. She reappears with her face covered in white foam, drenched in Edward's largesse like sprayed champagne, or a money shot.

. . .

Diana excused herself and left the table for the bathroom, leaving Oscar and I facing each other across the table: two chess players, battling over an imperiled queen; two CEOs, disputing a hostile takeover; two generals at a peace conference, arguing over a disputed territory.

It was his fault I was starting to think this way, I swear.

Oscar smiled and topped up my wine.

"So you have known Diana for a long time?"

"We were childhood friends," I replied, stretching the truth a little.

"Are you in love with her?"

"No! Of course not!"

Oscar swilled my denial around in his mouth like a dubious Rioja before nodding in acceptance.

"But you care about her very much," he said. "As a friend. That is why you are here, no? To protect her?"

"If you want to put it like that."

"You cannot put a price on loyalty. In business, in life…" Oscar tapped the tips of his fingers together thoughtfully. "But let me ask you this: If you are Diana's friend, if you care about her so very much, why aren't you telling her to listen to me?"

"Excuse me?"

"Let us be realistic for a second. This infatuation with the Russian boy will pass when she realizes that Yuri will not leave his wife. But by then, maybe it is too late. Maybe silly old Oscar has got tired of being sniffed at like he is dog food. Diana will have nothing – no man, no career. This is not so good. But if she can be persuaded to listen to my offer… well, tomorrow she is dancing in the Walker, next weekend we are watching the tide come in from my father's restaurant in Cadiz. Not only does Diana get her career, but she also gets a man who can take care of her." Oscar took a delicate sip of wine. "I am not so bad a catch, I think."

"You're blackmailing her!" I said incredulously. "What kind of catch does that make you?"

"I am passionate, it's true. And I am used to getting what I want. That is how I am a successful man. Perhaps you would not understand. But you *should* understand that I will get what I want, and if I were you, I would not want to be standing in the way. I would find some other place to stand."

There was a loud shout from the front of restaurant, an explosion of shattered crockery. I turned in my seat to see my blond bathroom assailant looming over the *maitre d'*, a hand wrapped around his throat. The man was wearing the same T-shirt as before, only with the colours reversed – this time the word 'Suomi' was printed in white lettering on a blue background. The look of blank rage on his face was also instantly recognizable. Catching sight of me peering over the booth, the man roared and shoved the *maitre d'* out of his way.

Oscar raised an eyebrow. "A friend of yours?"

I was already up and running. With the front exit blocked, I had no choice but to hurdle the steps into the open-plan kitchen, ignoring the angry shouts from the head chef as I barged past her. I was enveloped in hot steam, assailed by the rattle of pans and the sizzle of frying meat. Colliding with a sous chef, I knocked a tray of cutlets to the floor; he swore at me but I was already hurtling away down the gangway. I didn't need to turn around to see if my giant nemesis was following me – the cacophony of clattering saucepans and indignant protests sufficient indication that he had entered the kitchen. Dodging a surprised waiter, I turned left at the end of the gangway and sprinted towards the emergency exit.

I skidded outside, finding myself in a narrow alleyway. At one end lay a busy West End street, light and noise spilling out from bars and restaurants, rickshaws navigating the hooting traffic. I went in the other direction, plunging deeper into the darkness, wading through piled-up rubbish bags towards a wheelie bin resting open against the restaurant wall. Spurred on by the crescendoing crashes from the kitchen, I jumped inside the bin and pulled the lid down over my head. Here, amid the smell and the filth, I would be safe.

...

Wafting up through the muck and the stink, comes the voice of the underground. Jean-Paul Marat was a physician, a scientist and a philosopher, who felt that the French Revolution had failed to deliver on its promise of greater equality for the people. In September 1789 Marat began publishing his journal *L'ami du Peuple* on an almost daily basis, in which he excoriated the ruling classes and called for mass executions. He threatened to set fire to the King, and impale the deputies of the Assembly upon their seats. Marat's rage was implacable, much to the delight of his working-class audience. When the authorities came to arrest him, Marat fled to the cellars and sewers beneath Paris like Jean Valjean, or a subterranean Quasimodo. There he continued to write, railing against the dark forces that had sent him scuttling underground.

Although the suspension of the monarchy in August 1792 allowed Marat to emerge blinking into the political spotlight, joining the legislative assembly known as the National Convention, his time in the sewers had left their mark. He had exacerbated an existing skin condition, and now a rash spread up from his groin, itching with such intensity that at times Marat felt as though he was on fire. His already dishevelled appearance turned into the gruesome visage of a fairytale villain.

Marat sought relief by immersing himself in the bathtub, his brow wrapped in a vinegar-soaked bandana. Using a board bridged across his tub as a writing desk, he continued to declaim and decry, his wrath centering on a moderate political faction known as the Girondists. Whilst the precise nature of Marat's condition eluded contemporary diagnosis, in recent years medical scholars have identified their prime suspect: *Dermatitis Herpetiformis*.

...

I felt like an ingredient in a giant, rancid stew. The bin bags had been punctured, spilling out innards of brown, rotting vegetables, rancid meat fat and fish bones. The stench was almost overpowering. As I held my breath there were rustles amongst the rubbish, tiny eyes glimmering in the darkness. I forced myself to remain still. The kitchen door banged open and loud footsteps clumped down the alleyway. The door opened once more, and I heard someone protesting in aggrieved French. I held my breath.

Finally the alleyway fell quiet. In the stillness I became aware of the tick-tock of high heels upon the pavement. The footsteps came to a stop beside my bin, and then a woman said, in a voice creased with amusement:

"You can come out now. It's safe."

Peering out from under the wheelie bin lid, I was startled to find myself face-to-face with the Japanese girl from the hotel lobby.

"Hello," she said.

"Hi."

"Having fun in there?"

"Not really."

I clambered awkwardly out of the bin, swinging my leg over the rim and nearly slipping when my foot landed on a scrap of fish skin. The girl waited patiently as I extricated myself from the rubbish. Poised on perilously tall heels like champagne glass stems, she was wearing a buttoned-up black coat that reached down to her knees. Her bright blue eye shadow hauled my attention back to her face, where her long dark hair tumbled around a pair of unfeasibly large hooped earrings.

"I'm Keiko," she told me, with an abbreviated wave.

"I'm Edgar."

"I know."

I looked up and down the alleyway. "Are you sure he's gone?"

"The Finn?"

"I didn't catch his name."

"The massive blond guy who looks like the Terminator? He went stomping off down the street. I don't think he likes you."

"The feeling's mutual," I replied, with feeling. "I remember you from the hotel the other day. Thanks for the soap."

"You're welcome. It was a shame you didn't use it."

"I did!" I protested, fishing out a crab claw from my jacket pocket. "It may not smell like it now, but I used it all last night. It lathered up beautifully."

Keiko looked at me in astonishment, and then burst out laughing.

"What's so funny?"

"Nothing," she said, with a shake of the head. "Nothing at all. But you are in *way* over your head, Edgar."

"What do you mean?"

"Maybe you think you can help Diana, but you're in more danger than she is."

So our meeting in the hotel hadn't been a coincidence after all. I supposed my theory that Keiko was an itinerant soap saleswoman might have been a bit far-fetched. There was definitely something about her, though, a mysterious glamour, a spy's intimation that she kept powerful secrets in her confidence.

"How do you know Diana?" I asked. "Is she a friend of yours?"

"Friend would be stretching it," replied Keiko. "I know her, though – or at least I used to. It's been a while since our paths crossed."

"So why are you following her now?"

Keiko raised a sculpted eyebrow. "Who said I was following Diana?"

Which opened up a whole new world of possibilities, none of which seemed remotely plausible. It's fair to say I was struggling to keep up with the pace of events. I needed to clean up and mentally regroup. I also needed to check that Diana was OK. God knows what she had made of my sudden exit.

"It was nice seeing you again," I told Keiko. "But I have go back to the restaurant now."

"Too late," she replied. "She's just left."

My heart sank inexplicably. "With Oscar?"

Keiko shook her head. "He's still in the toilet, mopping the wine from his face."

"Really?"

"Diana made quite an exit. Why don't you walk me to my car? It's parked around the corner."

She led me out of the alleyway and into the crowded street, past the open stares of the drinkers on a terraced bar. We must have made for an odd couple – a beautiful Japanese woman on five-inch heels and an unkempt man reeking of rotten meat. To add insult to injury, I could feel the rash on my lower back growling as Keiko retrieved her keys from her bag and unlocked a brand-new green Mini.

"Is there any chance you could give me another bar of soap?" I asked, scratching the base of my spine.

"I suppose I can spare one more." Keiko opened up her bag and handed me a small pink rectangle in a wrapper. "But you might want to use it properly this time."

"What other way is there?"

Keiko considered replying before shaking her head and climbing into her car. When she wound down the passenger door window I bent down and peered inside hopefully.

"I'm guessing there's no chance of a lift?"

"Absolutely none whatsoever," Keiko replied.

"Fair enough. Will I see you again?"

"Probably. Provided you take a bath in the meantime."

"I think you can rely on that."

With a wicked grin Keiko gunned the engine into life, and the Mini wheeled quickly away from the kerb. I watched the car veer into the night, thoughtfully turning the bar of soap over in my hands.

THROUGH THE KEYHOLE

The hot tap let out a happy hiccup as I staunched its flow and settled back into the water. The bathroom was covered in a gossamer haze, the mirror blushing white under the steam's caress. I was a weary wanderer, my aching limbs joyously accepting the hot water's embrace. I was an indulgent Southern lady, giddy on whiskey and self-delusion. I was a giggling barbarian in a tent filled with dreams.

The stench from the restaurant bins had long been washed away, my dirty clothes churning around inside the washing machine. At the last moment I had decided to use my own soap instead of the bar that Keiko had given me. It was clear that her soap had some other, higher purpose – if only I could figure out what that actually was. My time outside of the bathroom, marooned on dry land, had posed all manner of puzzles and unanswered questions. Although Diana seemed convinced that Oscar had been behind Yuri's hit-and-run, I wasn't so sure. It seemed somehow too boorish, too obvious an act for the sophisticated Spaniard. I found myself wondering where Lilia had been when her husband had been run over. I had seen with my own eyes the violence of the ballerina's temper – had she become so enraged with Yuri's philandering that she had taken swift and brutal revenge? I couldn't escape the feeling that I was playing a role in a drama in which everyone had read the script but me, and I feared dramatic twists further down the line. The temptation to hide out until the curtain fell was overwhelming.

I had tidied up the bathroom after my altercation with The Finn, picking up damp towels from the floor and rebuilding the fallen stacks of the Ulpian Library. At least the ring-binder files on the shelf by the sink had been out of harm's way – books could be replaced, my notes could not. As soon as this case was over I would start my novel, I promised myself, resting a board across my tub like Jean-Paul Marat and scribbling away as I soaked.

"Edgar? Are you in there?"

Hauling myself out of the bath, I wrapped a towel around my waist and opened the door a crack. Gill was standing in the corridor, a bemused expression on her face. In her hands she was holding an open envelope filled with twenty-pound notes.

"What's this?" she said.

"Five hundred pounds."

"OK… and what's it for?"

"Rent. Is that enough, or would you like some more?"

"Ed, it's fine. I just…" She gave the money another disbelieving look. "Where did you get this from?"

"Diana. She hired me to help her out with something."

"Really?" Gill blinked. "She said she'd talked to you but I thought she was joking."

"Couldn't be more serious."

"Right." Gill looked lost for words, which was almost worth the £500 alone. "Well, that's great, Ed. Thanks very much."

"My pleasure. How was work?"

"It's Saturday. Even I'm allowed a weekend occasionally." She paused. "Do you really not remember Diana? She said you weren't sure who she was. She came with us on holiday when you were about twelve."

I shrugged. "At that age your friends all looked the same to me."

"Even Diana? I'm surprised you didn't have a crush on her. Everyone has a bloody crush on Diana."

"She's not my type. And I think I'd be at the back of a rather long queue."

"You have no idea. I'm not quite sure what you're doing for her, but do take care, Ed. I love Diana but she has a habit of getting herself involved in… complicated situations."

"So people keep telling me."

"OK. As long as you know."

Belatedly detecting a waft of perfume, I inspected my sister more closely. Gill was wearing an asymmetric purple dress beneath a leather jacket, with matching purple high-heeled shoes. There was a blush of pink in her cheeks, and a brush of red in her lips. She looked great. Suspiciously great.

"You're going out somewhere," I said.

"Maybe." Gill shifted awkwardly. "I'm meeting Richard for a drink."

"Gill!"

"I know, I know! Don't worry, I'm not getting back with him or anything like that. But this break-up's hit Richard really hard. He says he hasn't taken any more coke, but I know he's been drinking a lot and I'm worried he's back on the painkillers."

"Painkillers?"

"He was in a bad car crash a few years ago," sighed Gill. "It put him in hospital for weeks. Richard being Richard, he struggled to get off the painkillers."

"Jesus, Gill! The guy's a walking addict!"

"I know! That's why I'm worried about him. His leg still gives him trouble now, and every time it flares I'm scared he'll get hooked on the painkillers again."

"He's an actor. A professional liar! He'd pretend to be terminally ill if he thought it'd work. Don't believe a bloody word he says."

"Hark at my little brother, leaping to my defence!" laughed Gill. "Don't worry, Ed, it's just a drink. I think I can handle it."

"It's a drink you've dressed up for."

"It's Saturday night! I can have some fun too, can't I? We can't all live like hermits." She peered over my shoulder inside the bathroom. "Ray not in there with you?"

"What do you mean?"

"Nothing. He's a funny boy, though. Loyal. Like a big shaggy dog."

"He was asking me about you."

"Really?"

"Yeah. He thinks Richard's a tosser too."

"Well Ray hasn't met him either, so neither of you know what you're talking about." As she stuffed the envelope into her bag, Gill pulled out a postcard and handed it to me.

"I forgot – this came for you. Hand delivered."

Everybody was trying to give me things these days. In the past 72 hours alone I had acquired two bars of soap, £700 and a pair of scalded testicles. Thankfully this was just a postcard. On the front there was a painting of a naked woman sitting in a chair, towelling herself dry. Her back was turned to the artist, her face obscured, a flicker of red hair just visible above her towel. A dark shadow ran down the woman's back like a bruise.

Gill frowned. "I'm not sure I like that painting."

"It's *After the Bath, Woman Drying Herself*," I told her. "By Degas."

"I didn't know you were such an art buff," said Gill, impressed.

I'm not. But I know what I like.

. . .

Twenty-one paintings by Edgar Degas:

The Bath; The Tub; The Morning Bath; The Toilet; La Toilette; The hygiene; Woman in the Bath; Woman Washing in the Bath; Woman in her Bath, Sponging her Leg; Woman Washing Her Feet; Leaving the Bath; After the Bath; After the Bath, Woman with a Towel; After the Bath, Woman Drying Herself; After the Bath, Woman Drying her Neck; After the Bath – Woman Drying her Feet; After Bathing, Woman Drying Her Leg; After the Bath, Woman Drying Her Hair; After the Bath, or Reclining Nude; Woman in a Blue Dressing Gown, Torso Exposed; Breakfast after the Bath...

. . .

Long after Gill had left the flat I sat on the edge of the bath staring at the postcard. I recognized the handwriting on the reverse from the Degas postcard Diana had received. He may not have signed it, but Oscar Salazar's fingerprints were unmistakable. Next to my forename he had written a web address – there was nothing else on the card. A wave of foreboding came over me, and I let the water out of the bath and dried myself. By the time I went through into the living room the windows were dark; I closed the blinds and flicked on a lamp before setting up my laptop and typing the address into a web browser.

The screen went blank, and at first I thought I had made a mistake. Then a small box flashed up asking for a five-letter password. I clucked my tongue with annoyance, and typed in OSCAR. The screen flashed red, and the box reset. Wrong guess. Where was Ray when you actually needed him? I checked the postcard again to see if I had missed something but there was no password – only my name and the web address. As I stared at the woman towelling her hair a thought occurred to me: I typed in DEGAS, only for the screen to go red a second time. A message flashed up, informing me that I had only one attempt left. I had to think clearly. There would have been no point in Oscar sending me the card if he hadn't been sure I would get the password. It had to be something obvious. I looked again at the painting, and then my name on the card. Then, with a shrug, I typed in EDGAR. Immediately the password box dissolved and an hourglass icon appeared on the screen. I was in.

The hourglass stopped turning, and I found myself viewing a flat on closed-circuit television. The picture was split up into four quarters, each providing a fly-on-the-wall perspective of a different room: the lounge, the bedroom, the kitchen and the bathroom. The flat was dark and sullen, every room empty. I couldn't make out any clues to its owner in the gloom. Why had Oscar led me here?

I didn't have to wait long for an answer. The front door opened, spilling light into the room, and a woman entered, dropping her keys into a bowl by the door. Her face was obscured by the darkness, but I could see that she was dressed for a meeting, in a blouse and knee-length skirt. She kicked off her shoes and walked over to the lamp stand, easily navigating the dark lounge. Then she turned on the light.

Perhaps I shouldn't have been surprised. My heart pounding, I watched Diana as she straightened up and began to unbutton her blouse.

. . .

Degas was hardly the first painter to see the artistic potential in women bathing. His forebears of the Renaissance had long used Biblical figures like Bathsheba and Susannah to portray classical nudes with a religious seal of approval – naughty pictures slipped inside a hymnbook. Amongst Degas' contemporaries there were the saucy postcards of Anders Zorn's voluptuous nudes, Lawrence Alma-Tadema's schoolboy peeks of Roman bathers, and the stark black-and-white skin tones of Jean-Leon Gerome's Moorish bathhouses. But whereas many of these works indulged themselves in fantasy Degas was down-to-earth, clinical. He liked his female subjects to be hard at work; he saw more beauty in a yawning laundress than a reclining goddess. The one sight more appealing to Degas than a woman scrubbing herself in the tub was a woman scrubbing the tub clean afterwards. He presented his scenes as though he had just stumbled across them: the artist as sly onlooker, or something a little more unsettling:

> "Hitherto the nude has always been represented in poses which presuppose an audience, but these women of mine are honest, simple folk... Here is another; she is washing her feet. It is as if you looked through a key-hole."[6]

A perennial outsider, Degas made for a perfect voyeur – if only in artistic terms, at least. He claimed to have no personal life, and shunned company. Despite being regarded as being a forefather of the Impressionist movement, Degas rejected such labels. Unlike many of his lusty peers, there was no string of affairs. He kept himself at a rigorous distance from women – the better, one might assume, to observe them...

. . .

Diana took off her blouse without ceremony, tossing it over the back of a chair and revealing a small white bra underneath. Kneading her left shoulder with her right hand, she wandered into the bathroom and began to run a bath, pouring a generous helping of bubble bath into the steaming water. As the foam mushroomed Diana pinned up her hair and peered into the mirror, examining the shadows beneath her eyes and squeezing a couple of stray blackheads.

---

6 George Moore, *Impressions and Opinions* (Charles Scribner's Sons, 1891), p.318

I sat back in astonishment. "I've been keeping my eye on you," Oscar had told Diana. He hadn't been kidding. Somehow it appeared that he had managed to plant a network of cameras in her flat without her knowledge. Was it really possible? Diana sent a jet of cold water into the tub and swirled the foamy water around. Unzipping her skirt, she let it fall to the floor and stepped out of it in a matter-of-fact manner that gave me a guilty shiver of pleasure. Her underwear didn't match but I barely noticed, my eyes too busy devouring the long lines of her legs.

I tore my gaze from the screen just long enough to pick up my phone and scroll through my address book. But at Diana's name, my finger froze on the call button. For the life of me I couldn't understand why Oscar had let me in on his dirty secret. As soon as I called Diana his little game would be over for good. Was he so unmanned by what happened at the restaurant that he felt the need to show off, to brag about the size of his telephoto lens? Surely he knew that I'd tell Diana immediately?

Diana unhooked her bra, revealing two pale handfuls of breasts.

Of course I'd tell her immediately. In fact, I was going to call her right now.

A CASUAL OUTBURST OF RAGE

My bath lay empty, its taps strangled, the plug stranded in the middle of a vast white desert. Curtis sat becalmed by the side of the tub, slumped against a dish of congealing soap. I hadn't bathed since the discovery of the video feed from Diana's flat. I hadn't eaten. I hadn't slept. I hadn't changed my clothes. How long had it been? I had no idea. All my attention had been focused on the computer screen, on the four corners of Diana's world.

I watched Diana as she bathed, slipping her naked limbs into the deep water and enveloping herself in bubbles. She scrubbed her skin until it turned pink, then lovingly applied soft oils until every sumptuous inch of flesh glistened. After her bath I watched Diana as she dried herself off, trying in vain to keep my eyes from her breasts and the small patch of fuzz between her legs. She put on a white dressing gown and padded through into the kitchen to pour herself a glass of wine, and then I watched her as she watched a film in the lounge, her expression one of rapt concentration. Then I watched Diana as she slept, in a loose-fitting shirt and a small pair of shorts, the duvet thrown back in surrender to the sultry night, the softest of exhalations escaping from her lips.

I despised myself for every second. My mobile was never far from my hand; twice, I steeled myself to call her, only to be distracted at the last second by a sudden giggle or a glimpse of flesh. Not everything that Diana did was necessarily erotic – in the morning she munched loudly on her cereal as she watched music videos, and burped after a large gulp of orange juice; afterwards she hummed tunelessly as she washed up the dishes – but taken as a whole, as a *life*, it was utterly hypnotic. I scuttled away to my bedroom, where I knew that I wouldn't be disturbed. At one point I heard Gill return to the flat; when there was no reply to her knocks on the bathroom door, she must have assumed I was out, as she didn't bother trying my bedroom.

Deep down, I knew I had to put an end to this. I was tired, dirty, and consumed by self-loathing. I cursed Oscar for sending me the link. No doubt he'd already moved on to another girl, an auburn-haired TV presenter or a ginger gymnast, leaving me transfixed here alone. If only I could turn off the computer! Every time I tried to leave Diana did something to make me stay. Even now, I saw that the shower was running, and Diana was pulling her T-shirt up over her head...

...

Throughout the centuries women have filled their bathtubs with hope, viewing them not just as cleansing retreats, but magical chambers for renewal and regeneration. Skin could be more than cleaned; it could be smoothed and softened, made to look younger. Beauty regimes became zealous crusades that demanded greater firepower than mere tap water. The 16th-century French noblewoman and mistress of Henry II, Diane de Poitiers, bathed in pure rainwater, as did the celebrated courtesan and beauty Ninon de l'Enclos.[7] Mary Queen of Scots steeped herself in white wine, no doubt cursing that the invention of Buckfast was still some 300 years away. The Hungarian noblewoman Elizabeth Báthory, who at the trial of her servants in 1611 was implicated in the murder of some 650 young women, was even reputed to have bathed in the blood of her victims in the belief that it made her skin look younger.

Perhaps the most famous beauty ritual in history is that of Cleopatra, who is said to have luxuriated in baths filled with asses' milk. There is only one problem with this story – it is a myth, without a single scrap of evidence to prove its veracity. There *was* a woman in the ancient world who bathed in such a manner, but she lacked Cleopatra's renown. As Pliny the Elder wrote in his *Natural History*:

> "Asses' milk is also thought to be very efficacious in whitening the skin of females: at all events, Poppaea, the wife of Domitius Nero, used always to have with her five hundred asses with foal, and used

---

7 Anna Bonus Kingford, *Health, Beauty and the Toilet: Letters to Ladies from a Lady Doctor* (Frederick Warne and Co., 1886), p.26

to bathe the whole of her body in their milk, thinking that it also conferred additional suppleness on the skin."[8]

The woman's name was Poppaea Sabina. Emperor's wife. Wanton harlot. The cat who got the cream.

. . .

Something was troubling Diana. She paced up and down the living room, her brow furrowed. Seemingly coming to a decision, she picked up her mobile and called someone, her voice an inaudible murmur. When the call was finished she tried on a series of dresses before plunging for one with a plunging neckline and spent half an hour applying her make-up. Then Diana put her purse, phone and keys into her tasselled bag and strode out through the door. I wondered where she was going, who she was going to meet. It was hard not to feel sorry for her – that hurled glass of wine had probably spelled the end of her ballet career. Whichever way you looked at it I had let Diana down. She had asked me to stop Oscar but all I'd ended up doing was spying on her. I was like a stalker who charged for the privilege.

The shrill cry of the doorbell dragged me back to my own flat. I listened as Gill answered and there was a brief exchange at the door. A minute later she tapped on my bedroom door and poked her head into the room. Her eyes narrowed with suspicion at the sight of me.

"How long have you been in here?"

"A while," I replied, quickly closing my laptop. "I've been sleeping."

"Why aren't you in the bath?"

"I fancied a change."

"Very intrepid of you. That was Ray at the door. If I'd have known you were in here I would have asked him in. He was wondering where you were."

"I've been busy."

"So I see. You should call him. It's not like you have a million friends out there, Ed, and Ray's not completely hopeless."

"Unlike some people I could mention. How *did* it go with Richard?"

8 trans. John Bostock & H.T. Riley, *The Natural History of Pliny* (Henry G. Bohn, 1855), XI.96

Gill pulled a face. "Not well. I've never seen him like that before."

"Did he start popping aspirin in front of you?"

"You're not funny, little brother. And it was worse than that. He looked completely broken. At one point he even started crying."

"Sounds like quite a performance. I'll wait for the DVD."

"You know it's not *completely* beyond the realms of possibility that a man might be genuinely upset to lose me, don't you? Why do you always think that everyone's lying?"

"I'm just trying to look out for you, sis."

"If you wanted to help me you could have got the front door fixed. It still won't shut properly and anyone could walk in here. I suppose you're waiting for me to call someone out."

I spread out my hands. "I've been busy at work!"

Gill shook her head, but her mouth twitched with amusement. "And how is my little brother finding the professional world?"

"Complicated."

"That's Diana for you. I did tell you. Have you seen her recently? I've been trying to get hold of her but she hasn't returned my calls."

"I don't know where she is."

"Then there's another mystery for you to solve. In the meantime I've been called into the office. I'll see you later."

I waited until I was sure Gill had gone before opening up the laptop again. Diana's flat was pointedly empty. What was she going to do now? Come to think of it, what was I? I was guessing that my case was over, and there would be no more wads of money coming my way. It had bought me a month's grace with Gill, but that was all. I suddenly felt incredibly tired. I decided to wait until Diana came back – just one more glimpse, just to check that she was OK – and then I would turn off the computer.

. . .

The second wife of Emperor Nero, Poppaea Sabina was born in Pompeii around AD 30, some 50 years before Vesuvius buried her hometown in fire and ash. Poppaea was a child of the restless earth, possessed of a fomenting sexuality that threatened sedition wherever she went. As the Roman historian Tacitus wrote of her, with a disapproving cluck of the tongue:

"This Poppaea had everything but a right mind... She professed virtue, while she practised laxity... Wherever there was a prospect of advantage, there she transferred her favours."[9]

Poppaea was already twice-married by the time she caught the Emperor's eye. At fourteen she had wed a member of the Praetorian Guard, and then Otho, a good friend of Nero (and later, briefly, Emperor himself). Had Poppaea manoeuvred herself into Nero's orbit on purpose? Whether by accident or design, it wasn't long before she became the Emperor's mistress, and having obtained a divorce from Otho in AD 58, she married Nero four years later.

In this context Poppaea's lavish milk baths seem to make sense, the pampering of a haughty, spoiled woman. In the 1932 Biblical epic, *The Sign Of The Cross*, Claudette Colbert portrays Poppaea as a bisexual vamp – Elizabeth Báthory on a dairy diet. Yet there were dissenting voices amongst the condemnatory clamour, such as the historian Josephus, who argued that she tried to counteract her husband's vicious tendencies.

In AD 65, as Poppaea grew heavy with her second child, Rome was swept up in the feverish pageantry of the Quinquennial Neronia festival. But there was discord in the palace: perhaps the Emperor had been neglecting his wife for the stadium; perhaps he had participated in the races himself, only to come to grief. Perhaps his fingers had merely alighted upon a rotten grape in the bunch. As his once-trusted advisor Seneca had learned, as the life ebbed from his veins into the bathtub, dealing with Nero usually came at a price. Whatever the cause – if there was one at all:

"After the conclusion of the games Poppaea died from a casual outburst of rage in her husband, who felled her with a kick when she was pregnant."[10]

9 Wikisource contributors, "The Annals (Tacitus)/Book 13," *Wikisource*, <http://en.wikisource.org/w/index.php?title=The_Annals_(Tacitus)/Book_13&oldid=3709437> (accessed October 2, 2014).

10 Wikisource contributors, "The Annals (Tacitus)/Book 16," *Wikisource*, <http://en.wikisource.org/w/index.php?title=The_Annals_(Tacitus)/Book_16&oldid=4689487> (accessed October 2, 2014).

Following his wife's death Nero went into a spiral of grief and remorse. Instead of burying Poppaea, he had her stuffed with spices and embalmed, and installed in a mausoleum for public viewings.

. . .

The hunters have my scent in their nostrils – there is no hope of escape any more. Yet still I stumble blindly through the trees, branches whipping and clawing at my face. My breath comes in terrified hiccups, and my heart pounds against my ribcage. Tears are welling in my eyes – my foolish, treacherous eyes. If only I could burn them into darkness, or sew the lids closed over them.

The trees break, abruptly, and I am scrambling over rocks, mindful of the steep drop down to the gully floor. Unable to stop myself from glancing over my shoulder, I see the dark shadows flitting in and out of the trees behind me. It will not be long now. My voice breaks as I swear, cursing my misfortune, and the implacable wrath that hunts me. Shadows lengthen behind me, and then, upon the breeze, comes the violent fanfare of baying hounds...

I awoke to find myself tangled up in my duvet. My mouth was dry and my head was thumping. Night had fallen, and the flat was a silent tomb. At some point I must have muted the volume on my laptop, as Diana was now miming brushing her teeth in her bathroom. Save for the strip light above her head and a table lamp in her bedroom, her flat was completely dark. As I watched her lean forward and spit into the sink waves of self-disgust crashed down over me. I realized that – finally – I didn't want to see any more.

It was too late to disturb her now, but at least I could allow Diana the privacy of a night's sleep. I was reaching over to close the laptop when a movement stayed my hand. In another corner of screen, in front of the living room camera, the front door opened and a man crept inside the flat. My blood turned to ice. Dressed in all black and wearing a balaclava, the man moved with stealthy caution, slowly closing the door behind him before hugging the side of the wall.

Oblivious to the fact that she had company, Diana put her toothbrush back into the pot and began flossing her teeth. I scrabbled for my mobile phone, only to lose it in the folds of the bed sheets. As the intruder stole along the living room wall Diana dropped her floss in the bin and washed her hands. Finally my hands closed upon my mobile and I called her number, praying that I was in time.

In the bathroom mirror, I saw Diana frown. Her phone was flashing on the living room sofa; the intruder stepped swiftly back into the shadows of a bookcase. Drying her hands on a towel, Diana walked into the lounge.

"No!" I cried, helplessly. "Stay in the bathroom!"

Too late, I stopped the call. Diana had already reached the sofa when her phone went dark. The man sprang out from behind the bookcase – she threw up her arms and opened her mouth in a terrible, silent scream. Diana turned to run back into the bathroom but the intruder wrapped his arms around her, clamping a rag over her mouth. She fought like a wildcat, frantically pummelling him with her fists and feet, but the man refused to relent. Soon her kicks grew weak and then her body went suddenly limp.

"No!" I cried again, in a hoarse croak.

The intruder left the rag over her mouth for several seconds before he was satisfied his victim was out cold. Diana was a tall woman but he carried her as though she was a rag doll, or a parcel of meat from the butchers'. The man glanced around the flat as he left, to check he hadn't left any trace of his presence, deciding at the last minute to take Diana's tasselled bag with him before carrying her out of the flat.

Then the front door closed, and she was gone.

UNEASY LIES THE HEAD

On 13 October 1399, six years before he executed an archbishop and awoke to find his skin ablaze, Henry Bolingbroke strode bareheaded through the rain towards Westminster Abbey, past fountains flowing with red wine. The Lancastrian marched towards his coronation flanked by a retinue of loyal knights, members of a newly created order that had been only just been sworn in. The previous evening, in the Tower of London:

> "…all the Esquires who were to be made Knights on the next day, to the number of forty-six, watched all that night, each of whom had his chamber, and his Bath, in which he bathed; and the next day the Duke of Lancaster made them Knights at the celebration of Mass, and gave them long green coats with straight sleeves, furred with miniver…"[11]

Henry's new order – fittingly, for the son of Blanche – was called the Order of the Bath. Its creation was about more than just the formation of a loyal bodyguard. In its emulation of his beloved predecessor Edward III's Order of the Garter, it sought to confer Henry with a gleaming symbol of royal legitimacy. He was, after all, a usurper, who had swiped the throne from under the nose of the previous king, Richard II, who now resided in captivity.

Yet Henry was no presumptuous and avaricious upstart. In many ways he was a reluctant rebel who had been forced into action by his brittle, insecure cousin. Fearful of the Lancastrian's popularity and renown, in 1398 Richard had used a dispute with the duke of Norfolk as a pretext to exile Henry for ten years. A year later, upon the death of Henry's father, John of Gaunt, the

---

11 Jocelyn Perkins, *The Most Honourable Order of the Bath* (The Faith Press, 1920), p.26

king had declared the lands forfeit and seized the estate. At a stroke Henry had been disgraced, exiled and disinherited. Sitting on his hands was no longer an option. Whilst Richard waged a campaign in Ireland, Henry sailed back to England and set to raising an army. Men were not slow to come forward against the unpopular Richard, and the king returned to his realm to find his soldiers deserting him in droves. Presented with a *fait accompli*, Richard meekly acquiesced. For him there lay the prospect of imprisonment and a slow, wasting death in a cell in Pontefract Castle – for Henry a coronation, and accession to the throne.

But uneasy lay the head that wore the crown. Henry IV's was a gloomy, embattled reign, which could never escape from the shadow of its original sin. He spent the rest of his life in battle – against the Scots and the French; the harrying Welsh rebel Owen Glendower; the insurgents and the mutinous noblemen of his own country; and the crippling bouts of illness that left Henry a bedridden invalid with festering flesh. After his death, history shunned him. Subsequent monarchs had no wish to hear about the usurper who had taken it upon himself to subvert the natural order of kings. Showing too close or approving an interest in Henry IV came with a health warning. Two hundred years after his coronation, the lawyer and historian Dr John Hayward had the first part of his biography of Henry published. The first edition quickly sold out – to the outrage of Elizabeth I, who saw echoes of herself in Richard II. Hayward was thrown in the Tower of London, and all copies of the second edition of the offending biography were collected up and burned.

. . .

I stared in disbelief at the screen for what felt like an eternity, willing Diana to reappear. But as dawn's grey fingers stole into my bedroom, there was no movement inside her flat. Again and again I phoned Diana's number, watching helplessly as her mobile flickered like a distress beacon in the darkness. Why hadn't I warned her sooner? It wasn't like I hadn't known Diana was in danger. She had told me about the black people carrier she thought was following her, and I had seen Lilia try to attack her in the hotel lobby. Then there was Oscar Salazar. Had he grown tired of merely watching, and resolved to take by force what he couldn't acquire with flattery and blackmail?

It was clear I had to speak with the Spaniard. Going back over our conversation in La Baignoire Pleine, I remembered that Oscar had invited Diana to a ballet premiere. Checking the Walker's website, I saw that their new production of *Coppelia* was opening that evening. As a prominent patron of the ballet company, I figured that Oscar would have to be there. So I would be too.

The front door rattled loudly shut in the hallway – Gill had left for work. I gathered up a change of clothes and went through into her bedroom, which was as neat and clean as a cabin on the *Marie Celeste*. As I made for the door leading to the en suite bathroom I paused by my sister's bedside table, a framed family photograph catching my eye. It must have been taken over ten years ago – back when we still *were* a family. The four of us were gathered around a table in the back garden of our holiday home, dressed in T-shirt and shorts: my father flashing his charming, unreliable smile; my mother politely tight-lipped; Gill grinning; and then me standing slightly apart, a scowling adolescent goblin. As I stared at the photograph I wondered who had taken it. The answer came to me with a guilty lurch of the stomach: it could have been Diana.

I hurriedly put down the photograph and entered the bathroom. It was a small white space with just enough room for a toilet, sink and shower. Bright sunshine ricocheted off the tiles. Placing my clothes on the closed toilet seat, I took off my dressing gown and stepped into the plastic cubicle, shutting the door behind me and sealing myself inside. When I turned on the shower, it spat a mouthful of cold water down upon my head. I yelped, dancing from one foot to another beneath the icy waterfall like a *misogi* practitioner having a crisis of faith. Ramming up the thermostat, I felt the water temperature grudgingly rise, and hurriedly reached for a bottle of shower gel.

As I scrubbed myself clean all I could think about was escaping from this water torture chamber and plunging into a deep, hot bath, where my limbs could melt away and my mind drift on its gentle current. But this situation demanded action, and I had lost enough weeks and months in the bathtub's damp embrace. I couldn't afford to get trapped in there again.

. . .

The 27th president of the United States, William Taft, was a vast walrus of a man. Despite being a keen horse-rider and golfer, 'Big Bill' weighed in at over 330 pounds, and was so fat he couldn't sleep – he suffered from obstructive sleep apnoea. A natural jurist but a reluctant politician, few presidents could claim to have taken less pleasure from the office. Taft sought comfort in his meals, piling on the pounds despite his doctor and his wife's attempts to curb his appetite.

Taft became so hefty that – popular legend has it – one day he became wedged in his own bathtub. The story varies in the telling: it took four men to free the beached president; it took six; they had to grease him with butter to get him out; Taft broke the bath when they pulled him free. Perhaps it was an urban myth, but a telling hint that *something* had gone awry could be found in the new bathtub that Taft had specially designed for him. It was an astonishing structure, seven feet long and a metre wide, with enough room for four men to sit inside it. It was less a bath than an oil tanker, an early symbol of a nascent superpower, a bathroom Skylab.

Despite his miserable time in office, Taft sought re-election, only to be defeated by Woodrow Wilson. He dieted, his loss of 70 pounds making the front page of the New York Times. In 1921 he found his natural home when he was elected Chief Justice. His natural joviality restored, Taft later claimed to barely remember his time in the White House.

. . .

As I stood waiting outside Ray's house, blinking uncomfortably in the sunshine, a pair of starlings wheeled and banked above my head, sketching lazy patterns in the bright blue sky. A cat sunned itself on the warm paving stones in the front yard, purring contentedly as it cleaned its face. I tapped my feet impatiently, and watched a snail ooze across my path.

Finally the front door opened, and a sleepy face peered out.

"Oh," said Ray. "It's you."

After the baking heat outside, Ray's flat was like a cool secret garden. A soft autumnal smoke hung in the air, the coffee table covered in a bracken-like layer of tobacco. A snooker match was playing on the television, the commentators describing the action in hushed, respectful tones.

"I didn't think you liked sport," I said.

"Snooker's not really sport though, is it?" replied Ray. "It's tidying up. You break off, making a big mess of all the balls, and then you put them away into the pockets. Then you mess the balls up again, then you tidy them away again. Then you mess—"

"I get the picture."

Ray nodded sagely, and began sprinkling marijuana over a fresh cigarette paper. "I called round for you the other day but Gill said you were out."

"Yeah. I was busy."

"I was thinking I might ask her out," Ray said thoughtfully. "On a date."

"Who, *Gill*?"

"You think it's a bad idea."

"I do."

Ray nodded, brushing his hands clean. "You think she's still getting over Richard."

"Not really," I replied. "I just think she'd say no."

"Oh."

He rolled the joint into a thin cylinder and he held it up to the light, like a dopey-eyed Degas using his paintbrush to gauge perspective. Nodding with satisfaction, Ray lit the joint and inhaled deeply.

"It's not like you to be busy," he said thoughtfully. "What've you been up to?"

I took a deep breath, and told him. I had to tell someone. At first I sensed Ray was only half-listening, his mind preoccupied with the smooth glide of snooker balls across the baize, but at the mention of Diana undressing his eyes grew wider and from then on I had his full attention.

"Holy shit," he breathed. "Diana was kidnapped?"

"Yeah."

"What did the police say?"

I winced. Ray looked at me.

"You have told them, haven't you?"

"Not in so many words."

"Jesus, Edgar!" he groaned. "Why not?"

"What was I going to say?" I mimed picking up a telephone and said, in a sing-song voice: "Yes officer, I'd like to report a kidnapping. Yes, I witnessed it. How? I've been spying on my sister's old school friend on an illegal video feed. Lucky for her I was, isn't it?"

"I wouldn't put like that if were you," Ray said seriously. "You might get into trouble."

I put my head in my hands.

"This web feed you were watching," said Ray, opening up his laptop. "You still got the address for it?"

I took out the Degas postcard I had folded into my back pocket and handed it to Ray, telling him the password. As he opened an internet browser on his laptop and typed in the address I watched one of the snooker players as he smoothly potted a red into a pocket, before rolling in the black.

"Edgar," Ray said slowly. "Does Diana lives on her own?"

"As far as I know. Why?"

"'Cause there's a guy poking around there now."

"What?"

I hurried over to the laptop and looked over Ray's shoulder. On the camera in Diana's bedroom I could see a man rifling through her things, flinging open wardrobe drawers and checking beneath her bed. Having turned the flat upside down, the man stood in the centre of the living room, an expression of consternation on his face. He glanced down at the sofa.

"He's spotted something," said Ray, pointing at a small black object lying next to one of the cushions. "What is that?"

"Diana's phone," I replied grimly, aware of the torrent of my missed calls that would be recorded there.

The man looked up in the direction of the camera, and for a fleeting second it felt like he was staring directly at us. Then he picked up Diana's mobile and walked out of the flat, not bothering to close the door behind him.

"There's something familiar about that guy," said Ray. "I'm sure I've seen him somewhere before."

Remembering people has always been something of a problem for my friend, who can struggle to make faces out through the smoky haze that perpetually clouds his vision. But I knew exactly who we had been watching.

I might only have seen the man once before, in the lobby of a five-star hotel, but there was no mistaking his dark good looks and lithe, powerful frame. And for a hit-and-run victim who was meant to be in hospital nursing a shattered skeleton, Yuri Ivanov looked in pretty good shape to me.

A BAFFLING ROBE

I waited in the shadows across the street from the Walker Theatre, absent-mindedly scratching my elbows though my suit as I scanned the front of the building for movement. The night was warm and syrupy. Lights blazed out from the theatre foyer and through the floor-to-ceiling windows on the second floor. From deep within the building I could just make out the swelling rumble of the orchestra as *Coppelia* reached its climax.

I prayed the ballet was nearing its end. I was exhausted after my wakeful night, and the *Dermatitis Herpetiformis* was once again sniffing around my extremities. Thrown by Yuri's unexpected appearance in Diana's flat, I had spent several hours pondering the matter in the Scythian vapour bath that was Ray's front room. The Russian dancer had clearly faked his accident – but why? To end things with Diana? Then why turn up at her flat several days later and make off with her phone? Had he changed his mind, or was there someone else he was hiding from? As I breathed in the sweet mist that hung in the air, all manner of outrageous possibilities seemed plausible.

Lost in the drowsy caress of second-hand smoke, it was late afternoon by the time I remembered about the ballet premiere. I left Ray staring dully at the snooker and headed back home to change. On the stairs outside Gill's flat, I heard the sound of dark muttering on the landing. Peering around the corner, I saw a man in a paint-flecked jumper and tracksuit bottoms kneeling in the flat doorway, squinting at the lock.

"Hello?" I said, warily. "Can I help you?"

The man grunted, barely acknowledging my presence. He was in his late twenties, with a lean face darkened by a coarse shadow of stubble. Without looking at me, he pointed with his screwdriver at a toolkit by his knees and said, in a thick East European accent:

"Here to fix lock. Sister said you'd be here but no one in. Door was open anyway so I thought I make start. Nearly finished."

"Right," I said briskly. "OK."

Good old Gill. I knew she'd get round to fixing the lock eventually. Squeezing awkwardly past the workman, I went into my bedroom and began changing into my suit. In an ideal world I would have time for a quick sluice in the bath but there was barely an hour before the performance was due to start. I hurriedly buttoned up my shirt, cursing Ray and his hazy distractions. By the time I had adjusted my tie and slipped into my jacket the workman was packing up, shutting the toolbox and hiding its metal innards from view.

"I finish," he said, getting to his feet. "Lock work now."

"Great. Thanks." I hesitated. "Gill didn't tell you I was going to pay you, did she?"

The workman shook his head. "She said not to bother waste time. She pay already."

I smiled awkwardly. "OK, then."

I ushered him out through the door and closed it behind him, sighing with relief as the lock clicked shut. Peace of mind at last. I dashed into the bathroom to finish getting ready, unable to help myself straightening the ring-binder files on the shelf by the sink as I brushed my teeth. Searching for floss in the mirrored cabinet, I came across Keiko's bar of soap. I slipped it into my pocket with a shrug. Who knew when I might need an emergency lather?

Four hours later, as I lurked in the darkness opposite the theatre, my skin threatening a fresh mutiny, I wished I had stayed in the bathroom and used the soap there. To hell with Keiko and her coded hints, her knowing, enigmatic smile. I was in pain. Finally the Walker Theatre erupted with rapturous and prolonged applause, signalling *Coppelia's* conclusion. The audience came flooding down the stairs to the foyer, spilling out into the street. They were dressed in evening suits and ballgowns, bare shoulders draped with silk scarves and stoles, wrists and neck bedecked with glittering constellations of jewellery. But there was no sign of Oscar Salazar.

I stood and watched the crowd outside the ballet, biding my time.

. . .

In 1874 the writer Edmond de Goncourt spent a day at the Montmartre studio of Edgar Degas. He set down their encounter in his diary, struck by the painter's awkward, nervy disposition. De Goncourt watched bemused as Degas excitedly sketched out dance movements for him, standing on his tiptoes and rounding his arms as he teetered around the studio.

Degas lived for the ballet. He returned again and again to the same productions, and the subject dominated his dinner conversations. Time has mellowed his ballerina paintings, leaving them vulnerable to accusations of sentimentality, chocolate-box prettiness. This would be to misunderstand them completely. Degas liked to see women *work*, and he understood the years of great physical effort the dancers had undertaken to train their bodies and sculpt their movements... the stretch at the barre, the twist of the ankle, the arch of the back. Even when they weren't dancing, Degas' subjects were always busy: fiddling with straps and pulling up tights; massaging aching feet and fastening pumps; fixing their hair; balancing on tiptoe. There was something verging on the sadistic about the awkward poses he insisted upon capturing.

Many of the aspiring ballerinas of the time had been fished from impoverished Parisian homes, and the so-called *petit rats* had a reputation for loose morals. The tide of young dancers ebbing in and out of Degas' studio led to a visit from an inspector from a department of public morality. Indeed, Degas' portrayal of dancers during the longueurs of lessons and rehearsals shared more than a little with the listless prostitutes he painted in *Waiting for a Client*. When his sculpture, *Little Dancer, Aged Fourteen*, was unveiled at an Impressionist Exhibition in Paris, it scandalized critics with its starkly realistic portrayal of a *petit rat* – more Artful Dodger than Princess Aurora.

The year after Degas had staged his impromptu performance for de Goncourt, the Palais Garnier opened in Paris. Degas hustled and pressed for backstage access to the grand opera house, aspiring to the status of an *abonné*, the wealthy patrons who came and went with impunity. Gradually Degas insinuated himself inside the halls and classrooms, a constant shadow with a sketchpad. He became such a fixture that the dancers would listen to his critiques of their postures. It seems almost inconceivable that Degas harboured no sexual feelings towards the flocks of lithe young women he spent his days observing, yet whilst his brother Achille had an affair with a dancer the sexless Edgar remained steadfastly aloof. The brutal truth appeared to be that Degas didn't actually like women enough to sleep with them.

. . .

High-pitched laughter wafted over the road towards me as the patrons lingered outside the theatre, basking in the warm night air. As the crowd swelled I started to worry I might miss Oscar, so I crossed over and inserted myself in the middle of the throng. Judging by the breathless pronouncements, the premiere had been a roaring success. I peered over the top of the crowd, pretending to look for an old friend or a mislaid date. Instead I found myself staring into a pair of startlingly blue eyes set into a hard, beautiful face.

It was Lilia Kuznetsova.

The ballerina was standing alone, wearing a long white dress with a plunging backline. She did not look pleased to see me. Hastily I tried to turn away but she reached out and grabbed me, her fingers biting down upon my wrist.

"You again!"

"Excuse me?" I tried, feigning confusion.

"Don't play dumb with me," snapped Lilia. "I saw you skulking about in the lobby of that hotel, spying on Yuri and his little whore."

"There must be some mistake. I don't know—"

She pulled on my wrist with surprising strength, dragging me in close until her breath was hot upon my earlobe.

"Listen to me," she hissed. "Tell Valery to back off. The thing with Diana is over, finished. The deal stands and we will be in Kiev before the end of the summer. Do you understand?"

Around us, people were beginning to stare. Lilia didn't seem to care, but I could feel my cheeks growing hot with embarrassment. I nodded mutely.

"Hello, hello!" a stentorian female voice boomed. "Here's an unlikely conspiracy!"

Lilia's hand instantly detached itself from my wrist, and I looked up gratefully to see Margery waddling over towards us, swathed in a voluminous green pashmina.

"Hello, Margery," said Lilia, with a smile as warm as a Siberian winter.

"Lovely to see you again, my dear," said Margery, leaning in and kissing both of the ballerina's cheeks. "How long is it since you danced here? Four, five years?"

"A lifetime ago," Lilia replied, with a careless laugh.

"No doubt it feels that way to you, young lady, but to an old fart like me it seems like yesterday," Margery said jovially. "Even though you were just a slip of a girl it was clear you were destined for great things. And great things you've achieved, my girl! Your Odile brought tears to my eyes."

Lilia inclined her head in graceful acknowledgement.

"Edgar, isn't it?" said Margery, turning her attention to me. "I saw you last week in the café. How's your friend Diana getting on?"

"I don't know," I said. "I haven't seen her for a while." Seized by a sudden reckless urge, I turned to Lilia. "How about you, Lilia? Do you know where she is?"

"I have no idea," she replied, through clenched teeth. "Please, you must excuse me, I have to go. Goodbye, Margery."

"Give my best to Yuri," I said quickly, as Lilia tried to walk away. "I was sorry to hear about his accident. I hope it wasn't too serious."

Margery blinked. "What's this?" she said. "I haven't heard about any accident!"

"It was nothing," Lilia said quickly. "You know how rumours spread."

"Don't worry," I laughed. "I'm sure he'll be up and about before too long. Won't he, Lilia?"

The ballerina said nothing, her eyes burning with cold fury. She turned her back in a swift, regal movement and marched away through the crowd.

"Want to tell me what that was all about?" said Margery, eyeing me with amusement.

"Nothing, really. Just an in-joke."

"You are a dark horse, Edgar, and no mistake," she chortled. "You seem to make it your business to know the most beautiful girls at the ballet. My boy would be quite jealous. Have you ever seen Lilia dance?"

I shook my head.

"Then you haven't seen the best of her. Such grace, such poise, such precision! She's the best dancer of her generation, although perhaps not my favourite. There's something rather cold about perfection, I find."

"Do you know what she's doing in London?"

"I haven't the faintest idea," Margery replied. "Checking out the competition, perhaps? Lilia doesn't really do time off. Even though she's between productions I hear she dances every day at the Dauphine studios down in Kensington. The girl is completely driven."

"She doesn't like me very much."

"Guilt by association, old boy. It's fair to say Lilia does not have the highest of opinions where your friend Diana is concerned."

"You know about her and Yuri?"

"It's the talk of the season."

"You seem to know a lot about what goes on here."

"I'm on the board of trustees. They gossip like a bunch of old maids."

"So you know Oscar Salazar."

Margery nodded. "A sign of the times, my dear. Ballet likes to think of itself as timeless, but it has to change like everything else. Where once we would have had artists running the show, now it's hedge-fund managers and oligarchs. Still, it could be worse – say what you like about Oscar, but you can't doubt his love for the ballet. He knows the productions inside out: the history, the great dancers. Compare that to what's going on in the old Iron Curtain countries, the mobsters getting involved at the Maschenko Ballet for example—" She broke off, glancing over towards the foyer. "Speak of the devil."

I stepped back as Oscar Salazar appeared on the steps of the theatre, a sleek panther in a black suit and open-necked white shirt. He moved swiftly through the crowd, greeting every approach and compliment with a generous smile but never once, I noted, stopping moving.

"So glad you enjoyed the performance," he told a raven-haired woman in an evening gown. "Unfortunately I have to run. I have a pressing engagement, you understand."

He clasped her hand and kissed it gently in farewell, before turning on his heel and walking briskly away down the street.

"Edgar?"

I turned back to find Margery scrutinizing me, her expression at once forbidding and brushed with a strange sadness. "You've got the same look on your face that my boy gets when he's about to do something silly," she said. "You're not going to do something silly, are you?"

"Of course not," I said quickly.

"I'd think twice before meddling with Oscar Salazar. He's not a man to be trifled with, you know."

"Don't worry. I'll be fine."

I hurried off before she could call me back. As I slipped through the throng after Oscar I thought I heard Margery shout something, but her words were lost amidst the chatter and the traffic.

. . .

Cassandra, daughter of King Priam of Troy, was a beautiful redhead blessed with the gift of prophecy, and cursed never to be believed. In the aftermath of her city's fall, after a decade-long siege by Greek forces, Cassandra was claimed by the enemy commander Agamemnon as a concubine and taken back to his homeland of Mycenae and Argos as a spoil of war. Their homecoming is described by the playwright Aeschylus in *Agamemnon*, the first part of his tragic *Oresteia* trilogy. As they set sail a joyous fire lights up along the Aegean coastline, crackling beacons bringing news of the Greeks' victory and Agamemnon's return. But unbeknownst to the king, the beacons are a signal for the jaws of a trap to snap shut. For, as the chorus warns:

> "At home there tarries like a lurking snake,
> Biding its time, like a wrath unreconciled,
> A wily watcher, passionate to slake,
> In blood, resentment for a murdered child."[12]

The coiled serpent is Clytemnestra, Agamemnon's wife – the murdered child their daughter Iphigenia, whom the king was forced to sacrifice in order to appease the angry goddess Artemis. In her husband's absence Clytemnestra has taken up with his cousin, Aegisthus, in a lustful and incestuous affair fuelled by vengeance, ambition, and whispers of assassinations.

Upon Agamemnon's triumphant return to the palace, Cassandra sits quietly in the chariot as Clytemnestra plays the role of the doting wife. Cajoling

12 Wikisource contributors, "The Oresteia (Morshead)/Agamemnon," *Wikisource,* <http://en.wikisource.org/w/index.php?title=The_Oresteia_(Morshead)/Agamemnon&oldid=4049109> (accessed October 2, 2014).

her husband to step down upon a purple carpet, she tempts him inside with the promise of a soothing bath. When husband and wife disappear within the palace Cassandra is possessed by the god Apollo, who assails her with bloody visions of the past crimes of Agamemnon's House of Atreus. As the chorus struggles to divine the meaning of her jumbled outbursts, Cassandra sees Agamemnon under attack in the bathtub. Yet her warnings – like all Cassandra's prophecies – go unheeded by the chorus.

Distraught to the point of madness, Cassandra rushes inside the palace, even though it spells her own doom. Agamemnon's three hideous screams of pain from off-stage confirm the truth of her visions. A bloodied Clytemnestra appears, beside the bodies of Agamemnon and his concubine. Defiant to the point of disdain, she explains how she butchered her husband:

> "I trapped him with inextricable toils,
> The ill abundance of a baffling robe;
> Then smote him, once, again...
> And the dark sprinklings of the rain of blood
> Fell upon me"[13]

At this point her co-conspirator Aegisthus belatedly makes his entrance, accompanied by an armed retinue. With his cousin slain and the throne empty, the way is clear for him to marry Clytemnestra and become king himself.

...

Oscar prowled like a fox through the nighttime world of dormant shop fronts, overflowing bins and flickering streetlights. As the pavement grew quieter I became concerned he'd notice someone was on his tail, but as we turned left and continued past a row of park railings I realized that I was safe. This was not a man who ever looked over his shoulder – this was not a man who doubted. I drew back against the railings as Oscar stopped to light a cigarette, cupping his hand around the lighter's flame. It was then that I saw the woman.

---

13 *Ibid.*

She was standing outside a bar on the other side of the street, dressed in a short black dress that showed off a pair of toned legs. Her hair was pinned up beneath a hat with a delicate veil that dropped down over her face, tantalizingly obscuring her identity. At the sight of Oscar the woman sashayed across the road, took the cigarette from his hand and tossed it into the gutter before enveloping him in a long and tangled embrace. As they kissed his hand brushed against her hat, and I glimpsed of a flash of red hair, a stray spark from a bonfire. The breath caught in my throat.

The couple didn't hurry the kiss, bumping up against the park railings as they clasped and pawed at one another. It was Oscar who broke away first – the woman seemed momentarily affronted, but then he whispered something in her ear that made her laugh. They turned and walked hand-in-hand away down the street. I followed behind them, doused in dark suspicions. Had Diana been inspired by Yuri's fake accident and staged her own kidnapping? Was anything I had seen over the past few days actually real, or had it all been some elaborate theatrical performance?

At the corner of the park Oscar and the woman crossed the street and disappeared down a narrow side road. Ducking behind a phone box, I watched as they stopped outside a darkened building sandwiched between a brightly lit café and a neon sex shop. The windows were blacked out and there was no sign above the door, but I could see two smartly dressed doormen standing guard outside the entrance. Oscar gave the men a familiar nod as he approached, and I heard a bark of gruff laughter as he exchanged a joke with them before disappearing inside.

I hung back behind the phone box, scratching my inflamed elbows with dismay. Whatever was going on inside that building, someone was taking great effort not to advertise it. Lurid possibilities swirled in my mind – a high-stakes gambling den, an underground boxing ring, an exclusive swingers' club. None of these establishments were likely to admit me, but I *had* to find out the identity of the veiled woman. It was like a cold pool on a hot day – the only option was to plunge in.

I stepped out from the shadows and walked nervously past the café towards the doorway. The bouncers seemed to grow in size as I approached, until I could have sworn that both were seven feet tall. The slightly larger of the two was a black man with dreadlocks, the slightly shorter a wiry white man with a shaved head and protruding ears. Adopting what I hoped was a casual, almost careless air, I tried to walk straight past them.

A large upraised palm blocked my path.

"I'm sorry, sir," the dreadlocked doorman said courteously, in an American accent. "It's a private party tonight."

"It's all right," I replied. "I'm with Oscar Salazar. He's expecting me."

He looked me up and down, and exchanged an amused glance with the skinhead.

"I think we both know that's unlikely, sir," he told me, not unkindly.

"I'm not lying," I protested. "If I can just go inside and get him he'll vouch for me."

The doorman rolled his eyes. "No entrance to the club without a pass key, sir."

"Let him check his pockets, Walter," the other man said slyly. His accent sounded Russian. "You heard him! He is a big friend of Mr Salazar."

"No, it's all right," I stammered. "I'll just go—"

"Sergei said check your pockets," Walter said, in a tone that brooked no argument.

If I had been thinking straight I would have walked away, but I was so intimidated that I instinctively obeyed the doorman, taking out my wallet and forlornly examining my cash cards.

"Do we look like a bank to you?" Sergei said scornfully. He was having fun now, amusing himself on a slow night. "You need a pass key, idiot. Haven't you got anything else?"

I did. Unfortunately for me, it was Keiko's bar of soap. Dumbly I took it out of my pocket and handed it to Sergei.

The smile faded from the Russian's face and I tensed, ready to make for a run for it. But instead of howling with laughter or hurling the pink bar at me he handed it to Walter, who turned it over in his hands, thoughtfully inspecting the small heart carved into its face. With a shrug Walter pocketed the soap, stepped to one side and pushed open the door.

"You should have said earlier, sir," he said apologetically. "Welcome to Soaplands."

THE FLOATING WORLD

The story of bathing is also a story about dirt, a tale where purity and pollution are intertwined in a permanent embrace. When man first encountered water it was a wild, elemental force – the great slaker of thirst, the giver of life. Yet as centuries passed their relationship changed. Water became linked with recreation, and pleasure; and from there it was only a short distance to the sensual and the sexual. Bathhouses became brothels, spas turned into stews. In Japan, the Tokugawa shogunate of the 17th, 18th and 19th centuries saw the rise of *mizu shobai*, 'the water trade' – an elegant euphemism for the pursuit of nighttime pleasures. Networks of roadside inns beckoned in weary travellers with the offer of a hot bath and sexual relief, whilst in the cities red-light districts flourished. In the city of Edo, the early incarnation of Tokyo, the bustling district of Yoshiwara was a hive of tea shops, kabuki theatres and brothels, populated by a bohemian mixture of geishas and courtesans, actors and dancers. This metropolitan hedonism was known as *Ukiyo* – 'the floating world'. In the floating world, the search for pleasure was never-ending, as satisfaction was by its very nature impermanent: a snatch of perfume upon the air, a stolen glimpse of a curved leg, a courtesan's quick, shallow breaths upon the ear.

Although the government outlawed prostitution in 1958, *mizu shobai* endures in the hostess bars and the cabarets of modern Japan. The link between sex and water is as strong as ever. In the face of Turkish protests over the use of the term *toruko-buro* ('Turkish baths') to describe their brothels, a new soubriquet was chosen from suggestions entered into a national competition. The winner? Soapland.

...

The club's down-at-heel exterior was a charade, an extravagant in-joke. I found myself in a wood-panelled atrium, my feet sinking into deep, luxurious carpet. Expensive-looking oil paintings hung on the walls; antique lamps showed the way to a grand staircase leading up into the club. A sinuous baseline weaved down through the ceiling from the room above. In the corner of the atrium, a pretty girl was seated behind the cloakroom counter – she smiled as I hesitated, and gestured encouragingly towards the staircase. I slowly made my way up the steps to a set of double doors on the first floor. Taking a deep breath, I pushed through them.

Soaplands was a cavernous lounge draped in perfume and the soothing sound of trickling water. A cocktail bar fashioned from black marble ran the length of the near wall; women in one-piece bathing costumes mixed drinks against a gleaming backdrop of spirit bottles. High-walled booths ran along the back wall, shielding their occupants from view. In the middle of the room a smattering of small circular tables were arranged around a raised stage. Curiously, the men seated there all appeared to be wearing white bathrobes. A stunning blonde woman was dancing on the stage in front of them, naked save for a pair of pink bikini bottoms and a pair of high heels. A hosepipe was coiled around her feet like a snake – standing astride it, she bent down on the beat and snatched it up. The hose spurted into life as the dancer stood up and leant backwards, drenching her generous breasts with water. The men around the stage clapped and whistled; still in time to the pounding beat, the dancer drenched her blonde locks and her body, spraying water everywhere.

As I stared open-mouthed, a brunette in a sparkling swimming costume shimmered across the lounge towards me. Her skin was dusted in glitter, giving her the ethereal air of a water nymph.

"Good evening, sir," smiled the Naiad. "Would you like some company while you watch the show?"

"No, thank you," I replied, my voice cracking slightly. "I'm looking for someone. Oscar Salazar?"

"Of course," she said smoothly, slipping her arm through mine. "Follow me."

The Naiad led me through the lounge, her smooth bare skin against my arm. I couldn't help wondering what it must be like to kiss a water nymph, to press her damp lips against mine. Passing by the first booth, I discovered the source of the sound of trickling water – inside was a raised hot tub, tucked away to ensure maximum privacy whilst guaranteeing a view of the stage. Inside the tub an old man was sandwiched like a wrinkled hot dog between two statuesque girls. He cackled gleefully as we walked past, and buried his face in one of the girls' chests. In the tub in the next booth an overweight man in a sodden bathrobe was greedily kissing a topless girl; I hurriedly looked away.

In the third tub, sipping champagne, was Oscar Salazar. He looked as suave as ever, all white teeth and waxed chest, not a hair out of place. An attractive redhead in a bikini nestled beside him in the rippling water. It wasn't Diana. This girl was younger, with bobbed hair and a pouting expression that only deepened with pique at the sight of me. By contrast, Oscar registered my appearance without blinking.

"Here we are," the Naiad said brightly. "Perhaps when you're finished you'll come and find me?"

She gave me an unexpected peck on the cheek before withdrawing.

"Edgar!" said Oscar, raising his champagne flute. "Care to join us?"

"No, I'm good," I said hesitantly. "Um, thanks."

Oscar turned to his companion. "Allow me to introduce Audrey Du Maurier. She's one of France's premier ice skaters, a bronze medallist at the Winter Olympics no less. Audrey, this is Edgar. He... appears, from time to time."

Audrey ignored my awkward wave. "I've got to pee," she told Oscar abruptly, rising out of the water with a splash. As an afterthought she picked up a white bathrobe from the edge of the tub and slipped into it before padding away across the floor.

Oscar took a steady sip of champagne as he watched her depart.

"She is beautiful, no?" he murmured.

"Certainly seems your type," I agreed.

"Have you been to Soaplands before, Edgar?"

I shook my head. "This is my first time."

"You don't think I'm being rude if I say I'm not surprised? This place is very, very exclusive. *Dangerously* exclusive."

There was a loud round of applause behind me as the blonde in the pink bikini bottoms finished her act. She glided back towards the curtain, stepping daintily over the glistening pools of water and the limp, discarded hose. The lights around the stage plunged into darkness.

"What am I going to do with you, Edgar?" sighed Oscar. "I try and court your friend, you decide I am not good enough for her and try to stop me. I hold up my hands and say 'OK', and yet still you follow me around. Like an unwanted shadow, or an unrequited lover." He took another sip of champagne, his eyes never leaving mine. "Are you a homosexual, Edgar?"

"No!"

"I have no problem if you are. Just so long as you know I am interested only in women."

"I'm not here because of you. It's Diana."

"Ah! The gallant Don Quixote, still sallying forth in the name of his beloved Dulcinea!" Oscar exclaimed, raising his flute in a toast. "Diana is lucky to have such a faithful knight-errant."

"She's missing."

"Perhaps she has found a new love, and gone away. Ballet dancers can be notoriously capricious creatures, Edgar."

"You don't sound exactly heartbroken about it."

Oscar shrugged. "As you can see, I have moved on."

"Just like that? What about your father's restaurant in Cadiz?"

"The waiting list for a table there is six months long," Oscar said brusquely. "He won't miss the booking."

"I don't believe you," I told him. "After all that chasing and pressuring, you expect me to believe that you just gave up?"

"I withdrew, as a gentleman should. As far as I'm aware, Diana will be offered a role in the *corps de ballet* for the Walker's next production. In two days time I will set sail with Moira – my one faithful love. That is the end of the matter."

"You're going to hire Diana? What about Yuri?"

"I have become less certain that he will join our company. There are rumours that he has made a deal elsewhere."

"And what about the postcard?" I demanded. "Why did you send me that – just to mess with my head?"

"I have no idea what you are talking about."

"The Degas postcard with the link to the video feed. The secret video feed of Diana's flat that you had installed."

I thought I saw a fleeting shadow cross Oscar's face. Then he leant back in the tub with a soft chuckle.

"Don Quixote was a fantasist, you know," he said softly. "A joke who saw enemies everywhere, and mistook scullery maids for virgin goddesses. He was too crazy to realize that everyone was laughing at him. A word of advice, Edgar – if you keep tilting at windmills, one day you're going to get hurt. Even Quixote had a shaving basin for a helmet. You don't have any protection at all."

Before I could reply the stage lights blazed back into life, revealing a giant martini glass filled with foam.

"You should watch this act," Oscar said knowingly, pointing over my shoulder. "Maybe then you'd spend less time thinking about me."

A woman in a white G-string appeared from behind the curtain, sashaying across the stage on eight-inch heels. As she climbed gracefully up inside the glass, I realized with an electric jolt that I knew her. My jaw dropped open.

. . .

As the 19th century heralded the gradual opening of Japan to the wider world, one of the early intrepid visitors from the West came in the unlikely form of a theatre critic from the *Daily Telegraph*. In 1892 Clement Scott was commissioned by his editors to report on the World's Fair in Chicago. He opted to travel the long way around, taking in India, China and Japan on his way to the States. Upon his arrival in San Francisco, Scott began giving interviews expounding his views upon the country he had just left. The critic was, well, critical; he gave Japan a scathing review, damning the country for its immorality.

The main bone of contention for the upright theatre critic appeared to be the red-light districts he visited in Kobe and Tokyo. In his travel writings Scott described areas like Yoshiwara as "female slave markets"; the courtesans "soiled doves in cages":

"What a dreadful and appalling exhibition! Here you could stand and talk to the girls behind the wooden bars, penned in like so many animals; here bargains and arrangements are made; here you can throw down your glove to whomsoever takes your fancy."[14]

This state of high dudgeon was even more noteworthy for the fact that Scott didn't always appear to be such a chivalrous defender of women's rights. In fact he excoriated the women of Japan for their appearance and demeanour, accusing them of such varied crimes as coarse and greasy hair, shuffling gait, beefy cheeks and arms, and chronic grinning.

At the town of Kaikatei, Scott stayed at a roadside inn, one of the *mizu shobai* establishments where the lines between bathhouse, hotel and brothel were very faintly drawn. Tended to by a serving girl called O. Do-San, Scott was led to the baths, where he found himself "neck-deep in sulphur water that has bubbled into the bath... so scalding from the earth that you can scarcely bear it!"[15] Suitably reinvigorated, Scott dined and then relaxed amongst the female company in the sitting room afterwards. The atmosphere proved so congenial even Scott's perpetual moral outrage seemed momentarily dampened. Indeed:

"There is so much to see and do," he enthused, "'sampling' the mountain tea-houses and hearing the chatter of these bobbing and curtseying 'little maids from school,' who seem to interest and console the jaded and experienced traveller."[16]

Despite repeated complaints about the Japanese 'Circes' who worked in the bathhouses, Scott didn't leave Kaikatei the next morning. "I intended to stay a day," the weary Odysseus confessed, "but here, in spite of myself, I rested a good week."

. . .

14 Clement Scott, *Pictures Of The World* (Remington & Company, 1894), p.241
15 Scott, *Pictures Of The World*, p.200
16 Scott, *Pictures Of The World*, p.201

Keiko lay back in the foam-filled glass and raised her long, supple legs into the air. She spun herself around, her hair tipped back over the edge of the glass, a whirling revolution of limbs and breasts and damp flesh, then snapped to a halt, lifting herself up and arching her back. It was a performance that was dazzling and erotic and unsettling all at once. One moment Keiko was kicking her legs and blowing kisses at the audience, as innocent as a child in a paddling pool, the next she was up on her knees massaging her foamy breasts, her hands dipping suggestively inside her sodden G-string. Picking up a bubble blower from the side of the glass, she filled the lounge with clouds of iridescent bubbles.

I was so entranced by Keiko's routine I barely registered Audrey's reappearance behind me, sliding out of her bathrobe and back into the hot tub. She wrapped her arms around Oscar and began peppering his neck with kisses. The Spaniard seemed bothered by the sudden torrent of affection, knocking away Audrey's hand when it slipped beneath the surface of the water towards his shorts. Rejected, the ice-skater let out a squeak of irritation and sulkily folded her arms.

I was about to make my excuses and leave when the lounge doors burst open with a loud bang, and a man went staggering into one of the tables. It was Walter, the giant American doorman. As he went crashing to the floor one of the women behind the bar screamed, and then The Finn stomped into the lounge. Grabbing Walter's dreadlocks, he punched him in the face several times, before drawing back his foot and giving the doorman a savage kick in the ribs.

There was a hurried scrape of chair legs; a tide of white flannel robes headed for the exit. On stage Keiko stopped frolicking and knelt up in the glass, shielding her eyes from the lights as she tried to see the cause of the commotion. She frowned.

"Paavo?" she said. "What the hell are you doing?"

With a snarl The Finn clambered up on the stage, reaching up and grabbing Keiko by the arm. She shrieked as he tried to pull her out of the glass.

"Leave her alone!"

I looked around to see who had dared to speak up only to realize – with a mixture of horror and amazement – that it had, in fact, been me.

The Finn turned to look at me, his face registering something close to bafflement. Shoving Keiko back into the foam, he jumped down from the stage and stomped towards me. Fear wrapped me in a cold, sweaty embrace. There were hurried splashes behind me as Oscar and Audrey jumped out of the tub and fled. I wanted to join them but my feet were frozen to the floor. I didn't even raise my hands as The Finn wrapped a meaty fist around my throat and dunked my head into the hot tub.

Warm bubbles overwhelmed me. Through the pounding of my heart-beat in my ears I could hear distorted shouts and screams, but nothing disturbed the strong, adamant hand around my neck. How long had I been underwater – thirty seconds? A minute? In a surreal way, the utter hopelessness of my situation made it almost relaxing. There was literally nothing I could do except black out.

Which I did, seconds later.

ISLAND OF THE ENCHANTRESS

Even as I flee onwards through the trees I can feel my treacherous body change, assuming the form of prey. My ears quicken to sharp points, soft fur covers my skin; I reach up to find a pair of gnarled horns unfurling from my forehead. The baying of the pack upon my heels grows more intense, and I glance over my shoulder to see a roiling tide of dark flesh and glinting teeth engulfing the forest. I was a fool to run. How can a mere mortal hope to escape the dreadful vengeance of a goddess?

Then a pair of slavering jaws latches on to my leg, sharp teeth sinking into my flesh. I open my mouth to scream, and the sound that flees forth is the horrible, alien cry of an animal…

"Edgar? Are you OK?"

Keiko's anxious face swam out of the fog as I struggled back into consciousness. Lifting my head from a cold, hard surface, I discovered that I was lying in the middle of a vast mahogany table in what appeared to be an executive boardroom. Bottles of champagne kicked their heels in buckets of ice. Carved wooden cigar boxes had their lids propped open, proudly displaying their wares. The walls were covered with erotic photographs of naked women, their limbs wrapped around one another as they coupled and writhed.

I groaned as Keiko helped me into a sitting position, coughing up a thin dribble of water on to the table.

"Where are we?" I spluttered.

"The Executive Suite," said Keiko, picking up a sports bag and slinging it over her shoulder. "Some businessmen like the girls to dance on the meeting table for them. Come on."

I wiped the back of my hand across my mouth. "What happened? Where did everybody go?"

"They got out of here, like we need to. The shit's about to hit the fan and believe me, you don't want to be around here for that."

As I rolled off the table, I found myself being eyeballed by a large photograph of a stocky, bearded man with a naked blond women draped on either arm. Something about the man's face was familiar, but before I could place him Keiko was ushering me towards the door, ignoring my feeble, watery protests. Somehow she had found the time to put on a pink tracksuit and white trainers, although her skin was still dusted in glitter and her hair was damp from her turn in the martini glass. She chivvied and harried me through a warren of dingy corridors, a cornerman leading a punch-drunk boxer away from the ring.

Stumbling down a stairwell, I came out into a cavernous underground car park. Keiko hurried on ahead, fishing her keys out of her sports bag and unlocking the green Mini parked next to a pillar. I had barely climbed into the passenger seat before she jammed her foot down on the accelerator and the Mini screeched out of the car park and into the night. I slumped my head back against the seat, fighting back another coughing fit.

"It's all right," said Keiko. "We should be safe now."

"I thought I was going to die back there," I said weakly.

"So did I," she replied. "You took a real risk, you know."

"I didn't mean to… it's just, I thought he was going to hurt you."

Keiko gave me a cryptic look but said nothing. Keeping one hand on the wheel, she reached down and scrabbled through her bag. The Mini continued to zoom through the traffic lanes, even as her gaze flicked dangerously from the road, and I winced as she swerved around a black cab pulling away from the kerb. Then, with a triumphant "A-ha!", Keiko pulled out a plastic tray of chewing gum and popped a piece into her mouth.

"Nicotine gum," she explained. "I'm trying to quit."

"I'm just glad you've got both hands back on the wheel," I said. "One near-death experience is enough for me for one night."

"What are you worried about, you big scaredy-cat? I'm a great driver."

"I'll take your word for it." I said, as the Mini screeched to a disgruntled stop at a red light. "So what happened back there in the club – how am I still alive?"

"Search me," replied Keiko. "One minute The Finn looked like he was going to kill you, the next he let go and stomped out through the emergency exit. I don't know, maybe he took pity on you or something."

From what I had seen of The Finn so far, this seemed unlikely. "You knew his name. Paavo, right?"

Keiko nodded. "He used to be on the door of a club I used to work at."

"When you say a club, you mean...?"

She laughed. "Yes, a strip club, Edgar. It's OK to call it that."

"Right. Sorry."

"That's his real name – Paavo, though everyone calls him The Finn. He used to be a good guy, believe it or not. But then he got obsessed with one of the girls who danced at the club. It happens sometimes. The doormen get protective over certain dancers, and there are *always* girls who know how to play on that. But this one was something else. She wrapped The Finn round her little finger and she barely seemed to realize it. It was funny at first, but then Paavo starting getting seriously weird, picking fights with the customers when they asked her to dance for them. I mean, guys aren't supposed to touch us, but they're allowed to *look* at us. That's kind of the point."

I had the uneasy feeling that I knew where this story was going.

"Anyway," Keiko continued, chewing rapidly on her gum. "This guy started coming into the club all the time just to watch Paavo's girl dance, and one night Paavo lost it completely. He beat the guy up really bad, it was horrible. The Finn had to disappear before the police came – that was a couple of years ago, and the last time I saw him until a few days ago, outside the restaurant." She grinned. "You know, when you were hiding in that bin."

"Thanks for reminding me," I said ruefully. "This dancer The Finn was obsessed with – let me guess. Tall girl. Red hair. Background in ballet dancing. Name begins with a 'D'."

Keiko smiled. "Not bad, Mr Private Detective," she murmured. "Not bad at all."

Now that I thought about it, it made perfect sense. Diana had hinted that she had struggled to find work earlier in her career – why not use her dance training? Stripping might not have had the same cachet as ballet in certain circles, but I bet it paid a damn sight more by the hour. Thinking back to Diana's purse stuffed with money, I wondered whether she'd been stripping again to make ends meet. It would also explain why The Finn had taken such a psychotic disliking to me. Maybe he suspected that there was something going on between us, or that I was somehow involved in her disappearance.

Whilst I pondered this new information Keiko turned down a quiet residential street and parked outside a large Victorian townhouse. I peered out through the passenger window into the gloom.

"Where are we?"

"Home!" Keiko replied brightly, turning off the engine. "Do you want to come up for a bit?"

It was late; I was tired and sore, and there was a nastily familiar itch in the small of my back. I didn't know why Keiko's path kept crossing mine, and I wasn't sure I entirely trusted her. At this point, I wasn't sure if I trusted anyone. And yet still I found myself following her out of the Mini and up a dark staircase to the top floor of the house, where she unlocked the door and led me inside a spacious attic flat. I hovered awkwardly in the open-plan living room as Keiko disappeared into the bathroom, and I heard the taps churning out water into the tub.

"Mind if I take a bath?" she said, reappearing in the doorway. "I always need a long soak to wash the club off."

"By all means," I replied, taking a seat in an armchair.

"Are you sure you're all right?" she said curiously.

"I'm fine. Why?"

"I don't mean to be rude, but you keep scratching."

I glanced down to see my hand guiltily clawing at my elbow. I hadn't even been aware I was doing it. The *Dermatitis Herpetiformis* had returned with a vengeance, mercilessly attacking me when I was at my most vulnerable. I briefly considered lying to Keiko, but what was the point? She'd already seen me rise stinking from a rubbish bin and being drowned in another man's hot tub. It wasn't as if I had an image to protect.

"I have a skin condition," I said finally. "Nothing contagious, but I get these rashes on my body. They itch."

"That sucks," said Keiko sympathetically. "Isn't there any medicine you can take for it?"

"There's an antibiotic that clears it up, but I'm allergic. So I'm a bit stuck, really. It's why I spend a lot of time in the bath. The water helps."

Keiko nodded matter-of-factly. "Sounds like you'd better come through and join me, then," she said. She turned around and unzipped her pink track-suit top, tossing it to one side to unveil a smooth, perfect back, and disappeared into the bathroom.

Certain that I had misheard her, I stayed in my seat as the water continued to thunder into the bath in the next room. But then a manicured finger reached around the doorframe and beckoned me inside. Open-mouthed with amazement, I scrambled up out of the armchair and followed Keiko into her bathroom.

. . .

Pity poor Odysseus! Having spent ten years as part of the Greek army besieging Troy, he might have expected the city's fall to signal to end of his labours. But little could he know the epic journey that awaited him. Blown back and forth across the ocean by gusting tempests, bedevilled by mischance and ineffable wrath, the victorious hero was condemned to roam the ocean for a further decade like so much flotsam and jetsam – taunted by hopeless dreams of his homeland of Ithaca, and his faithful wife Penelope who waited for him.

Having fled from the land of the giant Laestrygonians under a murderous rain of boulders, Odysseus and his crew washed up on the island of Aeaea, home of the enchantress and goddess Circe, the beautiful sister of Pasiphae, King Minos's bull-lusting wife. Upon hearing the first exploration party outside her walls, Circe invited the men in and fed them a meal of cheese, barley meal and honey – before turning them into pigs, and leaving the mindless swine to grunt and paw in the muddy sties outside her house.

When Odysseus heard of his companions' fate, he resolved to rescue them. Aided by the God Hermes, he was able to resist Circe's enchantments and cowed her into submission with the threat of violence. The trembling goddess invited him to sleep with her and – after making her swear an oath not to try and trick him again – Odysseus duly obliged. Afterwards, as the satiated couple lounged in bed, the hero recalled:

"... the fourth [servant] brought in water and set it to boil in a large
cauldron over a good fire which she had lighted. When the water

in the cauldron was boiling, she poured cold into it till it was just as I liked it, and then she set me in a bath and began washing me from the cauldron about the head and shoulders, to take the tire and stiffness out of my limbs."[17]

What a bath that must have been! All those years of hopeless travelling, the hundreds of nights above and below deck, shivering in the lonely, brine-bitter wind, the nightmarish battles against giants and the Cyclops; the bitter companionship of despair – all washed away in a luxurious torrent!

Once he had persuaded the now-amenable Circe to return her swineherd to human form, Odysseus and his crew embarked upon a grand celebratory feast that lasted for an entire year. In the midst of the endless courses and toasts, all thoughts of home had apparently been forgotten...

...

It had been a long time since I had slept with anyone, well before the *Dermatitis Herpetiformis* had thrust a hair shirt of nettles over my head. And it had never been like this. We managed to squeeze into the tub together, laughing at the awkward overlap of our limbs and the foam spilling down on to the tiles, soaking the scattered piles of our clothes. I revelled in the exquisite softness of Keiko's touch as she washed my broken skin: a benevolent empress tending to a beggar. Kisses came pattering down upon me like raindrops, until the air was taut with electricity and we shared a sudden, urgent need: Keiko clambered on top of me right there in the soapy water, the storm building to a furious conclusion, her breathless cries like thunderclaps in my ear.

Afterwards we lay in bed together – *Hadaka no tsukiai*, companions in nudity. Keiko chewed thoughtfully on her nicotine gum whilst I reclined in a state of delirious, delicious exhaustion. I marvelled at the exquisite geometry of her figure, the contrast of her burnished skin against the white sheets. It made no sense at all, and I couldn't have cared less.

---

17 Wikisource contributors, "The Odyssey (Butler)/Book X," *Wikisource*, <http://en.wikisource.org/w/index.php?title=The_Odyssey_(Butler)/Book_X&oldid=4016489> (accessed October 2, 2014).

She rolled over and gave me an amused look, brushing the fringe out of her eyes.

"What are you thinking about?" she asked.

"Nothing." I grinned. "You, maybe."

"Only nice thoughts, I hope."

"Surprised thoughts, more than anything else. Women like you don't usually sleep with men like me."

"And what kind of woman am I?" Keiko asked archly.

"You know… beautiful."

She laughed. "Thanks very much. As beautiful as Diana?"

"What do you mean?"

"I think you know what I mean." She took the gum out of her mouth and reached over to her bedside table, where she pressed it in one of the empty blisters in the plastic tray. "Are you in love with her?"

"Diana?" I spluttered. "God, no! I think I'm the only person who isn't."

Keiko's eyes narrowed. "Hmmm… I'm not sure I believe you, Mister," she said, playfully poking me in the side.

"Ow! It's true, I swear!"

"Better had be."

"You don't like Diana very much, do you?"

"She wasn't popular in the club," said Keiko, with a small shrug. "She was never rude or anything, just… distant. As though she thought she was better than the other girls, but was too polite to say anything."

As I lay back on the pillow, I was struck by a sudden jolt. I had remembered where I had seen the moody-looking man in the Executive Suite before. He had been standing in the middle of Yuri and Lilia's wedding photo, inserting himself between the happy couple. I looked over at Keiko.

"Back in the boardroom, when I woke up on the table," I said urgently. "There was a picture of a heavy-set guy with a beard on the wall. Do you know who he is?"

Keiko rolled her eyes. "I do – unfortunately. His name's Valery Limonov. He owns Soaplands with Oscar Salazar, and had his portrait put on the wall to make sure no one forgets it. He comes into the club from time to time, usually with a bunch of escorts fluttering around him."

"What's he like?"

"Bossy. Rough. Likes to push the girls around. I try and stay well clear of him. Luckily for me he prefers blondes."

Things were slowly coming together. I guessed we were talking about the same Valery who Lilia thought I was working for. She seemed pretty frightened of him – was it possible that *he* had had a hand in Diana's disappearance?

"Why are you interested in Valery?" Keiko said curiously. "What's going on, Edgar?"

"She's missing," I said. "Diana, I mean. I think someone kidnapped her."

Keiko gasped. "Seriously?"

"That's how I ended up at Soaplands. I wanted to speak to Oscar about it. I didn't realize he owned the place."

"You think he had something do with it." It wasn't, I noted, a question.

"I *did*," I replied. "Now I'm not so sure. He's your boss – do you think he could have kidnapped her?"

"I don't know, Edgar!" said Keiko, with a hint of irritation in her voice. "I'm just a dancer. People don't tend to include me in their grand criminal schemes, you know?"

I was in danger of spoiling the mood, so I let it rest. But long after Keiko had drifted off to sleep beside me I lay awake, thinking.

The next morning Keiko insisted on driving me back to the flat, winding down her Mini's windows and letting in a stale city breeze as we stewed in traffic. Outside Gill's complex of flats she pulled over to the pavement but kept the engine running. I took the hint, and quickly climbed out.

"Will I see you again?" I asked her, through the driver's window.

"Who can say?" Keiko replied, with a brilliant smile. "Take care, Edgar. You're a nice guy but you've got yourself mixed up in a dirty business. I'd hate to see you get hurt."

With that she put on a pair of large sunglasses, blew me a kiss, and disappeared in a squeal of tyres. I buzzed open the gates, crossed the empty square and wearily climbed the stairs back to Gill's flat. Unlocking the door, I was surprised to find Ray in the living room, flicking idly through the TV channels.

"What are you doing here?"

"Waiting for you," he replied. "Where've you been?"

"Out." I was starting to feel a bit guilty that I had been distracted from my search for Diana, and I didn't feel like going into details. "How did you get in here?"

"Gill let me in. She had to go to work." Ray drummed his fingers on the sofa. "I had to promise her I wouldn't smoke. So I haven't."

"You must be keen to impress," I said. "I'll make sure she knows."

"Any luck finding Oscar?"

"In a manner of speaking."

I recounted what had occurred in Soaplands, quickly skimming over my further adventures in Keiko's flat. Thankfully Ray appeared too distracted by his desire for a joint to notice the large gaps in my story.

"Sounds like a busy night," he said. "What are you going to do now?"

I shrugged. "Take a bath. Think things over."

"Fair enough. I'll wait here."

The television blared through the wall as I trooped into the bathroom and examined my weary reflection in the mirror. As I bent down to turn on the bath taps, something caught my eye. A dark triangle was poking out from beneath the soap in the dish.

"Ray!" I yelled.

His chubby face poked around the door, a quizzical expression on his face.

"You called?"

"Have you been in the bathroom?"

"No. Why?"

"Someone has."

Reaching down into the dish, I retrieved a soggy Polaroid from beneath the bar of soap. The black-and-white photograph was obscured by a layer of milky scum; I gave it a vigorous shake and wiped it down with a towel. Then, holding it up to the light, I examined it.

. . .

In the summer of 1885, whilst on holiday in Dieppe with some friends, Edgar Degas posed for a photograph on the front steps of a house. Seated, he gazed humbly down at the ground with his hat in his hands. Behind him stood three women clutching flowers, mimicking Muses, whilst on the step below the artist a pair of young boys played the role of praying choirboys. The composition was a parody of Jean-Auguste-Dominique Ingres's grand painting 'The Apotheosis of Homer', in which the ancient Greek poet (accompanied by two moody women clutching a sword and an oar – manifestations of the *Iliad* and the *Odyssey* respectively) was raised to divine status. Although a local photographer was drafted in to take the final shot the conception – and the artistic braggadocio – was all Degas'.

Ten years later, aged 61, Degas bought his own camera and began experimenting with the nascent medium. His compositions were meticulously planned – there was nothing spontaneous about his snapshots. There was an element of memorialization in his work: Degas' eyesight was failing, and he had suffered the death of his brother Achille and sister Marguerite in close succession. This might explain why the majority of Degas' surviving photographs (which number fewer than fifty) are of his friends and peers. Perhaps surprisingly, he took very few of his favourite subject matter: dancers. Only three glass negatives remain, carefully stored away in the Bibliothèque nationale de France in Paris. However, the photographs developed from these negatives are among the most powerful and unsettling of any of Degas' work – scratchy shadows of white flesh and blurred limbs; nameless, unknown women trapped in awkward poses for eternity.

. . .

It took me several seconds to recognize Diana. She had been photographed in an anonymous hotel room, dressed in a simple white dress that proffered a generous glimpse of her upper back. Her dress strap had fallen down her left shoulder, and she was struggling to pull it back up whilst raising her right arm in an attempt to shield her face from the camera. The dancer's upright posture had melted into the uncertain slump of a vagrant, her hair messily pinned up and her eyes staring vacantly out into the middle distance. Everything about the scene suggested a strangled cry for help, or a stinging reprimand.

Wordlessly I handed the photograph to Ray. He let out a low whistle.

"At least she's still alive," he said. "She looks in a bad way, though."

"I'm guessing she's been drugged."

"Jesus." Ray tapped the photograph absently-mindedly against his cheek, looking around the bathroom. "The big question is, how the hell did it get in here?"

"I've no idea. The last time I used the bath was before Diana went missing."

"Wasn't your front door broken?"

"It got fixed a couple of days ago. I guess the kidnapper could have taken the photo and dropped it round whilst I was at yours, but the timing's pretty tight. I can't see it."

"Which means…"

"Which means someone's broken in since then. Unless you or Gill left it, and I'm thinking that's unlikely."

"Why go to all that trouble?" asked Ray. "Why not post it? Just to rub our noses in it?"

I shook my head irritably, trying to think. I sat down on the edge of the tub, examining the photo once more: the studied composition, the unmistakable echo of Degas, the item's careful positioning in the heart of the bathroom…

"He's not rubbing *our* noses in it," I said slowly. "He's rubbing *mine*. He's challenging me."

Ray frowned. "Challenging you to what?"

"To find Diana. Don't you see? He set up this photo to look exactly like one I would know, by an artist I've just happened to spend years reading about. Do you think that's a coincidence?" Crouching down beside the Ulpian Library, I picked out a biography of Degas and waved it under Ray's nose. "Look where he left it!"

"Hang on," said Ray. "Are you saying this guy kidnapped Diana to get at you?"

"Maybe not. But now that he's got her, he's sending me messages in a language he knows I'll understand."

"If you say so," Ray replied, unable to disguise the scepticism in his voice. "It's a challenge. So what now?"

"We need to find this hotel room."

"Easier said than done. It could be anywhere." Ray peered closer at the photograph. "Hang on a minute. There's something on the table behind it. Some kind of box."

I snatched the Polaroid off him. "It's a carton from a fast-food place." I squinted, trying to make out the tiny handwriting. "Volcano Chicken?"

"Oh, that's near King's Cross," Ray said immediately. He returned my incredulous stare with a modest smile. "Sometimes I get hungry, you know…"

Unbelievably, it appeared that Ray's susceptibility to the munchies had actually come in useful. He had already got his phone out and was scrolling down through the screen.

"So you're looking for hotels around King's Cross," he mused. "It doesn't necessarily narrow it down. You've got the Travelodge, the Holiday Inn, The Morrison, The Eastern… there's got to be about fifty here. This is hopeless!"

"Actually, it's not," I said – even as my heart sank at the terrible implications of it all.

THERE WAS RAIN IN OUR WINDOW

Clouds were rolling in overhead as the bus crawled through a bleak land-scape of tower blocks and backstreets pubs towards King's Cross. The heat had brought the city to its knees, squeezing the life from its narrow airways. As we passed the prison on Pentonville Road, a loud rumble warned of an approaching storm. The electric crackle in the air was aggravating my *Dermatitis Herpetiformis*, and I shifted restlessly in the seat as the bus inched between red lights. Beside me, Ray looked equally glum. He had been desperate to go back to his flat for a smoke and I'd had to promise to put in a good word with Gill in order to get him to come along. For some misguided reason, Ray seemed to think this might actually help him.

The first raindrops began to fall as we stepped off the bus on to the pavement. Ray glanced up at the leaden sky and gloomily turned up his collar.

"You never said anything about rain," he grumbled.

"You want me to apologize for the weather?"

"It's your fault we're on this wild goose chase," Ray said defiantly. "If it was up to me we'd be inside and dry."

"All right, Ray," I replied, holding out my hands. "I'm sorry it's raining. Can we please go to the hotel now?"

There was a crack of thunder above our heads, and the rain came cascading down in a thick grey sheet. Businessmen sprinted towards King's Cross station beneath improvised umbrellas of newspapers and briefcases. I led Ray in the opposite direction, away from the strangled snarls of the traffic on Euston Road. Following a map on Ray's phone, we navigated a passage through the backstreets, shoulders hunched against the driving rain, until I saw a hotel sign poking out into the street ahead of us.

"I still don't understand how you can be so sure that this is the right place," Ray said gloomily.

"Look, it's easy, when you think about it," I replied, summoning all the patience I could muster. "Diana's kidnapper left a clue in my bathroom, near all my books about bathing – a photo mimicking the work of an artist famous for his paintings of bathers. Are you telling me you aren't sensing a pattern here?"

"I'm not stupid," muttered Ray, as we walked up the steps beneath the sign of the Morrison Hotel, "but what's this got to do with bathing?"

. . .

Jim Morrison sat on the terrace of the Café de Flore, sipping whiskey in the Parisian sunshine. It was June 1971 and the Lizard King was on the lam, having fled from the US whilst appealing against a six-month jail sentence for profanity and indecent exposure. During a heaving, feverish gig in a converted aircraft hangar in Miami, Morrison had been accused of unzipping his trousers and displaying his Crawling King Snake to the crowd. Even by Morrison's standards, he had been drunk – swearing, haranguing the crowd and forgetting lyrics. "I'm talking about love!" he screamed repeatedly, exhorting the sweaty audience to hold each other. Yet despite the lurid and outraged claims, the most damning evidence produced in court amounted to dazed witness testimony and some ambiguous photographs. It was enough to find Morrison guilty. Sensing a censorious mood in the air, he stuffed a suitcase with notebooks and poetry recordings and fled to Europe to join his girlfriend Pamela Courson.

The exiled singer was at something of a crossroads. The Doors were on hiatus, having called a halt to their live shows after Morrison had suffered a breakdown during a gig to promote *L.A. Woman* in Louisiana, carrying out a sit-down protest and refusing to sing any more. The drink was making him pile on the pounds, and he was coughing up blood. Seemingly uncomfortable in his own skin, he was stockpiling alter egos like excuses: Mr Mojo Risin'; James Douglas Morrison; the Lizard King; the dreaded, drunken Jimbo.

As he considered his options on the café terrace, Morrison became aware of a discordant note carrying on the breeze. In the street outside a pair of

American buskers were butchering Crosby, Stills, Nash and Young's back catalogue. By now the drink was kicking in, and as Morrison wandered down to watch them slaughter 'Marrakesh Express' he was struck by a sudden brainwave. The lubricated singer introduced himself and carted the star-struck buskers off to a studio, where he paid for 45 minutes of recording time.

The session was not a success. Bored sound engineers lounged around in the background whilst Morrison and his new band struggled to tune their instruments and bickered over what songs to play. There were several minutes of out-of-tune noodling, with Morrison's slurred encouragements as backing vocals. Finally, exasperated by his cohorts' ineptitude, Morrison launched into an impromptu performance of 'Orange County Suite' – his poetic tribute to Pamela Courson, which had failed to make the cut on a couple of The Doors' records. Giving the whole thing up as a bad job, Morrison cut the recording session short, ending up with a quarter-hour tape by a band entitled Jomo and the Smoothies. The drunken shambles would be the last thing Morrison ever recorded.

...

We stood in an empty lobby, dripping water on to the carpet. The Morrison Hotel was proudly, almost deliberately anonymous. There was no one behind the desk and the armchairs in the reception area were empty. I had the sense that there would always be a room free here, no questions asked. Anyone would be welcome, provided they had the right amount of coins in their pocket – cheating couples and lonely salesmen, petty criminals on the run…

"OK, let's pretend for a second you're right, and this is the right hotel," said Ray, under his breath. "How are we going to find what room they're in? Do you think he's booked in under A. Kidnapper, plus guest?"

Even I had to admit that this was a fair point. I gnawed on my lip, thinking. I needed to get in character. I needed to channel the Lizard King.

"Everything has a meaning," I said. "Even the room number. Let's go and check out Room 17 first."

We headed for the stairs with the watchful step of intruders, passing through deserted corridors decorated with flocked wallpaper shadowed with damp. From time to time muffled noises challenged the silence: voices raised in argument, a slamming door; the weary drone of a hoover somewhere on the upper floors. But we never saw a soul. Our pace slowed as we crept along the second floor, until we came to a stop outside the door to Room 17.

"It's open," Ray whispered.

My heartbeat quickened at the sight of a crack of light between the door and the frame, and I pressed myself against the wall. Instinctively I knew that we had come to the right place. But having reached the end of the kidnapper's trail, I felt my confidence begin to ebb away. Who knew what lay on the other side of the door? Could Diana really be waiting for us, or had I led us both into a trap?

There was no turning back now. Gesturing at Ray to step back, I slowly pushed the door open.

Like all cheap hotel rooms, Room 17 was at once alien and familiar, covered in secondhand stains and hand-me-down odours. Raindrops were smeared across the window like tears. Everywhere I looked I saw violence's grimy fingerprints. The floor was carpeted with broken glass, bloody sheets torn from the bed; the bedside table sprawled on its side like a drunk in the street.

"This doesn't look good," said Ray.

"You can say that again."

Squatting down by the bin, Ray pulled out a fast-food carton with the Volcano Chicken logo emblazoned upon it in fiery red lettering.

"You were right," he said. "They were here."

They had been. But were they still? I stared at the door leading through to the bathroom, a solid fist of dread in my stomach. I had been right about Morrison Hotel. I had been right about the room number. I just hoped to God I was wrong about what lay beyond that door.

...

Maybe it was all the blood he was coughing up, but Morrison's time in Paris was overshadowed by the spectre of death. He badgered a friend into taking him around Père Lachaise, the Parisian cemetery where Balzac and Wilde were buried, and mused that he wanted to be laid to rest there. Heroin from

China had become dangerously fashionable: Morrison's girlfriend Pamela Courson was an addict, and 'China White' was a constant presence in the dark alcoves of the Rock n' Roll Circus, a hip club on the Left Bank where the walls were covered in murals of Morrison's rock alumni dressed in clown suits.

On the night of 3 July Morrison took Courson to the movies, taking in the Robert Mitchum noir western *Pursued*. They had a late-night meal at a Chinese restaurant and headed back to their apartment at 17 rue Beautreillis around one o'clock in the morning. What happened next is a muddy tangle of accusations, conflicting testimonies and rock mythology. According to accounts by Courson (before her death in 1974 from a heroin overdose), in between whisky sips and lines of heroin she and Morrison played The Doors' records and sang together. As Courson slipped in and out of consciousness Morrison started vomiting blood. He stumbled into the bathroom, where Courson helped run him a bath. He filled saucepans with clots of his own blood before the nausea appeared to pass. Drugged, drained, Courson left her boyfriend and went back to bed to pass out.

She rose the next morning to find Morrison dead in the bathtub, the water the colour of rosé wine, a slight smile playing upon his lips. The French coroner – who appeared to be in a mystifying hurry – quickly attributed the death to heart failure, and no autopsy was ever performed. Morrison's body was buried on 7 July at Père Lachaise cemetery, alongside the poets and the artists he had so admired. With confirmation of his death still to reach the U.S., only a handful of mourners attended his funeral.

. . .

The bathroom door creaked open with a waft of stale air. Edging inside, I flicked on the light, which let off a harsh buzz as it cast a jaundiced eye over the scene. The bathroom was a wet grotto with mildewed tiles and a stained ceiling, the shower curtain drawn around the bath. Through the filmy plastic shroud I could make out the unmistakable silhouette of a slumped figure. I crept forward and reached out for the curtain, mouthing a silent prayer over and over to myself.

Yanking back the shower curtain, I let out a shocked cry.

The Finn lay sprawled in the tub, his mouth open in a final, futile battle cry. Stuffed into the tight coffin of the bath, his giant limbs had taken on almost comical proportions. He was wearing a black bomber jacket that was caked in blood, a sticky trail emanating from the bullet wound in his chest.

"Jesus Christ!"

Startled, I whirled round to see Ray backing away from the bathtub, the colour draining from his face. "Is he... you know?"

"Certainly looks that way."

"Shit," whispered Ray. "Shit! What happened to him?"

"Looks like someone shot him."

"*Shit!*" said Ray again. "How can you be so calm?"

"I'm not calm. I'm relieved. I was worried it was going to be someone else."

"You thought Diana—?"

I nodded. "I guess we're not done playing yet."

"Speak for yourself," said Ray, with a nervous laugh. "If you want to keep playing 'Where's the Corpse?' with some maniac then that's up to you, but I am officially off this case." He hovered in the doorway. "You coming or what?"

"Two seconds."

Ray bolted from the bathroom, leaving me to share a final moment alone with The Finn. Even after all that had passed between us – the implacable, inexplicable violence he had committed upon my person – I took no satisfaction from seeing his dead body. Pulling the shower curtain back around him felt like the least I could do.

On my way back through the bedroom, I caught sight of something poking out from beneath the bed. It was a tan leather tassel. In his haste to leave the crime scene, the kidnapper had overlooked something. I crouched down and pulled out Diana's bag from under the bed. It was filled with make-up: lip gloss and lipstick, concealer, a compact. Feeling a small plastic object through the bag's lining, I unzipped a side pocket and found a memory stick at the bottom. I slipped it into my trouser pocket, put the handbag back beneath the bed and left the room.

Ray was already at the end of the corridor, repeatedly jabbing the button to call up the lift. He motioned at me to hurry up, almost manhandling me into the lift when it finally arrived. The doors were closing when I saw a man appear at the other end of the corridor. Dressed in dark clothing, he prowled gracefully to the door of Room 17 and pushed it open. My eyes widened in surprise. As the doors slammed shut and the lift lurched downwards I turned excitedly to Ray.

"Did you see that?"

"What?"

"That was Yuri! We have to go back up there!"

I reached over to press the button for the second floor, only for a hand to shoot out and fasten around my arm.

"Listen to me very carefully," Ray said quietly. "We are not going back up anywhere. We are getting out of this place as soon as we can."

"But Yuri—!"

"Have you lost it completely?" shrieked Ray. "There is a fucking *corpse* up there, Edgar! This is not a game!"

The lift shuddered as it reached the ground floor, and the doors reluctantly opened. I had to pull Ray back to stop him from sprinting through the lobby, and we didn't speak until we had put several streets between us and the Morrison Hotel. Ray was so agitated that I had to take him to Volcano Chicken to calm him down. We sat in moody silence at a counter by the window, staring out on to the rain-drenched street while Ray picked listlessly through his chilli wings and large fries.

"So what do you think happened back there?" he asked finally.

"I'm not sure," I replied. "Whatever our guy was up to, I don't think The Finn was part of the plan. The kidnapper is precise and methodical, and Paavo's a psychopath. He always seems to turn up sooner or later – maybe he was following Diana and waited until they were settled in the hotel room before surprising them."

"They could have been working together," Ray suggested. "Maybe they had a falling out. Over money. Or her."

We sat in silence, digesting the grisly prospect.

"I've never seen a dead body before," Ray said mournfully. "I can't stop thinking about it. And you know what the stupidest thing is? It's the bloody duck I can't get out of my head."

He shook his head, and took a long sip from his coke. I rubbed my temples wearily. It felt like a migraine was coming on. "What are you talking about?"

"You didn't see it?"

I had been so relieved that the body in the bathtub hadn't been Diana's that I hadn't examined it properly. I shook my head.

"It was the strangest thing," mused Ray, biting on a chip. "This giant guy, covered in blood, and in his hand he's holding this plastic yellow duck."

There was a sinking feeling in the pit of my stomach, as though someone had pulled out the plug.

"A plastic yellow duck," I repeated dully.

"Yeah – like a bath toy. You know, like the one you've got."

40-21-35

I tipped the bathroom upside down, demolishing the Ulpian Library and ransacking the ring-binder files on the shelf, but it was no use. Curtis was nowhere to be seen. The kidnapper must have swiped him when he had broken in and left the photograph in the soap dish – I had been so distracted by the haunting image of Diana that I hadn't noted the duck's absence. The stakes were getting too high; I couldn't afford to make those kinds of mistakes. Not only had I been at a murder scene, leaving my careless fingerprints all over Diana's bag, but one of my things had been clutched in the dead man's hand. Add that to my repeated run-ins with The Finn, and I would be a natural suspect for his murder. No wonder the kidnapper had left a trail of clues for me to follow. With one Degas photograph he had set a simple trap for me, and I had blundered right into it.

As we left King's Cross Ray insisted that we go to the police, or at least tell Gill what was going on. He grew sulky when I refused, and we parted on bad terms. Maybe it wasn't such a bad thing. Grateful as I was for Ray's help, I was getting sucked deeper and deeper into a murky whirlpool and it wasn't fair to drag him down with me. So I said nothing about Curtis or the memory stick I had taken from Diana's bag, and let Ray return to his flat to lose himself in sweet smoke.

Giving up on the hunt for Curtis, I took my laptop through into the living room and inserted the memory stick into the USB port. The stick contained a single video file. As the cursor hovered over the icon, my mind began conjuring up all kinds of terrible possibilities: a tearful hostage's plea, a ransom demand, a snuff video. Had the kidnapper really overlooked the memory stick, or was this just another sly trick?

Clicking 'play' before I could torture myself with any more unpleasant possibilities, I was rewarded by Diana's smiling face flashing up in front of me.

. . .

In November 1957, two months before her marriage to the Hungarian body-builder Mickey Hargitay, the movie star Jayne Mansfield bought a mansion at 10100 Sunset Boulevard in Beverly Hills. Mansfield embarked upon a radical redecoration, drenching the 40-odd rooms in her favourite colour: pink. A heart-shaped fireplace was installed. A fountain squirted pink champagne. Hargitay built a heart-shaped swimming pool for his wife, with the inscription 'I love you Jayney' inlaid into the floor of the pool.

Needless to say, the bathroom didn't escape Cupid's violent onslaught. The walls, ceiling and floor were covered in pink shag-pile carpet. Never camera shy, Mansfield was happy to be photographed in her small, heart-shaped bathtub, dipping a demure toe into the water, a small pink towel barely covering her spilling breasts; or admiring her reflection in the mirror; or submerged in the water, with a modest covering of bubbles; talking on her (pink) telephone. Mansfield's curvaceous figure seemed somehow invented for the bath – her overgenerous frame always tilted slightly forward, in case anyone was in danger of overlooking her chest.

Given the dubious merits of her roles in such modest successes as *Will Success Spoil Rock Hunter?* and *The Girl Can't Help It* – a scattershot rock-and-roll comedy with gender politics from the late Middle Ages – it seems to me that Mansfield's greatest performances were those captured on camera in the Pink Palace. Her tub was as small and shallow as a birdbath, a pedestal rather than a sanctuary; her own bathroom turned into just another movie set.

. . .

I was watching some kind of a home movie – the picture wobbled unsteadily as the camera lurched uncomfortably near to Diana's face. Her hair was cut shorter, in a playful bob, and she looked several years younger. Although she was smiling, as the camera zoomed in I thought I detected a slight tightness in her jaw, a grit of irritation in her eye. She shied away from the lens, pushing the cameraman back.

"I'm not ready for a close-up yet," she said.

The camera dutifully panned out. Diana was stretched out on a bed in matching red underwear. The room was bright with sunshine, a vase of yellow and orange flowers providing a vivid splash of colour against the whitewashed walls. A sliding door leading out on to the balcony was half-open, letting the breeze toy with the white drapes. At the bottom of the picture the cameraman's bare feet were just visible, poking out of a pair of black trousers. He appeared to be sitting up on the bed, his back against the headrest.

"You're determined to film this?" asked Diana.

The camera nodded up and down.

"Even if I ask you nicely not to?"

Diana sighed as the camera nodded again. "As you wish."

She sat up and unclipped her bra, laying a protective arm across her breasts as it fell to the floor. Diana glanced up at the camera, offering it a teasing hint of a smile that made my skin prickle with anticipation. Then she let her arm drop. The cameraman chuckled softly.

"I thought you'd enjoy that," Diana said archly.

A gust of wind swept into the bedroom, sending the drapes into a billowing fury. Diana got off from the bed and walked over to the balcony, closing the sliding door. She turned around and slowly slid her red thong down her legs, her eyes never leaving the camera as she bent over. Stepping out of her discarded underwear, Diana crawled naked on her hands and knees across the bed and unbuckled the man's trousers. He grunted as she worked them free, eliciting a grim grin from Diana. Pulling down his boxer shorts, she pushed a lock of hair behind her ears, leant down and began to

. . .

CUT! First drawn up by a Presbyterian Elder in 1930, The Motion Picture Production Code (also known as the Hays Code) was a reaction to those who felt that movie-making was spiralling into a pit of lust and depravity. In the hope of protecting the public from vulgarity and obscenity, sex and profanity – Hollywood's Four Horsemen of the Apocalypse – it laid out a set of guidelines for errant movie producers. Under the Hays Code, scenes involving everything from excessive kissing and undressing to certain dances were to be cut.

The publication of the Code was greeted with a combination of disdain and outright amusement, and for a time filmmakers such as the flamboyant Cecil B. DeMille were able to simply ignore it. Like that other great American showman, P.T. Barnum, DeMille recognized the bubbling potency of the bathtub, and reputedly included a bathing scene in every film he made. His 1932 Roman epic *The Sign Of The Cross* – boasting Claudette Colbert as Poppaea Sabina, Nero's wife – presented him with the perfect opportunity. In the name of historical authenticity, De Mille claimed (probably mischievously) that he used actual asses' milk to recreate Poppaea's lavish baths. The finished scene is thick with sexual tension: the empress admiring herself as she luxuriates in the pool, the swell of her breasts visible just below the milky surface; Poppaea's imperious command that her attendant Dacia take off her clothes and join her in the pool; the close-up on Dacia's bare legs as she slowly follows her mistress's bidding. The scene is even more impressive for the fact that overnight the milk had turned under the glare of the lights, producing a stink so foul that Colbert nearly fainted.

However, unbeknownst to DeMille, the licentious days of empire were running out. Two years after *The Sign Of The Cross*, Joseph Ignatius Breen became head of the new Production Code Association (PCA), which was granted the power to approve films for release. This belatedly provided a framework by which the Hays Code could be enforced, the censor's scissors tutting and trimming celluloid with abandon. American cinema entered a prolonged period of stunted adolescence, at once prudish and prurient, which spied indecent couplings in dance steps and threw up its hands in horror at the thought of blacks and whites kissing, or homosexuals existing.

It wasn't until the early 1960s, and the rise of television and increased competition from more permissive foreign films, that the censors were persuaded to relax their grip upon the scissors. This easing of conservative values triggered a race – a kind of competitive striptease – amongst American filmmakers to see which famous actress could be persuaded to appear nude on camera first. In 1962 Marilyn Monroe went naked for George Cukor's *Something's Got To Give*, but filming was disrupted by the star's health problems and the film remained unfinished upon her death. In this race, it would be another blonde bombshell who would eventually breast the tape...

The 1960s hadn't started well for Jayne Mansfield. Her film roles had tailed off and she had been reduced to appearing in low-budget foreign language films, her bosom a cheap punchline for talk-show hosts. The 1963 sex comedy *Promises! Promises!* offered her an opportunity to reclaim the spotlight – provided she was willing to take off her clothes. In the film she frolics in a foam-filled bathtub singing 'I'm In Love', her legendary breasts on show for the 0.14% of the population who hadn't yet seen them. Photographs of the naked Mansfield on set were published in *Playboy*, resulting in an obscenity charge for Hugh Hefner.

Despite the renewed publicity Mansfield's career continued on a downward spiral – her final billed role was only four years away. Perhaps the most damning indictment of the Hays Code is that her nude scenes in *Promises! Promises!* are a marked regression of the sophisticated sexuality of Colbert's performance thirty years earlier. Obvious in their adolescent titillation, simultaneously innocent and tawdry, there is something rather desperate and strangely sad about them.

...

The man continued to film Diana as she pleasured him, running his free hand through her red hair, his breaths growing hoarse with pleasure. I watched with a combination of horrified fascination and guilty desire. Although I told myself I was only watching to see if the man revealed his identity, I wasn't sure I would have had the strength to stop the film even if he had.

Diana broke off, looking up straight into the camera.

"Let's cut to the chase, shall we?" she said.

Taking the man's erection in her hand, she straddled her legs around him and mounted it with a small gasp. The camera wobbled and shook as she began to ride him, her eyes closed, her head thrown back. Diana refused to look down at the man, batting his hand away when he reached up to grope her breast. As she drove herself deeper and deeper upon him, I saw not just Diana but Bathsheba, reluctantly acceding to her king's demands; and Poppaea Sabina, recklessly courting Nero's volatile affections; and Vivian in a Beverley Hills penthouse, charging by the hour. Unexpectedly, I also thought about Keiko, and the gentle balm of her touch on my skin as she washed me.

The couple began to rock faster and faster and Diana finally lost patience, snatching the camera from the man's hand and hurling it to the floor. The world spun sickeningly, and I was left staring at the whitewashed ceiling as the pair of them built to a frenetic crescendo of pants and groans, the bed creaking beneath them. Then the man let out a shuddering explosion of breath, and the room fell silent.

Nothing moved for thirty seconds or so, and then a giant hand loomed over the lens and the man picked up the camera, sweeping over Diana's leggy debris as she lay sprawled and flushed across the bed.

"Happy now?" she asked huskily.

The picture went black before the man could reply. Rewinding the video and slowing it down to a frame-by-frame crawl, I was able to freeze the man's reflection in a wall mirror as he turned back to film the bed. But it was more of a smudge than a portrait, a vague suggestion of white skin and tousled dark hair. It could have been Oscar Salazar. It could have been anybody.

As I peered closer at the man in the mirror, my phone suddenly went off in my pocket. I pulled it out, staring at the screen in disbelief.

Diana was calling me.

THE COMMON'ST CREATURE

I gazed dumbly at my phone as it rang. The ringtone seemed to herald a message from the other side, a tinkling bell at a Victorian séance. Finally I snatched it up and held it to my ear. For several seconds there was nothing but the crackle of the line and the sound of heavy breathing, and then a man's voice said:

"I'm going to kill you."

He spoke slowly and deliberately, as though his mouth was struggling to frame the words. In the background I heard a glass clink, and the glug of liquid as it poured from the bottle. My mind racing, I thought back to the day after Diana's disappearance, when Ray and I had watched a man going through her things in her flat, before pocketing her mobile phone.

"Yuri?" I said hesitantly. "Is that you?"

There was a long pause, and a cough.

"Yes," he said. "It is Yuri. It is good that you know who will kill you."

"Why do you want to kill me?"

"You have taken my Diana."

"*Me?* I had nothing to do with it!"

"I saw you in the lift of that hotel," Yuri said obstinately. "And Lilia said she saw you in the lobby when I was with Diana, and outside the theatre. Everywhere we go, you go too. I know you are working for Valery."

"You've got it all wrong!" I protested. "I'm working for Diana! She hired me to try and stop Oscar coming on to her, only someone broke into her flat and kidnapped her. Now I'm trying to find out who. When I saw you in the hotel, I thought it might have been you."

"Me?" roared Yuri, with grand indignation. "I would never harm a hair on her head! I love Diana! She is my Odile!"

"If you love her so much, why did you pretend you'd been run over?"

"I had no choice," Yuri mumbled. "There are people after me, shadows on the street. A big black car, like a hearse, following me everywhere I go. But then I found out my Odile was gone." Yuri choked back a sob. "I had to come out of hiding to find her. I will not rest until she is back in my arms."

"Let me help you try to find her," I said. "Listen to me carefully. You've got Diana's phone. Have you checked her records?"

"Records? What records?"

"Her list of dialled calls. The night she was kidnapped she arranged to meet someone on the phone but I don't know who it was."

"How come you know this?" Yuri said suspiciously.

"It doesn't matter."

"I see," said Yuri, with a tinge of drunken triumph. "You were watching her too – spying on my Odile through your little peepholes."

Either he was a more perceptive drunk than I had given him credit for, or Yuri knew about the cameras. Had he been watching Diana too?

"I will find out who took Diana," Yuri declared grandly, "and when I do I will kill them. Screw you. Screw the Maschenko. I will kill them dead. I will have revenge."

"OK, but let's find Diana first," I told him. "We can worry about killing people afterwards."

"Worm," Yuri said scornfully. "You are scared. You are half a man."

"Yes, but—"

"A slimy slug."

"OK, but if you could just check—"

"Piece of shit."

"Yuri!" I shouted. "Who did Diana call?"

I was talking to dead air. He had hung up.

. . .

Having belatedly excused himself from Circe's inexhaustible hospitality, Odysseus was forced to travel to the Halls of Hades in order to consult the blind Theban prophet Teiresias. The North Wind blew his ship all the way to the River of the Ocean, where Odysseus disembarked and made a sacrificial offering to summon forth the underworld. As the spirits of the dead flooded around him, he encountered his old comrade Agamemnon, with whom he had laid siege to Troy. At the sight of Odysseus, Agamemnon burst into tears. Having survived the perilous journey home, the Greek king had accepted an invitation to feast at the palace of his cousin Aegisthus. There, the unsuspecting Agamemnon and his men were butchered "like sheep or pigs for the wedding breakfast."[18] As he lay dying, the blood ebbing from his wounds, the king was forced to watch as his treacherous wife Clytemnestra slew his beloved Cassandra before his eyes.

Such is Agamemnon's tale of woe in the *Odyssey*. Yet some two and a half centuries later, in Aeschylus's play *Agamemnon*, the king suffers a different fate. Agamemnon meets his end not at the dining table but in the bath, and it is Clytemnestra not Aegisthus who brings the axe down upon him. So why did Aeschylus break with tradition, and dare to contradict Homer?

Agamemnon is only the first part of a trilogy of plays known as the *Oresteia*, which plot the tragic downfall of the House of Atreus. It is driven by Clytemnestra's quest for vengeance upon her husband. Her wrath is three-headed like Cerberus – that of a grieving mother, a spurned wife, and a frustrated lover. But how can she hope to kill the great warrior and war hero? Even Homer's Aegisthus needed the pretence of a feast to catch Agamemnon off-guard. Clytemnestra's instrument of misdirection is the bathtub – an alluring Venus flytrap. Once immersed in the warm water Agamemnon is unmanned, the great warrior stripped of his weapons and armour and left naked and vulnerable to a woman's onslaught.

Just as the Kowalskis' bathroom lies offstage in *A Streetcar Named Desire*, so Aeschylus places the murder scene out of sight. The audience can only listen to Agamemnon's chilling screams as he is set upon – their helplessness serving as a sombre reminder from Aeschylus of the futility of interfering with the will of the gods.

. . .

---

18 Wikisource contributors, "The Odyssey (Butler)/Book XI," *Wikisource*, <http://en.wikisource.org/w/index.php?title=The_Odyssey_(Butler)/Book_XI&oldid=4016488> (accessed October 2, 2014).

I tried to call Yuri back but all I got was an answerphone message, a ghostly reminder of Diana's soft, knowing voice. I pictured the Russian sitting alone at a table in the gloom, his head sinking deeper towards his chest. In his drunken stupor, he had let slip a couple of interesting clues. First was the mention of the black car following him, which I guessed had to be the same people carrier that had been on Diana's tail. And then there was the Maschenko, which I remembered Margery mentioning outside the Walker Theatre. Googling the name, I discovered it was a ballet company based in Kiev – which just so happened to be where Lilia had been supposed to travel before she had heard about Yuri and Diana. In the past year, the Maschenko had been taken over by a wealthy Russian businessman promising a revolution that would turn the ballet into the biggest in the world. His name? Valery Limonov, joint-owner of Soaplands. Slowly the different threads of this case were starting to come together, the connections becoming clearer. I knew I needed to learn more about the shadowy Valery, but Diana was missing and Yuri was no use. There was only one person left I could try and talk to. Luckily for me, Margery had told me just where I could find her.

Evening was falling by the time I arrived outside the Dauphine Studios, an unassuming two-storey building off Kensington High Street. As I approached the front entrance I heard the lock buzz and a young dancer emerged from the front door. I jogged over and caught the door before it shut, offering the girl a quick reassuring smile. There was a brief flicker of hesitation as she looked at me, then she nodded and walked away across the car park.

Inside the building was a maze of empty corridors. Everyone appeared to have gone home, and instead of the harsh admonitions of the instructors, the resounding surge of the piano and the light rainfall of feet upon the floor, all I could hear was the strip light buzzing above my head and the distant strains of orchestral music. It felt like an uneasy childhood dream of being trapped in school long after everyone else had gone home. I followed the faint trail of music through the building, up to a dance studio on the second floor, where I looked in through the open doorway.

Set against a backdrop of darkening sky in the windows, the studio was lit up with bright spotlights that bounced off the full-length mirrors that ran the length of the back wall. Lilia Kutznetsova was dancing alone to a portable

CD player in the corner in the room. Dressed in a ballet top and tights the colour of winter frost, she shimmered across the studio, her slippers squeaking on the smooth floor as she pirouetted and leapt. Lilia moved with the glittering, perfect precision of a droplet of water falling from an icicle. I had a sudden sense of what Degas must have felt standing in the wings of the Palais Garnier, an admiring onlooker lost in the beauty of the dance.

Catching sight of me in the mirror, Lilia faltered. She spun round.

"Who's there?" she called out.

I stepped out of the doorway and gave her a forlorn wave. Lilia made a small noise of contempt and turned back to face the mirror.

"For a moment I was worried," she said coolly. "But it is only you."

"I'm sorry to barge in," I said apologetically. "I had to talk to you and I heard you were practising here every day so…"

With a sigh Lilia padded over to the CD player and stopped the music. As I cautiously entered the room she unfurled a slender leg on to the barre and stretched out to touch her toes. The half-empty water bottle by the stereo suggested she had been dancing for some time, but Lilia looked as though she had barely broken sweat.

"If you're looking for Yuri then you're wasting your time," she told me, without looking up. "I haven't seen him for days."

"It's you I wanted to talk to. I spoke to Yuri earlier on the phone."

Lilia paused in the middle of her stretch. "Yes?" she asked, her voice tight, controlled. "And how is my husband?"

"Fine," I replied quickly. Lilia stared at me in the mirror, and I found myself suddenly examining my feet. "Actually, he sounded pretty drunk," I admitted.

"How very predictable," she said.

"If you don't mind me saying, you don't sound that bothered."

Lilia shook her head slightly, and swapped legs on the barre. "Yuri is an artist, a great artist. Nobody denies this. But great artists are not simple men. They are not 'easy-going guys'. I understand this. Whether I am bothered or not has nothing to do with it."

"What about Diana?" I said. "She seems to bother you a lot."

"Is that who you wanted to talk to me about? Because you're wasting your time."

"Actually, I wanted to ask you about Valery Limonov."

This time it was Lilia who avoided eye contact in the mirror.

"Who?" she said.

"A Russian businessman who owns the Maschenko Ballet in Kiev. You accused me of working for him outside the *Coppelia* premiere."

"I don't know who you're talking about," Lilia said.

"That's funny, because he was at your wedding. I've seen the photographs."

Lilia stopped stretching.

"I told Valery it was a bad idea to put those pictures in the newspaper," she said finally. "But he insisted. He said he had paid for everything, so why shouldn't people know about it? He is a hard man to argue with."

"He paid for your wedding?"

"How else could we have it in the Caribbean? I have a little money saved but Yuri has nothing. He is not good with money – he needs me to take care of things like that. So I approached Valery and made him a proposition."

"You and Yuri would dance for him at the Maschenko Ballet. With a nice wedding as a down payment."

"In Kiev Yuri and I will dance all the great roles. Together we will make the Maschenko the most famous dance company in the world. Believe me, Valery will get his money's worth."

"But only as long as you and Yuri are still together," I said slowly. "So when Yuri continues this affair with Diana…"

"…it threatens everything. I try to tell him this but he will not listen. When I tell him all he can say is that I am jealous. He is a fool who believes his whore is a perfect princess that can do no wrong."

"Diana's not a whore," I said quickly.

"She used to take money from men to have sex with her. Maybe you have another word for that." Lilia shrugged. "I do not."

. . .

By the 16th century, Europeans were bathing in increasingly mucky water. Mixed bathhouses provided the perfect location for romantic trysts, lovers entwining in the anonymous fog of steam. In England, bathhouses became known as 'stew-houses' or 'stews', bywords for immorality and sexual impropriety. In Act 5, Scene III of Shakespeare's *King Richard II*, the usurper Henry Bolingbroke seeks news of his dissolute son Hal, who has fallen in with a bad crowd. It is the Duke of Northumberland, Henry Percy, who replies, telling Bolingbroke that he has recently spoken with Henry's son about an upcoming joust in the city of Oxford. According to Percy, Hal plans to head to the stews to take a glove from one of the bawdy girls there, which he will sport as a mark of support in the jousts.

Shakespeare could be forgiven for having a certain familiarity with the insalubrious stews. In 1599 the Globe theatre, which staged many of his plays, was rebuilt in Southwark on the south side of the Thames. Handily situated beyond the reach of the civil authorities of the City of London, Southwark was a notorious Tudor vice den of taverns, bear-pits and prisons, its streets populated with a pungent collection of criminals, prostitutes and actors. The theatre was situated around the corner from such infamous stews as Holland's Leaguer, which sets the unworthy mind to wondering whether after a bad review or a calamitous rehearsal, or a simple bawdy moment, the Bard had ever popped in for a soak and a rubdown, and a nibble upon a succulent stewed prune.

To add an extra pinch of spice to the mix, the brothels of Southwark stood on land owned by the Bishop of Winchester, earning local prostitutes the tag 'Winchester geese'. Stephen Gardiner, bishop during Henry VIII's reign, had close ties to the king and was rumoured to have supplied him with a few plump birds. Yet many of the bawdy geese were possessed of a fearful bite – syphilis. A particularly vicious outbreak of the disease in 1546 forced Henry VIII to put the lid on the stews, banning prostitution. The theatres managed to survive another century until their entertainments incurred the displeasure of the ruling establishment – in this case the Puritans, who shut down the Globe in 1642.

...

"All the other dancers knew it," Lilia said defiantly. "Ask them if you like."

I didn't need to. I had video evidence. A ghost of a smile passed over Lilia's lips. She picked up her water bottle and took a victorious sip.

"Maybe – in the past – she was some kind of an escort," I accepted. "But this thing between her and Yuri seems genuine."

"I told you that Yuri is a complicated man," said Lilia. "I cannot stop him chasing every girl that pushes her breasts out at him. Sometimes I can look the other way. But this isn't just insulting. It is *dangerous*."

"You think that Valery might do something violent if your deal is threatened?"

"In the blink of an eye."

"Even kidnap Diana?"

Lilia let out a fragile, high-pitched laugh. "Kidnap? He would put a bullet through her head. Valery is a gangster, not a businessman. He thinks that if he invests in the ballet, then people will think better about him. That he is some kind of patron, with taste and style." Lilia smiled mirthlessly. "He knows nothing."

I scratched my head. It was clear I'd gotten myself mixed up in something that was far bigger than I realized, and it was a struggle to make sense of it all. "I don't know about Valery and the ballet," I said. "All I'm trying to do is find Diana."

"It would be best for all of us if you don't," Lilia said bluntly.

"What if she's in danger?"

"She makes her own bed. I will not cry for her. But Valery has threatened to hurt Yuri if he doesn't end the affair, and I am scared about what he will do." I was shocked to see tears glittering on Lilia's pale cheeks. She quickly wiped them away. "If Valery hurts Yuri I'll kill him," she said fiercely. "I know where he hides out in that grubby bathhouse of his. I'm not scared of him."

"What bathhouse?" I said. "Where can I find Valery?"

Lilia laughed. "You don't need to look for him. He will come looking for you. And then you'll be sorry, believe me." Pulling a jumper over her ballet top, she began packing her things into a bag. "Now if you have finished with your questions, I am going home. Maybe I am lucky, and my husband has remembered that he is married. Are you going to follow me home too?"

I shook my head.

"Then good night."

Lilia slung her bag over her shoulder and padded out of the room, the sound of the door closing behind her echoing around the studio. I went over to the window and watched as she hurried through the deepening shadows of the car park, unlocking a yellow sports car and climbing inside. As the sports car hurtled away my phone began to ring. It was Yuri again.

"I check records," he said, his words more shapeless than ever. "I found out who my Odile called."

"Who?"

"I will kill him. I will make him beg for mercy, and then I will kill him."

"Kill who, Yuri?"

"Oscar," he slurred. "She called Oscar Salazar."

Who had told me he didn't care about Diana any more. Who had lied to me.

"Don't do anything stupid, Yuri," I warned.

There was a sharp intake of breath, and the scrape of a chair leg as Yuri stood up.

"Yuri? What's wrong?"

"The black hearse," he said hoarsely. "It is here!"

I heard a door slam, and a glass smash. There was a loud yell on the other end of the line, and then the phone went dead once more.

A HONEYED SHELL

The clock tower above the dock tolled a genteel eleven as I walked down a set of steps in the shadow of Tower Bridge. Sunlight played upon the frothy swell of the Thames. Outside the cafés on the dock front, people were drinking coffee and sunning themselves, watching the soothing bob of the boats moored in the water. An invisible veil of quiet was draped over the scene.

I rubbed my eyes wearily, trying to ignore my complaining skin. It had been a long night without sleep, and I hadn't been able to bathe. It was all Gill's fault, I thought grumpily. My sister had called me the previous evening, just after I had left the Dauphine studios. She started shouting before I could even say hello.

"What the bloody hell is going on, Edgar?"

"What do you mean?"

"Where's Diana? Apparently she disappeared days ago! And you never said a word to me!"

I made a mental note to give Ray a severe talking to the next time I saw him.

"It's all in hand," I said, as confidently as possible. "Don't worry about it."

"Don't worry about it? Edgar, the *police* have just come round to the flat. They want to talk to you."

I cursed silently.

"They're talking about some kind of incident in a hotel room. It sounds serious."

"It wasn't anything to do with me!"

"The police don't seem to think that way. You need to speak to them right away and make sure they know you're innocent."

I grunted noncommittally.

"Edgar, I'm not messing around!" Gill said urgently. "Do it *now*. Ray says you've got these crazy ideas about what's going on but this isn't some kind of abstract puzzle. My friend is missing and I'm really worried about her."

"OK, OK! I'll speak to them tomorrow."

"And if you do get into any problems, call me," added Gill. "I'm a lawyer, remember?"

"How could I forget?" I said glumly. A sudden thought occurred to me. "Listen, if the police come round to the flat again don't let them into the bathroom, OK? I've got years' worth of valuable notes in there and I don't want PC Plod stomping around and mixing everything up."

"Of course, Edgar I will," said Gill, with heavy sarcasm. "Because protecting your notes is a priority for me right now."

I shouldn't have expected her to understand. She was worried about her friend and my work wasn't important to her. But with the police on my tail, I could hardly go back to Gill's flat and pack away my things. And now that I was giving Ray a wide berth, I had nowhere to go. Unwilling to use up the last of the money Diana had given me on a hotel room, I found an all-night café and slumped at a table. Nursing a coffee I went over everything I knew about Oscar Salazar, trying to piece together every word he had to me. As the dawn lightened the café windows, two memories of the Spaniard stuck in my mind: his plans to sail away with Moira, his 'one true love', and the internet photos I had seen of Oscar aboard his yacht, his hair ruffling in the sea breeze. If I could stumble across the right dock, maybe I could catch him before he left England.

It was a long shot, but then long shots were all I had left. I felt increasingly like Agamemnon, surrounded by a vicious host of Clytemnestras, each hurling their own intricate, strangling nets around me. It was only a matter of time before one of them brought their axe down upon my head. As I left the coffee shop and travelled across the city to Tower Bridge I felt shadowy eyes watching me from the anonymous streams of commuters, and I kept seeing the outline of black people carriers on the roads.

Now, ducking through an archway, I came out into a larger dock, where the yachts were a mixture of floating palaces and streamlined arrows. A network of wooden gangways connected up the boats, closed off to the rest of the dock by small electronic gates. I peered through the tangle of lines and masts at yacht names as I walked past: the *International*, the *Corsair*, the *Betty Blue*. And then I saw it, a luxurious white behemoth at the end of the row. Oscar Salazar was leaning over the edge of his yacht, surveying the sunlit quay through a pair of wraparound shades. He waved as I approached the boat, and pointed to the open electronic gate.

"Edgar! Come aboard!"

Just once in my life, it would be nice to surprise this man. Gritting my teeth, I walked through the gate and down along the gangway, before climbing aboard the *Moira Shearer*.

. . .

As he scoured the Mediterranean for the errant inventor Daedalus, whom he blamed for replacing his queen's robes with a hollowed cow's shell, King Minos knew that it would take extreme cunning to winkle out his former charge. After all, this wasn't the first time that Daedalus had laid low – he had only appeared on Crete after being exiled from his homeland of Athens, where he had murdered his apprentice and nephew Perdix in a fit of jealous rage.

Amid great fanfare Minos announced a competition, promising a priceless reward to anyone who could achieve the apparently impossible task of threading a conch shell. When word of this challenge reached the court of King Cocalus in Sicily, where Daedalus was sheltering, the king knew he had the one man capable of answering Minos's challenge. Daedalus, the author of his own labyrinth back on Crete, duly devised a solution. Smearing the empty shell with honey, he tied a thread around an ant and let the creature follow the trail through its winding passageways – Theseus with a sweet tooth.

With the shell threaded Cocalus proclaimed that he had solved Minos's puzzle, unaware that he was betraying his prize asset. Minos set sail for Sicily at once, intent upon reclaiming the inventor. Little did he know the lengths to which Cocalus would go to protect Daedalus, or the fate that would await him in a bathtub filled with burning hot water...

. . .

"Drink?"

A table had been laid on the deck of the yacht, a bottle of champagne cooling in an ice bucket. Two glasses, two chairs – the door to the cabins below slightly ajar. Had my arrival sent someone scurrying below deck? For all Oscar's casual bonhomie, it looked as though I had interrupted a rather intimate breakfast.

"It's a bit early for me," I said, taking a seat opposite Oscar. "But thanks."

"You don't mind if I…?"

"Be my guest."

Oscar reached over and pulled the champagne bottle out of the bucket. Easing out the cork, he carefully filled his glass with sparkling liquid.

"Now then, my persistent friend," he said. "What brings you to my yacht?"

"It's about Diana."

"Ah, Don Quixote!" exclaimed Oscar, rolling his eyes. "Still he pines for his mythical Dulcinea, galloping through the landscape of his own lunacy."

"I know you met her the night she disappeared," I said obstinately. "Which makes you the last person to see her. You lied to me at Soaplands. You told me you didn't care about her any more."

"And I don't! I can barely recollect her name. I am done with redheads; Oscar Salazar has finally learnt his lesson. At first the passion, the fire, it is exhilarating, but sooner or later the flames get out of control. I am tired of burning my fingers."

"Is that what happened with Diana? She burned you?"

"I know what you are thinking, but it wasn't like that," Oscar told me. "After La Baignoire Pleine I had decided to move on – that much was true. It was Diana who called *me* afterwards."

"To apologize for the scene in the restaurant."

"I am not easily embarrassed. But she wasted an excellent Tempranillo. There is a principle involved."

"So what happened next?" I asked. But I already knew the answer. After all, I had watched Diana as she changed for their meeting, selecting the dress with the lowest neckline. If nothing else, I respected the lengths to which she would go to protect her dancing career.

"We met up," Oscar told me. "This time the wine stayed in the glass. Diana was very penitent. She offered to make certain... amends."

"I'm guessing you didn't tell her you'd been spying on her?"

Oscar smiled faintly, running his finger around the rim of his champagne glass. "I admit that I saw this website, and maybe I sent you the postcard with the link. But I didn't put the cameras there."

"Then who did?"

"Who knows?" Oscar put down his glass and leaned forward. "Do you know the story of *Coppelia,* Edgar?"

I shook my head.

"A young country boy called Franz becomes infatuated with a woman he sees sitting on the balcony of a house in his village. Blinded by her beauty, he doesn't realize that she is a life-size doll created by an inventor called Dr Coppelius. The doctor invites Franz into his home with the aim of sacrificing him and bringing the doll to life – only the intervention of Swanhilde, Franz's true love, saves his life."

"OK," I said slowly. "But I don't see how—"

"I had other plans the night that Diana danced the *Giselle* solo," Oscar explained. "I wasn't going to go. I received an anonymous note the day before the gala telling me it was in my interest to attend. I confess, I was intrigued, so I went."

Of course. Originally it had meant to be Lilia dancing the *Giselle* solo, before she had been summoned to the Ukraine to meet Valery. Diana had stepped in at the last minute.

"Someone wanted you to see Diana dance," I said slowly. "Someone who knew you'd fall for her."

Oscar shrugged. "My weakness for ladies with a particular hair colour is common knowledge. So I go to the gala and I meet Diana and naturally I am impressed, but all the time I am asking myself – who sent me here? Maybe I was being paranoid, but I felt someone was watching us as we talked. Little eyes, peeping." Leaning forward, Oscar continued in a whisper. "Do you see my point now, Edgar? *I* am Franz – nothing more than an innocent country boy, at the mercy of my own desires. You are chasing the wrong man, Edgar.

Somewhere out there is a cunning, deceitful inventor, a Dr Coppelius – he is your real foe, not me."

A breeze picked up off the river, ruffling Oscar's hair and sending goose pimples rippling across my skin. I leaned closer.

"Are you talking about Valery Limonov?"

Oscar clapped his hands together with delighted amusement. "Edgar, you continue to surprise me!" he said. "But this time I fear you are barking up the wrong tree. It's true that Mr Limonov and I share certain commercial interests. For sure, he is not an easy man to get along with, but sometimes this is the price of doing business. No, I am talking about a clever, subtle mind – and you could never accuse Valery of possessing those qualities. He prefers the direct approach."

As the businessman smiled at me, another piece of the puzzle fell into place. "It was *you* who told Valery about Yuri and Diana!" I exclaimed. "You must have found out that he had approached Yuri and Lilia to dance for his company. Maybe Valery's 'direct approach' could get Yuri out of the picture, and leave the way clear for you."

Oscar shrugged. "Valery had an investment to protect. I presumed he wouldn't sit idly by."

"Did it not occur to you that he might try to hurt Diana?"

"It's true I might have underestimated Valery's determination to see the deal through. Although for what it's worth, he says he had nothing to do with Diana's disappearance."

"And you believe him?"

"I've no reason not to." Oscar laughed. "You look so disapproving – like a disappointed mother. I am not a man of violence, Edgar, I do not trade in broken bones and gunshot wounds. As soon as I learnt that Diana had gone to you for help it would have been easy for me to arrange some... *mishap* to befall you. Instead I send Keiko along as a distraction."

I stared at him. "Excuse me?"

"You didn't realize she came on my behalf? My friend, let us speak honestly: what are the chances of a woman like that speaking to you of her own accord?" Oscar gestured at my crumpled clothes. "I mean, look at you..."

Of course he had sent Keiko. It made perfect sense. From the first moment she had appeared in the hotel lobby, a beautiful enigma wrapped in the scent of jasmine, I had sensed danger. Oscar was right – ordinarily there was no way Keiko would care about me, enough to talk to me and help me and kiss me. I wasn't hurt, I told myself fiercely. I wasn't hurt at all.

"You look upset," Oscar said lightly. "Really, there is no cause. You should be grateful to me."

"And what about The Finn?" I said, through clenched teeth. "Should I be grateful for him too?"

"What about The Finn?"

"You're telling me he wasn't working for you?"

"The man's a psychopath," said Oscar, with a dismissive wave of the hand. "You can't do business with people like that."

"Someone killed him."

"How unfortunate. I had nothing to do with it."

I believed him – but then again, Oscar had already proved he was a convincing liar. Sipping his champagne, he settled back into his chair, gazing out over the dock through his sunglasses. He seemed to be weighing something up, making another calculation in his head.

"I didn't sleep with her, you know," he said finally. "Diana. She suggested we went back to my apartment, but I said no."

"It's none of my business."

"Of course it isn't. But maybe you should understand anyway: I *never* fuck the girls."

I blinked. "None of them?"

"They always want to," said Oscar, with a nonchalant shrug. "But I say no. It keeps me sharp. Hungry. Do you know how crazy a girl gets if she offers herself to you and you say no? It requires inner steel not to cave in, iron will. It keeps me sharp, focused. How do you think I am so successful at business?"

"So you date all these beautiful women," I said dubiously, "but you don't sleep with them because you have *inner steel*?"

"You don't believe me?" For the first time I detected a dangerous gleam in Oscar's eye. "You think maybe I have some kind of problem – my little man can't rise to the occasion? There's a girl on this yacht right now, in my cabin. She's as beautiful as dawn on the ocean. You want to come down and watch me fuck her?"

As Oscar's offer hung in the air, I was distracted by the sunlight catching on a silvery object on the deck of the yacht. A foil tray of nicotine gum.

. . .

The summer of 1888 found Vincent van Gogh in Arles. His move to the south of France from Paris had reinvigorated him, the sun-bathed country-side brightening his palette. His paintings were drenched in startling new hues of yellow and mauve. Harbouring hopes of founding an artistic community in Arles, van Gogh invited his friend Paul Gaughin to visit him. The Frenchman prevaricated, claiming ill health. As he waited that August, van Gogh passed the time by painting a vase of sunflowers. He also wrote to his friend Emile Bernard, a 20-year-old artist with a happy knack of making influential friends. Over the course of their letters, the subject had turned to Edgar Degas, whom Bernard claimed was impotent. Van Gogh – who knew Degas through his art-dealer brother, Theo van Gogh, and greatly admired him – was having none of it. As far as Van Gogh was concerned, Degas had made a conscious decision not to sleep with women. He had chosen his art over his love life, his ascetic detachment allowing him to paint better. Chastity sharpened the pencil, argued van Gogh. A chaotic and passionate love life drained the artist of his creative juices. He advised Bertrand to focus on mealtimes and military drills rather than bedroom escapades.

The long-awaited Gaughin finally arrived in Arles on 23 October 1888. But van Gogh's hopes of the two men establishing an artistic haven proved to be a bitter pipedream. The two men quarreled incessantly; an enraged van Gogh threatened Gaughin with a razor blade. Fleeing to a brothel, he cut off his left ear, wrapping the severed lobe in a piece of newspaper and presenting it to a prostitute. In May 1889, the defeated van Gogh left Arles for the asylum.

. . .

"I'll take that as a no," said Oscar. "Your loss."

The interrupted meal. The ajar cabin door. The glittering foil of the gum packet. Lots of people used nicotine gum. It didn't have to mean it was

Keiko. So why did I feel a dull ache in my chest? *You want to come down and watch me fuck her?* I had been so caught up in the desperate search for Diana that I hadn't had time to think about Keiko, or what I felt about her. I guess this sour pain meant that I had liked her even more than I had realized. She had warned me I was caught up in a dirty business – I guess I had just hoped that she was cleaner than everyone else.

Oscar picked up an olive from the bowl on the table and popped it in his mouth, visibly enjoying my discomfort.

"We are sailing back to Spain today," he told me.

"Your father's restaurant in Cadiz?"

"There will be a table for two waiting for us." He stood up and offered his hand. "Farewell, Edgar. You are an odd little man, but in a strange way I have enjoyed locking horns with you. Please accept my sincerest wishes for success in your further endeavours."

As I accepted his handshake I felt my fingers being enveloped in a crushing grip.

"If the authorities do become involved in this affair I trust you will keep my name out of any investigations," Oscar murmured. "It would not do for a man of my position to be tainted with all this... unpleasantness. And truly, what am I guilty of? A red-blooded passion for redheads? Hardly a crime."

"I'll do what I can," I gasped, extricating my hand from his grasp with a wince.

"Good boy. Or I'll send men after you who'll make The Finn look like a ballet dancer. *Si?*"

I nodded dumbly. Oscar laughed, slapping me on the back a little harder than was necessary. Clambering down from the *Moira Shearer*, I walked back along the gangway and out through the gate. I felt utterly defeated. It had been days since I had had a proper night's sleep. My skin was bristling angrily, threatening outright rebellion. The police were after me. Maybe Gill was right, and it was time to go and give myself up. I trudged away from the dock, glumly glancing over my shoulder to see Oscar Salazar finish his glass of champagne and disappear down to the cabin below.

DO NOT DISTURB MY CIRCLES

I stood outside Ray's flat, drumming my fingers on the doorframe as I anxiously scanned the street. A lawnmower grumbled in the garden next door. Across the street, a pair of panting joggers came to a halt beneath the shade of a tree. A toddler stared down at the remains of a dropped ice cream on the pavement, a look of complete and utter desolation on his face.

"OPEN THE DOOR, RAY!" I screamed, hammering on the door. "I HAVEN'T GOT TIME FOR THIS!"

He appeared with surprising speed, flinging open the door and dragging me into the cool hallway.

"Shh!" he said, pressing a finger to his lips. "Don't want to wake the neighbours."

This seemed unlikely, given it was well after midday, but I knew it was pointless telling Ray that. His front room was thick with the pungent stink of marijuana, a homemade bong standing proudly in the middle of the coffee table. Empty pizza boxes and biscuit wrappers were strewn across the floor. It looked as though I had interrupted some kind of raucous Scythian feast. I went over to the window and opened a crack in the curtains, peering out into the street.

"What are you looking for?" Ray said curiously.

"A black people carrier." I replied, snapping the curtain shut again. "Why, have you seen one?"

"I haven't," said Ray, settling down on to the sofa. "Then again, I haven't really been looking. I finished a website late last night. I'm still celebrating." He gave me a sideways look. "Looks like you had a late one too."

"I didn't get much sleep. It's a long story."

"Jump in the bath if you want."

"I haven't got time," I replied, scratching my lower back.

"Jesus. It must be serious."

"Deadly. And I need your help."

"No, no, no," said Ray, shaking his head. "I told you – I'm off the case."

"Ray, you're my only hope! The police are looking for me and I can't go back to Gill's flat. You owe me one for going blabbing to her. I'm never going to hear the end of this, you know."

"You didn't leave me any choice!" Ray said indignantly. "I was worried about you. This isn't a game any more, Edgar. Someone's dead, someone else has been kidnapped. This is serious shit."

"All the more reason to try and solve it now," I pressed. "Listen, can you show me that video you found of Diana dancing at the charity gala? I need to see it again."

He let out a long sigh. "If I find you this video, will you promise to leave me alone after that?"

"You have my word. I won't even speak to you again, if that's what you want."

Ray nodded, seemingly mollified. He opened a new browser on his laptop and began searching for the video. Within a couple of minutes he had retrieved it and Diana was dancing on stage once more, her skirt billowing out around her as she spun faster and faster on the point of her toes.

"What are you looking for?" he asked.

"I'm not quite sure," I admitted. "I feel like I'm missing something obvious, and I need to go back to the beginning. It all started here, at this gala, when Diana danced *Giselle*."

There was a thunderous ovation as Diana came to the end of her solo, dropping into a graceful curtsey. Abruptly the picture jumped to the aftermath of the show, the camera roaming amongst the audience as it panned across the crowded tables. The sound was a jumble of indistinct conversations and snatches of laughter. Last time we had stopped the video here, but now as it ran on I caught sight of a flash of red hair and there was Diana, still dressed in Giselle's peasant girl costume, clutching a bouquet of roses. She was talking to Oscar Salazar, who looked like a matinee idol in his dark tuxedo. As he gave her a dazzling, predatory smile Margery waddled over and kissed Diana on both cheeks.

"I know her!" said Ray. "She was in the cafe at that theatre, wasn't she?"

I gave him an incredulous look. "You forget everything I tell you five seconds later, but you remember *Margery*?"

"Some stuff sticks," replied Ray, spreading his arms out innocently. "I can't explain it."

Margery plunged headlong into conversation with Oscar who, judging by the frequent sidelong glances in Diana's direction, wasn't paying complete attention. When another lady came up and spoke to Margery Oscar seized his opportunity, leaning in to whisper something in Diana's ear. She laughed gracefully.

"Whoah, check out Mr Angry there," said Ray, pointing at a face in the background. "What's his problem?"

Behind Margery's shoulder, sitting at a table on his own, a young man in a tuxedo was watching the three of them chat, his eyes as black as coals, a programme gripped tightly in his hand. As he glared at them Margery turned round, as though sensing she was being watched. A look passed between them that I couldn't decipher, and the young man got up and walked away.

"What was all that about?" Ray muttered.

"I don't know. But there's definitely something going on."

"Do you recognize him?"

There was something undeniably familiar about the man's features, but I couldn't place him instantly. I had to replay the video again and again – long after Ray had lost interest and returned to the heady delights of his bong – before I realized that I had in fact met the man before. I stared at the screen, unable to quite believe it. Because if you added a little bit of stubble to his clean-shaven face, changed his suit into a paint-splattered jumper and tracksuit bottoms, and swapped his programme for a screwdriver, you'd have a spitting image of the workman who had fixed Gill's front door.

. . .

By the 1910s, night was closing in around Degas. His failing eyesight had ended his career as an artist, and he had been forced to move out of his Montmatre studio. His reputation had suffered during the Dreyfus Affair of the 1890s, during which the artist had sided with the anti-Semitic right and broken off relations with his Jewish friends. Never a sociable animal, he had become something of a recluse, spending his days wandering alone through the streets of Paris. In 1915 Degas was approached by the film director Sacha Guitry, who asked him to appear in *Ceux de Chez Nous*, a documentary celebrating the contemporary giants of French painting. Though Renoir, Monet and Rodin all agreed to participate Degas – characteristically – refused. The enterprising Guitry filmed him anyway, setting up his camera on the street outside Degas' apartment. The artist walked blindly past, not even noticing the camera. Whilst his contemporaries appeared in Guitry's film at the easel, vigorously creating their masterpieces, Degas was shown to be just another old man in the street, a doddery victim of an early paparazzo.

. . .

"So let me get this straight," Ray said slowly. "You're saying the guy who kidnapped Diana is a Polish workman."

"No! Well, yes... I mean, he came round and fixed the lock on Gill's front door, but I think he was only pretending to be a workman."

"OK." Ray paused. "But he is Polish?"

"I don't know! I doubt it."

"I see."

"Do you, Ray? That's how he was able to leave the photo of Diana in the soap dish. He left it there for me to find. I've been so stupid – why didn't I see it?"

"To be fair, you've had a lot on your plate recently," Ray offered supportively. "What with all the spying and strippers and that."

I gave him an icy stare.

"So what now?" he asked.

I tapped the screen. "I need to find Margery. I think she knows more about all this than she's been letting on."

"But I can stay here right?"

I patted Ray on the shoulder. "Of course you can. I'll take it from here. Have fun."

He nodded sagely, and reached out for his bong. Leaving my friend to his celebration, I slipped out of his flat and girded myself for another trip into the city.

. . .

Born around 287 BC, the great mathematician and inventor Archimedes grew up in Syracuse on the island of Sicily, which at the time was trapped between the two warring states of Rome and Carthage. The First Punic War had seen Sicily brought under the Roman aegis, although Syracuse remained an independent region, part of a wider confederation of Greek states. The eruption of the Second Punic War in 218 BC left the city in a precarious position. When Syracuse chose to align itself with Carthage, in 214 BC Roman forces swept down to the east coast of Sicily, catching the city between the pincers of a massed army and a seaborne armada of sixty galleys. The Romans were led by General Marcellus, a veteran of the First Punic War who had spent the previous two years battling Hannibal's incursions into Italy.

Syracuse had two major lines of defence – the forbidding geography of the crags and cliffs surrounding the city, and Archimedes. In order to protect his beloved city the inventor turned his mind to the fashioning of terrible machines of war. Shouldering Oppenheimer's burden 2,000 years before the atomic bomb, he became an engineer of death, a destroyer of worlds. Mathematical symbols became slashes and sword thrusts. Archimedes designed catapults, mangonels and trebuchets to hurl boulders into the enemy ranks with unerring accuracy. To combat Marcellus's fleet, he devised a giant claw that reached down into the water and bit into the prow of attacking ships, before hoisting them out of the water and dashing them upon the waves. Archimedes' Claw was a startling demonstration of the principle that had led the inventor to claim that – given a long enough lever – he could move the Earth.

With their assault foundering in the face of the mathematician's wrath, the Romans had little option but to lay siege to the city. It lasted for two years, until 212 BC, when they were able to take by cunning what they had failed to take by force. Taking advantage of a Syracusan festival to the goddess Artemis, the Romans sent a small squadron of men over the walls and inside the city. Wise to Archimedes' potential value, Marcellus had given specific orders that the inventor was not to be harmed. Archimedes remained hard at work in his studio drawing diagrams in the ground, heedless to the uproar that signalled the Romans had taken control of his city and that his cause was already lost.

When a soldier burst into his studio, demanding that he present himself before his new conquerors, Archimedes refused. The soldier – mistaking the famed mathematician for just another curmudgeonly old man – ran him through on his sword. Archimedes fell to the ground, taking his last ragged breath surrounded by the figures and equations he had scratched into the dirt: his defiant, belligerent signature.

...

There was an expectant hush in the café of the Walker Theatre, the held breath of the audience between the raising of the curtain and the performance's first note. Margery was sitting alone at her table, peering through a pair of large spectacles as she tapped a text into her mobile phone. When I took a seat opposite her she held up a finger to ask me to wait, grunting with satisfaction when she eventually pressed send.

"Sorry about that," said Margery. "Sometimes I think it'd be quicker if I popped a letter in the post. The bloody buttons on this thing are so small!" She placed her phone back on the table. "Now, what can I do for you, Edgar?"

"I wanted to ask you about the charity gala two weeks ago."

"You'll have to be more specific, my dear. Those things are two a penny."

"The one where Diana danced the *Giselle* solo."

"Ah."

"You were there."

"Indeed I was."

"Did you go on your own?"

Margery shook her head, a trace of a smile on her lips. "No, I had company."

"I think I saw him on a video of the gala," I told her. "A young man, maybe my age? He looked angry when he saw Diana talking to Oscar. I really need to know who he is, Margery."

I waited as she thoughtfully stirred her coffee, her gaze fixed on some point in the middle distance.

"In some ways, I only have myself to blame," she said finally, with a small, apologetic smile. "He hated going to the ballet, you see, especially as a teenager. Perhaps if he'd been a girl, it might have been different. But he was a boy, a boy without a father, a boy who blamed his mother for everything that had gone wrong. We fought all the time. So when he agreed to come with me to see the *Nutcracker* I was so happy, Edgar! I thought it was a peace offering, that my boy was doing something for me. I didn't know he'd seen a picture of Diana in one of the programmes. When I saw him gazing up at the stage at her, utterly oblivious to anything else, I could have happily wrapped my fingers around Diana's neck and throttled the little bitch. I knew I'd lost my boy, you see. It's a terrible blow for a mother to take."

"He became obsessed with her."

"He's always been a boy with strong passions," Margery said defensively. "He shares that with his father. And don't you try to tell me that Diana didn't lead him on. Don't tell me she didn't know what she was doing. I know that she fucked him."

So did I. I had seen the video.

"Your son's kidnapped Diana," I told Margery.

"That's perfectly possible."

"Do you know where he might have taken her?"

"There could be any number of places. Will you go to the police?"

"Not yet. At the moment they think I did it, and I haven't got any real evidence to prove them wrong. Your son's done a pretty thorough job. I know you love him, Margery, but if we don't stop him there's a real chance he's going to do something very bad. Is there any help you can give me?"

"I'm afraid I'm completely in the dark."

"If you did know something, would you tell me?"

"I very much doubt it."

"Will you not even tell me his name?"

"I think I've been more than helpful, given the circumstances."

"Who were you texting when I came in?"

Margery smiled thinly.

"I imagine you think me quite callous," she said, matter-of-factly. "I don't expect you to understand. When there is something you truly love, you'd be amazed the lengths you'd go to protect it. The depths to which you'd stoop."

I understood her better than she gave me credit for.

"You don't seem surprised," I said. "That I found out about you."

"I guessed you'd figure it out eventually," said Margery. "I don't know why, I just had you pegged as a natural detective."

I wanted to be so angry with her. She could have warned me about her son from the start. Maybe we could have stopped him before he had kidnapped Diana, and none of this would have happened. Margery's tight-lipped silence could have cost Diana her life. I wanted to be so angry with her – this lonely, middle-aged woman sat in a café, adrift in an ocean of youth and vigour – but there was something about her frank, unapologetic protectiveness that I found almost... well... *admirable*.

There was a murmur of voices on the stairs, and a group of young dancers fluttered past the café in formation. Margery smiled and waved at one of the girls. She turned her attention back to our table in time to catch me wincing and scratching at my back.

"You look like you're suffering a bit," she said.

"I have a skin condition," I replied. "This heat isn't good for it."

"You poor thing!" Margery said sympathetically. "For me it's hay fever. The faintest whiff of pollen and my eyes are burning, my nose is on fire and I'm sneezing like billy-o." Fishing into her handbag, she produced a handkerchief the size of a picnic blanket. "Speaking of which."

As she loudly blew her nose everything came to a jarring halt. Before my eyes the years fell away from Margery, and she was suddenly a slender dancer in her twenties, her cheeks flushed from exertion and her red hair tied back, blowing her nose as she complained about her hay fever. *"It's all the flowers Oscar bought me,"* Diana had said to me. *"My flat's like a pollen time-bomb."*

Abruptly I stood up from the table.

"Edgar?" said Margery, folding up her handkerchief. "Was it something I said?"

She had no idea. I had told Ray I was missing something obvious, and Margery had just showed me what. I stumbled out of the café and ran down the stairs, cursing my stupidity with every step.

UNDERNEATH THE MASTIC TREE

One of the earliest detective stories appears in the Bible, and concerns an innocent young woman dragged into a sordid world of lust and lies. The daughter of Hilkiah the priest and the wife of Joakim, Susanna was a pious beauty who attracted admiring glances as she walked through her husband's garden in Babylon. One warm afternoon she ordered her maids to bring her oil and soap and leave her to bathe. Susanna disrobed, unaware that there were serpents coiled in her garden. Two pairs of lecherous eyes watched her slowly lower herself into the water; two mouths ran dry at the sight of the droplets dappling her soft flesh. The men, local elders, had become infatuated with her – now they spied upon her bath, overcome with lust. When Susanna had finished and went to leave the garden they sprang from their hiding places and demanded she sleep with them. Susanna refused, and screamed for help.

In the ensuing furore, the mendacious elders claimed to have witnessed Susanna sleeping with a man who wasn't her husband. She was put on trial before her family and friends. Her protestations of innocence went unheeded, and she was found guilty of infidelity. But as Susanna was being led to her execution, a young boy's voice rang out from the crowd. The boy, Daniel, who had been possessed by a divine spirit, admonished the adults for condemning Susanna without evidence. He had the two elders separated and then cross-examined them for himself. When Daniel asked one of the men what tree Susanna had been standing beneath, he answered a mastic tree, but the other elder claimed it had been an oak. This discrepancy was more than minor confusion – no one could mix up the shrub-like mastic with a majestic oak. With the elders' lies exposed Susanna was spared, and it was the two men who were put to death for perjury.

Part of a series of additions to the Book of Daniel written in Greek rather than Hebrew, the tale of Susanna is considered by some Bible scholars to be apocryphal, and is excluded from certain Protestant canons. However, the great painters of the Middle Ages eagerly seized the opportunity to paint a classical nude. Rubens and Tintoretto, van Dyck and Rembrandt all depicted Susanna bathing – an innocent, naked beauty startled by the hot breath of lechery upon her neck.

...

I was furious with myself. All the time that I had spent watching Diana, I had been so distracted by *her* that I hadn't been paying enough attention to her surroundings. Back in the theatre café she had told me and Ray that Oscar had turned her flat into a veritable botanical garden with his gifts of flowers, but there hadn't been a single leaf or stem visible on the video feed. I had an uneasy feeling that I had made a basic error of assumption right from the outset. What if the flat Oscar and I had been spying on hadn't been Diana's at all?

As I hurried through the foyer of the Walker Theatre and out into the parched street I fished out my mobile phone from my pocket and rang Gill.

"What do you want, Edgar?" she said brusquely. "I'm pretty busy here."

"Sorry," I said. "I needed to ask you something."

"Have you talked to the police yet?"

I winced. "Not exactly, no."

"Edgar!" Her voice dropped to a hiss. "Don't you know how serious this is? This is a *murder* case. You can't just stick your head in the sand and hope that they'll forget about you!"

"I'm not sticking my head in the sand. Precisely the opposite – I'm trying to solve it. The police should be grateful that I'm helping out."

"For God's sake don't say that when you do speak to them. They'll lock you up on a point of principle."

"Listen, have you been to Diana's flat?"

"Of course. Why?"

"I need the address."

There was a long pause on the line. "I'm not sure that's a good idea," said Gill.

"Why not?"

"I think you're in enough trouble as it is."

"Do you want Diana back safe?" I countered. "Because I'm the only person who can find her, you know. Talk about the police all you want, but they don't understand what's really going on here. I'm the one who knows who's behind this, not them. If you want your friend back, then you've got to trust me, Gill. I promise I won't let you down."

There was a long pause down the phone line. I held my breath.

"OK," Gill said reluctantly. "But I'm coming with you." She gave me a street name in Southwark, near the south bank of the Thames.

"Got it," I said. "See you in half an hour."

I rang off and headed down the steps into a tube station. August had turned the Underground into a sweaty sewer, trains grinding to a halt in the tunnels between stations as though they had run out of breath. Faces glistened; tempers frayed. On the train a woman stared at me with open disgust as I scratched my backside, trying in vain to calm the volcanic wrath of my *Dermatitis Herpetiformis*. Closing my eyes, I dreamed of bubbling volcanic springs and ice-cold mountain streams, echoing ocean caves and still ponds in late spring.

Finally the train crawled into London Bridge, opening its doors with a blast of hot halitosis. I stumbled out on to the platform and was immediately swallowed up into an impatient crowd. Buffeted and jostled, I fled up through a network of tunnels and escalators and emerged blinking into the afternoon sunshine. I headed east along cobbled riverfront streets, through the shadows of old dock warehouses converted into expensive offices and apartments. The streets narrowed and twisted back on themselves, creating a brickwork maze. Here and there were reminders of the borough's past — winches and cranes, old wharf signs daubed on the brickwork in bright white lettering. As I passed beneath wooden balconies painted in rich purple hues, I fancied I could hear the long-dead echoes of the hoots and cackles of the Winchester geese as they offered their wares to their Elizabethan clientele.

Gill was waiting for me outside Diana's apartment block. Even by my sister's high standards in this regard, she looked unhappy with me.

"You're late," she said.

"Northern line."

"Right."

"At least you got out of work at a decent time for once."

"I told my boss it was an emergency."

"How did that go down?"

"Like a lead balloon."

I peered up and down the deserted street. "Has a black people carrier gone past whilst you've been standing here?"

"I don't know, Ed!" said Gill, exasperated. "It's a street – cars go up and down it all the time. I wasn't writing down number plates or anything."

"Just checking," I replied defensively. "I think someone might be following me." I examined the imposing façade of the apartment block. "This place must have cost her a fortune! How did she afford it?"

"There was some kind of property guy who had a thing for her. Let's just say she got a good deal. Are you really telling me Diana's been missing all this time and you haven't even checked her flat yet? Nice work, Sherlock."

"Don't call me that!"

Gill grinned maliciously.

"Any idea how we can get in?"

"I think Diana said her neighbor had a spare key," said Gill, pressing the buzzer for the flat next door. "Hello?" she said, into the crackling intercom. "We're friends of Diana Mayweather's – could you let us in please?"

Diana's neighbour was an affable Middle Eastern businessman who recognized Gill from a party Diana had thrown a few months back. When Gill explained that her friend had gone missing, he frowned and told her he had seen a man leaving her flat that morning. My pulse quickened. Once again, it seemed, Margery's son was one step ahead of me. There had been no keys inside Diana's bag in the Morrison Hotel – he must have already taken them. The neighbour gave Gill the spare key to Diana's flat, and she smiled and thanked him. It suddenly occurred to me that my sister would make a pretty decent private detective herself. Better than me, at any rate.

Gill slipped the key into the lock.

"Ready?"

I nodded.

She opened the door and instantly stepped back, wrinkling her nose at the smell that wafted out. With its high ceilings and large rooms, and the sunlight flooding in through the windows, Diana's flat should have been a bright, airy dream. But instead it was a sarcophagus, steeped in decay. Everywhere I looked there were dead and dying flowers in vases, their stems brown and petals wilting. The rooms were drenched in the stench of a romance gone sour, extinguished candles and crossed-out love letters. As I examined a framed photograph of a very young, gap-toothed Diana in a pink tutu, a single nagging question ran through my mind: if this was Diana's real home, then what had she been doing in the flat I had been watching on the internet?

We walked up a spiral staircase into the bedroom, which I immediately recognized from Diana's home movie. The duvet was still pulled back from when she had last slept here, the floor covered with old tights and vest tops. As we carefully sifted through Diana's things I told my sister about my conversation with Margery, careful not to mention any names. The case was very delicately poised, and I didn't want Gill running off to the police as soon as my back was turned.

"So this nutter's been obsessed with her for years?" she exclaimed. "Yuk! Diana doesn't half attract some creeps at times."

"She's not the only one," I said, with a pointed look.

"Oh, come off it, Ed!" scoffed Gill. "Richard wasn't perfect, but he wasn't a psycho!"

"I guess he did have that going for him," I admitted. "You're setting the bar pretty low, though."

There was nothing out of the ordinary in the bedroom, but then I hadn't expected there to be. I was interested in what lay behind the closed door at the end of the hall. As I neared Diana's bathroom I could feel my heart pound, my hands trembling with anticipation as I turned the door handle.

But I was in for a disappointment. Having spent hours admiring Diana showing and bathing, I couldn't help but feel let down by her real bathroom. It was a mess: surfaces cluttered with half-empty bottles of shampoos and conditioners, long red strands of hair lining the tub, a musty pile of towels heaped on the floor beneath the rail. I inspected every tiled inch, convinced that Diana's kidnapper had left some clue or message waiting for me. But there was nothing out of the ordinary. As I crawled across the floor on my hands and knees, inspecting the side of the bath, Gill looked on with bemusement.

"You know there's nothing here, don't you?"

"There has to be," I insisted. "Everything is about the bathroom now."

"Seriously, Edgar, I'm starting to worry about you."

"You sound just like Ray."

"And if all the people who care about you are saying the same thing maybe you need start listening to them. Take a step back and take a long look at yourself."

I froze mid-crawl, cocking my head to one side. Scrambling to my feet, I peered into the bathroom mirror. My face stared quizzically back at me. Unlike the rest of the room, the mirror looked as through it had been cleaned recently. Peering closer at the surface, I thought I could make out a series of faint streaks on the glass, almost invisible to the naked eye.

Gill sighed. "When I said 'take a look at yourself', I meant it metaphorically," she said.

"*Mene mene*," I muttered, ignoring her. "Maybe that's it."

"What?"

Manoeuvring my sister to one side, I closed the bathroom door and turned the bath's hot tap on full before fitting the plug into the plughole.

"Ed!" groaned Gill. "This really isn't the time."

Ordinarily I would have been desperate to jump in, but that would have to wait. As a fiery puddle filled the bathtub and the air grew warmer I concentrated on the mirror. Gradually steam from the bath began to settle upon its glassy surface, skirting around the shapes of letters and numbers, bringing a ghostly message into view. I clenched my fist in triumph.

. . .

As the armies of Persia marched upon his city walls, the Babylonian king Belshazzar threw a lavish feast, making blasphemous use of sacred Jewish vessels his father Nebuchadnezzar had taken from Solomon's Temple in Jerusalem. But the carousing and clink of gold goblets were interrupted by a terrifying vision: a ghostly apparition of a man's hand, writing a message for the king upon the palace wall.

Quailing at the sight of this disembodied envoy, Belshazzar struggled to comprehend its message of 'Mene, mene, tekel, upharsin' – an apparently meaningless list of currencies. He summoned astrologers and soothsayers, offering great power and riches for any man who could decipher the message, but the wisest heads in Babylon were baffled. In desperation the queen suggested Belshazzar seek out Daniel, who had interpreted Nebuchadnezzar's dreams for him. When he arrived at the palace Daniel not only rejected Belshazzar's offer of a reward, but chastised the king for his arrogant blasphemy. Only then did he turn his attention to the graffiti. In essence, Daniel explained, the different coins signified three processes: numbering, weighing and dividing. God was telling Belshazzar that he had been judged and found wanting, and his kingdom would be split asunder as a consequence. In this way Daniel coolly predicted the demise of the king's empire to his face.

Later that night Belshazzar was slain, and Darius the Mede became king. A warning from history to pay heed to the writing on the wall...

. . .

The message consisted of two words, presumably traced by the kidnapper's finger hours before we had arrived. Gill's brow wrinkled as she leant forward and read it.

"Room 46?" she said. "What does that mean?"

I had no idea. I was just glad I had found it. Knowing the rules of the game Margery's son was playing was one thing, but applying the right knowledge at the right time was a little more tricky. I would never have admitted it to Gill, but I had a sneaking admiration for my adversary. It had taken me two years of study to become an expert on bathing – how he had learned it so quickly? It was hard not to be impressed.

I wiped away the message with a flannel before turning off the taps and pulling out the plug, watching wistfully as bathwater gurgled down the pipes. When we left the flat I waited downstairs while Gill returned the key to Diana's neighbour. She was chewing on her lip as she came down the stairs, a thoughtful expression on her face.

"So what's this guy's game?" she said. "OK, he's so obsessed with Diana that he kidnaps her. But why run around setting up this little treasure hunt for you?"

"I don't know," I replied, truthfully. "I think he wants more than just her. I think he wants, I don't know… respect."

"Respect?" echoed Gill, exasperated. "You're all little schoolboys at heart, aren't you? Desperate to prove you can pee up the wall the highest. Well this time Diana needs *you* to win, little brother. So come on, put your thinking cap on. Where is this Room 46?"

I buzzed open the door and walked out into the street, lost in thought. "Somewhere with a large number of rooms. Some kind of swimming baths, maybe? No, they have numbered lockers but not numbered rooms." I turned to my sister, who was staring down the street. "How about a—?"

"Run," said Gill, out of the corner of her mouth.

I blinked in surprise. "Sorry?"

"Get out of here!" she hissed, with a surreptitious elbow in the ribs.

A police car was nudging down the road towards us, its emergency lights switched off. The driver appeared to be checking the building numbers as he went past. I put my head down and walked quickly away in the other direction, trying to look as casual as possible.

As I neared the estate agent at the bottom of the street, I saw a shadow cross its window. A black people carrier was driving down the adjoining road, its reflection rippling across the glass like a shark. Instinctively I turned to sprint away in the opposite direction, only to see the police car pull up outside Diana's apartment. I was trapped. The safest option was definitely the police, but I didn't have time for questions and cross-examinations. Once they had picked me up there was the strong possibility of a jail cell looming. Gill was staring at me quizzically, wondering why I had stopped. I shot her a look of pure helplessness back.

The people carrier had slowed to a halt at the bottom of the street, its engine humming. As I walked towards it a wiry bald man with protruding ears leapt out from the passenger seat. It was Sergei, the doorman from Soaplands. Glancing into the people carrier, I could make out the sizeable outline of Walter, his companion, behind the wheel. The American's face was bruised, postmarks of his beating at the hands of The Finn.

"Look who it is!" Sergei called out, gripping my arm like a vice. "You remember our friend Edgar?"

"Hop in, Ed," Walter replied in a deep American baritone, leaning towards the passenger window. "We'll give you a ride."

Behind me a policeman stepped out of his car and rang the bell to Diana's apartment. It was my last chance to cry for help. I didn't know what the doormen wanted with me, or where they might take me. It was a step into dangerous, unknown waters, but one I had to make if I had any hope of finding Diana. So with a heavy heart, I kept quiet as Sergei bundled me inside the vehicle and slammed the door shut.

AN X-SHAPED CROSS

As his faithful wife Penelope struggled to repel the tsunami of suitors flooding her palace in his absence, Odysseus belatedly resumed his journey back to Ithaca. An unenviable choice awaited him. His ship had to cross a narrow strait beset by two monstrous hazards, so close that neither could be avoided at the expense of the other. On one side of the strait, in a cave halfway up a towering rock perpetually swathed in black cloud, lay the lair of Scylla. A nightmarish vision with six heads, each with three rows of teeth, Scylla preyed on passing ships, her long necks snaking down to the sea as she gobbled up mariners. On the other side of the strait, in the shadow of a small crag with a fig tree hanging over it, lay a whirlpool called Charybdis, a force of elemental fury capable of reducing whole fleets to kindling.

Faced with a choice between the devil and the deep blue sea, Odysseus opted to sail past Scylla, reasoning that the loss of six men was preferable to the potential loss of the entire vessel in Charybdis's hungry maw. As their ship nudged tentatively into the strait, Odysseus and his crew anxiously scanned the horizon for signs of trouble:

> "We entered the Straits in great fear of mind, for on the one hand was Scylla, and on the other dread Charybdis kept sucking up the salt water. As she vomited it up, it was like the water in a cauldron when it is boiling over upon a great fire, and the spray reached the top of the rocks on either side."[19]

19 Wikisource contributors, "The Odyssey (Butler)/Book XII," *Wikisource,* <http://en.wikisource.org/w/index.php?title=The_Odyssey_(Butler)/Book_XII&oldid=4016486> (accessed October 2, 2014).

As the crew stared transfixed at the churning water, Scylla attacked, snatching up six men in her jaws and taking them back to her lair to devour them. Agonized screams and crunched bone echoed around the crags as the ship fled for the open sea.

Odysseus's relief upon leaving the strait of nightmares behind him was to prove short-lived. Upon reaching the Island of the Sun, his crewmembers ignored Circe's warning to leave alone the herds of cattle and sheep belonging to Hyperion the Sun God. When their ship set sail an enraged Zeus sent a hurricane to attack it, bombarding the stricken vessel with lightning bolts. The crew were washed overboard and drowned, leaving only Odysseus clinging to the wreckage.

With sunrise he saw that he had survived Zeus's wrath – only to drift back towards the dread strait, and directly into Charybdis's embrace. As the vortex sucked down the remains of his ship Odysseus leapt clear and grabbed hold of a low branch of the overhanging fig tree. He clung on for an entire day, until with evening the whirlpool spat up the shattered timbers of Odysseus's ship, and the exhausted warrior was able to latch on to the flotsam and drift away to safety.

...

The people carrier followed a labyrinthine trail through Southwark away from the river and back towards the main road. Walter tapped his fingers on the steering wheel as he drove, humming softly to himself. In the seat beside me Sergei lit up a cigarette, taking short, irritable drags. The atmosphere in the vehicle was heavy with acrid smoke and sullen menace. The size of the risk I had taken was only now sinking in. There was no telling what these two might do with me. I wanted to save Diana, but I couldn't that from a hospital bed – or the bottom of a river.

We drove on in silence, joining the queue of traffic shuffling across Tower Bridge. The pimples on my backside were itching with such intensity that the leather upholstery beneath my backside felt as though it had been coated in lye. I squirmed in my seat, earning me a look of open contempt from Sergei. As we edged along the bridge he opened the window and flicked his cigarette end into the road; I stared wistfully out at the watery expanse of the Thames. Gritting my teeth, I willed the people carrier on as it threaded a route through the city and up to the giant roundabout at Old Street where we headed east, eschewing the main roads for narrow, litter-strewn side streets.

Finally Walter parked the people carrier outside a series of boarded-up shop fronts. The American stayed in the car whilst Sergei climbed out and gestured curtly at me to follow him. Above the nearest doorway a security camera monitored the street, next to a white sign with Cyrillic lettering. Sensing my unease, Sergei grabbed my arm and propelled me over to the doorway. He pressed the buzzer, glancing casually up into the camera. Immediately the door clicked open.

Given the rundown street outside, I was surprised to enter an airy foyer furnished with wicker seats, cherubic statues and leafy plants in terracotta jars. The walls were filled with abstract paintings – giant blocks of blue colour. A bored-looking woman was flicking through a magazine behind the counter. Sergei marched past her down a long corridor. He stopped and rapped sharply on a door, before opening it and shoving me into the room beyond.

I stumbled into a small, wood-panelled sauna lined with benches. A thick pall of steam rose up from an iron stove in the corner of the room, the heat a sweaty bear hug. A short, stocky man with a beard was sitting on one of the benches, a thick white towel around his waist and another draped over his head. He was weighed down with gold jewellery – a heavy chain around his neck, gleaming rings on his fingers. His stomach was a sagging paunch, but his arms were knots of pure muscle. I waited awkwardly as he gazed at me through the steam.

"Sit," he said finally, in a guttural Russian accent.

I took a cautious seat on the bench beside him.

"You are Edgar," the man said. "Do you know who I am?"

I had seen his photograph in a Russian newspaper, celebrating a Caribbean wedding. I had stared at his moody portrait in Soaplands' mock boardroom. I knew who he was, all right. "You're Valery Limonov."

He nodded. "Good. You are not a complete idiot."

Valery removed the towel from his head and sat back on the bench, exhaling loudly. He was in no hurry, content to let the suffocating room temperature reduce me to a quivering puddle. In a futile attempt to staunch the sweat pouring down my back, I undid a couple of shirt buttons and rolled up my sleeves.

"Do you know why you are here?" he growled.

"No. Is there some kind of problem?"

There was a loud crack as Valery flexed his knuckles. If Oscar Salazar was a rapier then the Russian was a mace – or something even less subtle, a broken bottle or a hurled brick. His fists were permanently clenched, his arm muscles tense with potential violence.

"Is it hot enough for you?" he asked.

I nodded frantically. Valery stood up anyway, walking over to the iron stove and pouring a ladle of water on the hot coals. Immediately we were enveloped in rolls of enervating steam. My head swam, a wave of dizziness washing over me.

"Yes, there is problem," he told me. "Big problem."

"I'm sorry to hear that," I stammered. "If there's anything I can do to help you, I'd be only too happy."

The Russian gave me a brooding stare. "Maybe there is something you can help with." He got up, adjusting the towel around his waist. "Come look."

A strong hand grabbed my shoulder, and I was manhandled out through another door into fresh, gloriously cold air. Spots exploded in front of my eyes like black fireworks, and it took me several seconds to clear my head before I was able to take in the scene before me. We were standing in the middle of a deserted men's changing room, surrounded by metal lockers. In front of us was a row of open shower cubicles, and slumped in a naked heap on the tiles of the middle cubicle, was Yuri Ivanov. His hands had been tied together and the rope had been looped around the shower apparatus high above his head, forcing his arms up into the air. His face was bruised and there was a gob of dried blood by his lip.

"Jesus!" I said, with a low whistle. "Is he OK?"

"He is fine," Valery said dismissively. "In Russia ballet training is very tough. It builds not only strong muscles, but strong will. This for him is nothing."

"If you say so," I replied, with a dubious glance at the bloodied, crumpled dancer.

"It is his own fault," said Valery. "He tried to go back on a deal we had agreed. I cannot allow that."

"He and Lilia are supposed to dance for the Maschenko Ballet."

"Winter season, they join us. They show the world that no one understands ballet like the Russians. They show the world that Valery Limonov is not just a rich man, but a cultured one. That he understands beauty, and art."

Yuri's eyes snapped open. He stared balefully at his captor.

"That he understands beauty and art?" he repeated, with a little mocking laugh. "What do you know about ballet? Nothing! You can put a diamond necklace on a pig, it's still a pig."

Valery strode over and turned on the shower above Yuri's head, drenching him in cold water. Yuri cried out, turning his face away from the torrent.

"Fuck you!" he cried, spluttering.

"This attitude is a problem," Valery admitted to me, over the roar of the shower. "He makes things worse with his mouth. He does not learn. How can I make him learn? I would break his legs, but then he cannot dance. It is difficult question."

"It's a poser, all right," I agreed politely.

Valery turned off the shower, booting the groaning Yuri in the ribs for good measure. This act of minor violence seemed to amuse him, and there was a smile on his face as he came over and put his arm around me.

"You, on the other hand," he said, pinching my cheek. "I don't care whether you dance or not."

The sweat froze on my clammy skin. I could only watch as Valery stomped over to a wooden bucket in the corner of the changing rooms, his flip-flops slapping against the tiles, and pulled out a bunch of dried leaves and branches tied together at the bottom. He held it up to the light admiringly.

"You know what this is?"

"It's a *venik*," I replied, in a thin, halting voice.

Surprised, Valery nodded with approval. "You know about the *banya*."

"The Russian bathhouse. Yes, I've read a bit about it."

"Is that so?" The *venik* made a swishing sound as he swatted the bunch through the air. "Then you know its purpose. You sit in the *banya* and hit yourself with the *venik*. Good for circulation."

"As long as they're soaked first," I said, eyeing the dried branches. "They need half an hour in warm water to soften them."

"Soften them?" replied Valery. He chuckled. "What use are they to me soft?"

His golden rings glinted in the light as he raised his arm, and then he struck me full in the face with the *venik*.

. . .

After the death of Jesus his twelve apostles scattered like seeds upon the wind, intent on spreading word of the Christian faith. Once fishermen and minor officials, now emissaries of God, they went forth: to the heartlands of European civilization, Greece and Rome, and to Persia, Armenia and India. According to Hippolytus of Rome, the intrepid Andrew headed north to Scythia in the hope of converting the barbarian tribes. Through the sweet fog of the Scythians' tents, he preached to a congregation of stoned sinners. The results went unrecorded, although it's not hard to imagine Andrew finding his vision of miracles and saviours reaching surprisingly receptive minds, his tale of fishes and loaves greeted with nodding heads and rumbling stomachs.

Andrew pressed on, skirting around the Black Sea and then heading north, following the course of the Dnieper River. At the site of modern-day Kiev he foretold the rising of a great city, and planted a cross upon the later location of St Andrew's Church. Apparently Andrew went as far north as Novgorod in modern Russia. According to a history of the region known as the *Primary Chronicle*, compiled in Kiev in AD 1113, the apostle was particularly struck by the local bathing practices. He looked on as the men emerged from their steaming wooden bathhouses, stripping off and beating their bare skin with reeds. After whipping themselves half-senseless, they doused themselves with freezing water. The simple act of cleaning had been transformed into a rigorous regime of daily punishment.

Was there a touch of envy in Andrew's admiring account of this stoic flagellation? Did the apostle view the act of suffering as the most potent and powerful display of faith? There seemed to be something almost masochistic about the way in which the Apostles courted persecution and death. Almost to a man they were brutally and sadistically executed for preaching their gospel: Bartholomew was skinned alive, Simon Peter crucified upside-down in Rome; James, son of Alphaeus, was stoned and then clubbed to death; Thomas was speared.

Andrew's end came at Patras in modern-day Greece. Sentenced to crucifixion, he asked to be bound to a *crux decussata* – an X-shaped cross – as he deemed himself unworthy to die in an identical manner to Jesus. This X-shaped cross, or saltire, leaves its imprint on the flag of Scotland, one of three countries to claim Andrew as a patron saint – along with Greece, and Russia.

...

The force of the blow sent me reeling backwards, spitting out a mouthful of leaves and bits of twig. Valery hit me again, pummelling me to the ground where he kicked and thrashed me. I curled up into a ball and buried my face in my arms, praying for the buffeting to end. Finally, panting heavily, Valery tossed the stripped *venik* to one side. His towel had slipped down during the beating, exposing a tangled thicket of pubic hair. As he pulled up the towel and tightened it around his waist I stayed in a ball on the tiles, coughing. There was too much adrenaline coursing through my system to feel any pain yet, but the cuts on my face were bleeding and my leg was throbbing where the Russian had stamped on it.

"Get up," Valery said hoarsely. "Or I'll get a fresh *venik*."

I pushed myself up on to my elbows and crawled to my feet, leaning against a locker for support. Underneath the shower Yuri broke out into thin, bitter laughter at the sight of me.

"Look at the pair of you," Valery said scornfully. "Call yourself men? All this over some stupid whore."

"She's not a whore!" cried Yuri.

"Of course she's a whore!" exclaimed Valery. "She used to let men pay to fuck her; now she lets men pay to spy on her. Didn't you go to the flat like I told you? Didn't you see all the cameras there?"

"Diana knew about the cameras?" I said, through gritted teeth.

"Of course!" Valery roared with laughter. "That was whole point! She pretended to live in the flat so men could pay to watch her over the internet.

Sad, lonely men who will never know what it is like to fuck a beautiful woman."

And me and Oscar Salazar. It seemed that once again I had underestimated Diana's commercial operations. I had supposed her to be the victim of a predatory voyeur, but all along she had been in sitting pretty in a web of her own creation.

"When my business partner told me about this woman I asked some people some questions," explained Valery. "Strippers, escorts, hookers – I know this world. Now Diana only lets the men watch her on their computers, but when she was younger and needed the money they could do what they liked."

"I'm not listening to your lies," Yuri said obstinately. "Diana would never do that kind of thing."

"She would," I corrected him. "And she did."

The two men stared at me. "There's a video," I explained.

"She was a call girl?" breathed Yuri, in disbelief.

"Very high-class," said Valery. "Millionaires, princes, oil tycoons. Chances are, I fucked her myself once."

"You bastard!" spat Yuri, struggling to break free from his ropes. "I'll kill you."

"No, no, no," Valery said calmly. "Save your energy. You have many dances to perform for me. Many ballets."

"Not until I know that Diana's all right! I don't care what she's done – I still love her!"

"You see what I am dealing with?" Valery stretched his arms out, appealing to me. "He thinks you might have made this girl disappear. Is that true?"

"I didn't touch her!" I said indignantly. "She hired me to help *her*! At first I thought Oscar kidnapped her and then I thought it might be Yuri or Lilia, but now I know who did it. I just have to find him."

"Good. You have twenty-four hours. Or I will have someone put a bullet *here*." Valery jabbed a finger into my right temple. "Now get out of my sight."

He didn't need to tell me twice. As I scuttled out of the changing rooms, wiping the blood from my face, I left Valery standing over Yuri. "You will dance for the Maschenko. You will dance for me. You will dance for all of

Russia. Do you hear me?" He grabbed his captive by the chin, forcing the prone ballet dancer to look at him. "You will dance!"

The sound of a ringing slap was cut off by the door closing behind me. It was hard luck on Yuri, but the only thing I could do to help him was to find Diana – which meant I had to pick up the trail to Room 46. The message on the mirror hadn't been accompanied by any kind of key, so I guessed I was looking for a public building, somewhere I could easily enter. A large building with many rooms.

As I passed back through the bathhouse foyer, my eyes lingered on the abstract blue paintings on the wall.

Like a museum, say. Or a gallery.

THE NINTH BOOK ON ARCHITECTURE

I limped across Trafalgar Square, a burning king whose own body was rising up in rebellion against him. Children clambering over the bronze lion statues stopped and stared as I passed. Smiles froze; fingers paused on camera buttons. I was tired and dirty, my face covered in cuts where the *venik* had lashed me. My skin was a suit of fire. As I walked through the square I tried to block out the fountain's beckoning trickle, scared that I would lose my head and plunge into its shallow water – anything to end the infernal, ceaseless itching.

Ahead of me, swollen rain clouds hung in a grey frame around the National Gallery. I skirted around the crowd gathered around a juggling street entertainer and hurried up the gallery steps, feeling a spit of rain upon my neck. The entrance hall was heaving with tourists and schoolchildren, and I had to fight my way over to the help desk to retrieve an information leaflet. As I studied the map, a slight smile flickered across my lips. My hunch had been correct – the gallery's rooms *were* numbered. And Room 46 was exactly what I had suspected it might be.

I limped through the gallery hallways, my breath quickening with anticipation. Intent upon following the map, I barely glanced at the British portrait paintings of the Middle Ages before turning right and making for the bright dappled colours of a Cezanne. There I manoeuvred around the edge of the scrum assembled around van Gogh's sunflowers, my gaze fixed upon the small windowless room that lay at the far end of Room 45.

Room 46. The works of Edgar Degas.

I had spent two years staring at these paintings in the damp-wrinkled volumes stacked in my bathroom, their colours and textures dulled by reproduction. But nothing could prepare me for the real thing. I was besieged, overwhelmed. To my left, *La Coiffure*, a portrait of a maid combing her mistress's hair. Drenched in bloody red hues, it looked more like a crime scene than a domestic snapshot, as though the maid was wielding a razor blade instead of a comb. *Miss La La at the Cirque Fernando*, a dazzling portrait of a female acrobat rising up to the rafters of the circus hall, a rope clenched between her teeth. On the facing wall, *Ballet Dancers*, a gaggle of girls in white tutus gracefully stretching out their arms. And hidden away in the corner of the room, *After the Bath, Woman drying herself* – the naked redhead perched on the edge of the tub, her face hidden from view as she vigorously towelled herself dry. It felt as though the entire story of Diana's disappearance was being told on the walls of the softly lit room.

I sat down on the wooden bench and gazed at each painting for several minutes in turn, oblivious to the steady stream of people interrupting my view. It was only when a herd of schoolchildren in bright green baseball caps appeared, giggling at the glimpses of bare flesh on canvas, that the spell was broken. I shook my head. Diana's kidnapper had sent me here for a reason, not just to stare at paintings. But for the life of me, I couldn't work out what it was. Apart from paintings and tourists, there was nothing else in the room. I got down on my hands and knees and peered underneath the bench, hoping to see some secret message taped to its underside, but all I found were a couple of blobs of chewing gum. Feeling a gallery attendant's suspicious gaze upon my neck, I quickly sat back down.

I put my head in my hands and massaged my temples, fighting back the urge to dig my nails into my elbows and knees and gouge out chunks of itching flesh. The endgame to this mystery was fast approaching and I was still one step behind my adversary. I needed to silence my rash. I needed my books. I needed my watery chamber of contemplation. I needed my bath. I needed to *think*.

. . .

Bathing is as much about the mind as it is the body. Throughout history there have been moments when the act has given birth to great ideas and moments of pure inspiration. Perhaps it is a product of the bath's considered stillness, the glassy surface of the water encouraging reflection. Perhaps the soothing heat that cajoles muscles into relaxing also encourages the mind to untangle and unknot itself. Whatever the reasons, some of the answers bathing has provided have touched the divine.

Around the year 1499, Nanak Dev went for his daily bathe in the Kali Bein in the Punjabi region of India. Thirty years old, he had long shown an interest in spiritual matters, debating and arguing with religious leaders, urging the importance of inner purity over materialist displays of faith. That morning, in the cool embrace of the Kali Bein, Nanak was touched by an ecstatic revelation. When he failed to return home a search party discovered his clothes in a pile on the riverbank, and assumed that he had drowned. Three days later, to their amazement, Nanak reappeared. Pressed to explain his absence, he said nothing, and remained mute for an entire day. Finally he cleared his throat and spoke, professing a belief in a single God and rejecting the division between Hindu and Muslim. Nanak founded a new religion: Sikhism. Accepting the title Guru Nanak – and thus becoming the first in a succession of ten Sikh Gurus who helped guide the nascent religion's disciples until 1708 – he left his job and undertook a series of epic journeys that took him not only the length and breadth of India but north to Tibet and west to the Arabian peninsula, where he preached the values of sharing, honesty and devotion to God.

...

As I racked my brains a human tide washed through Room 46, their anoraks slick with rain, immersed in the electronic guides playing through their headphones. Even without a clock on the wall I felt the passage of time keenly. Every minute felt like a fresh defeat. After a while the suspicious gallery attendant lost interest in me, and I looked up to see him peering through the open doorway into the next room. Above the low murmur of the crowd and the shuffle of feet I became aware of a distant clicking sound, high heels on wooden floorboards.

Then Keiko appeared in the doorway.

She was wearing a summer coat over a pair of white shorts and a small grey T-shirt, her hair tied back and a pair of sunglasses pushed up over the top of her head. A large red-and-white striped golfing umbrella was furled at her side. Upon Keiko's entrance, every head in the room turned in admiration at this living artwork – a creature more vibrant and more beautiful than anything Edgar Degas had been willing to admit existed in real life.

"Surprise," she said evenly, taking a seat beside me. Her scent enveloped me, a subtle hint of jasmine among raindrops. At the sight of my cut face, Keiko's eyes widened. "God, Edgar, are you all right?"

"I'm fine," I said, an apologetic note in my voice. "It's been a difficult couple of days. What are you doing here?"

"I was worried about you. I wanted to check that you were OK."

"How did you find me?"

"I called Oscar and asked him," Keiko replied, matter-of-factly.

"And he knew I was here?"

Keiko nodded. "He's had you followed since you started on the case."

Well, that solved one mystery, at least – no wonder I had never been able to catch Oscar unawares. From day one his people had been on my tail, and I had never once suspected their presence. Then again, I suppose Oscar could afford to hire the best.

"You called him?" I said. "I thought you were both in Spain."

"*Spain?*" Keiko frowned. "Er... why?"

"I was on Oscar's yacht yesterday. I saw your nicotine gum. He told me he was going away with a girl who wasn't a redhead, so I thought—"

"—that I'd hopped into bed with him." Keiko grimaced. "I see."

"What was I supposed to think? He told me you'd been working for him. A 'distraction', he called you. Every time I saw you – in the hotel lobby, outside the restaurant, you were there because he'd told you. Weren't you?"

Keiko blew out her cheeks, and nodded.

"At first he wanted me to try and break up Diana and Yuri," she said. "But when he found out Diana had hired you, Oscar phoned to tell me to concentrate on you instead."

"Well he must have been over the moon with you, because you did a bloody good job, didn't you?" There was a shrill edge to my laughter. "I hope you got paid enough for it."

"Edgar, listen to me. *Listen to me.*" Keiko grabbed my face and turned it around so that I couldn't help staring into her large brown eyes. "Yes, I let Oscar talk me into getting mixed up with something I should have stayed well away from, but at the time it didn't feel like I doing anything wrong. It felt like I was just… I don't know, a magician's assistant or something… all sequins and smiles, making the audience look the wrong way. But when I found out what had happened to Diana I didn't want anything more to do with it. The reason you saw my gum on Oscar's yacht was because I'd gone there to tell him I was done with our deal, and that I was leaving Soaplands."

"And what about the night in your flat?" I said, struggling to move my mouth with my face still in Keiko's grip. "Us?"

"That had nothing to do with Oscar or anybody else. That was just about me and you."

The doubt must have shown in my eyes, because Keiko abruptly let go of me. When she spoke again her voice was low and hard. "Look, whatever Diana does with her body is her own business but she's not me, all right? I might take off my clothes for money, but no one buys my body. Don't think people haven't tried."

She looked down at her feet, which were visible through her sandal straps. Her toes were small and delicate, their nails painted in a soft shade of pink.

"I'm sorry, Keiko," I said wearily. "I didn't mean to offend you. I'm just having a bit of trouble with the idea that you might actually like me. I mean, you're this beautiful, amazing girl and I'm…"

"What?"

"Me. I mean, look at me! I'm a complete mess!"

"Men!" Keiko exclaimed, exasperated. "Half the time you don't think at all, and then when you do, you ruin everything! I'm not here because Oscar wanted me to be, or because I feel sorry for you, or for any other reason than the fact that I care about you and I wanted to make sure you were OK."

"But *why*?"

"I don't know. Because I gave you a pass to a strip club and you used it to clean yourself. Because you barely knew me but when The Finn tried to hurt me you got in the way, even though you knew he might kill you. Because maybe I can see that inside that itchy shell of skin there's a nice guy threatening to get out – even if you can't."

"Really?"

"Really!"

"Wow." I couldn't help smiling. "You do know there's a good chance you're wrong on that score, don't you?"

"There's always that," Keiko conceded. "My friends are always telling me I've got dreadful taste in men."

She grinned. A warm tingling swelled up from the tips of my toes, covering my whole body, every inch of scarred skin and damaged flesh.

"He's dead, you know," I told her. "The Finn."

Keiko stared at me. "You're kidding me."

I shook my head. "I found him in a hotel bathtub. He'd been shot."

"That's horrible!" she said. "I know Paavo was a messed-up guy but he wasn't always that way. Before Diana he was OK. He always looked out for the girls."

"I'll take your word for it," I said, remembering the sensation of liquid fire raining down upon my scrotum.

"I never really understood why he kept attacking you," said Keiko. "Paavo was massively over-protective of Diana but you were trying to help her, not hurt her. It doesn't make any sense."

"I don't think sense matters where The Finn is concerned. Didn't he get sacked for beating up some guy who was involved with Diana?"

Keiko nodded. "It was horrible. This guy used to come in all the time to watch Diana dance and Paavo couldn't stand it. One night they started arguing and he just lost it. It took three other bouncers to pull him off. The other guy was in hospital for weeks – I think he had trouble walking afterwards. I remember saying to one of the other girls at the time that was it, I was getting out." Keiko smiled ruefully. "How many years ago was that?"

I stared at the painting of Miss La La at the Cirque Fernando, ascending like a glittering angel to the heavens, basking in the gasps and applause of her audience. Something was nagging at me, a distant echo of another conversation. Pieces from different jigsaw puzzles unexpectedly slotting together. I scratched my head in disbelief.

It couldn't be. Could it?

...

TOM BECKERLEGGE

King Hiero II of Syracuse had a problem. He had ordered a craftsman to fashion a crown from gold he had provided, but upon inspecting the finished item the king suspected that the artisan had substituted some of the gold for silver. Both precious metals weighed the same, so the issue could not be resolved with a simple pair of scales. The crown was destined for the forehead of a god or goddess's statue, and was thus too sacred to be sliced upon and probed. Vexed, Hiero turned to a young mathematician to solve this knotty conundrum – Archimedes.

Just 22 years old, Archimedes must have felt that a heavy weight had been placed upon his shoulders. The surest way to differentiate between gold and silver was to measure their density, but how was he to do that? As he wrestled with the problem, Archimedes took a trip to the public baths. What followed was recorded many years later by the Roman writer Marcus Vitruvius Pollio, in the introduction to Book IX of his *De Architectura Libri Decem* ('Ten Books on Architecture'):

> "While the case was still on his mind, [Archimedes] happened to go to the bath, and on getting into a tub observed that the more his body sank into it the more water ran out over the tub. As this pointed out the way to explain the case in question, he jumped out of the tub and rushed home naked, crying with a loud voice that he had found what he was seeking; for as he ran he shouted repeatedly in Greek, 'Eureka, eureka' ['I have found it, I have found it.']"[20]

By dropping the crown in a tub full of water – and its equal weight in silver, and then gold – Archimedes was able to measure the amount of water each mass displaced and thus prove that Hiero had indeed been cheated by the opportunistic craftsman. Later mathematicians such as Galileo were skeptical of the tale, noting the imprecision of Archimedes' method, but the Syracusan's streak through his city remains a timeless symbol of the mad ecstasy of inspiration – the thinker as a damp exclamation mark.

...

20 trans. Morris Hicky Morgan, *Vitruvius: The Ten Books on Architecture* (Harvard University Press, 1914), pp. 253-4

"Hello?" said Keiko. "Earth to Edgar?"

I barely heard her. The chatter of the schoolchildren; Keiko's beautiful round face, caught in a slight frown; the faint suggestion of her perfume – all of it faded into the background.

"Whatever Diana's done he's been there," I said slowly. "At the ballet, at the strip club, he's always been near. He makes sure he's close by."

I was a Guru climbing out of the river, rising out of the waters of revelation. I was a small boy touched with a god's wisdom, opening my mouth and feeling truth flood out like purest birdsong. I was a mathematician with the answer to an impossible problem.

"I don't understand," said Keiko.

"You're not supposed to," I replied, agitated. "*I* wasn't supposed to. Don't you see? The gallery... these paintings, they're just another distraction!"

"Why?"

"It's not 'why' that's the question, it's 'where'. Where am I *not* supposed to be?"

"You've lost me."

I was too giddy to explain myself properly. For the first time since this case had begun, I had all the facts at my disposal. I knew who was behind Diana's kidnapping. And now I knew where they would be. Adrenaline surging through my body, I leant over and kissed a startled Keiko before rising to my feet.

"Hey!" said Keiko. "Where are you going?"

"To the bath!" I called out over my shoulder, and strode towards the exit.

Outside the National Gallery, rain was bucketing down on to the damp flagstones of Trafalgar Square. I raised my face to the sky, letting the water splash upon me like a benediction. My clothes were soon soaked but I didn't care. I hurried down the steps, suddenly urgent with the thrill of inspiration, and began sprinting across the square towards the subway entrance to the Underground. I ran on, my face wreathed in ecstasy, dripping wet, bathed in naked triumph, impervious to the confused glances and open stares of passers-by. Nothing mattered to me except the joy of discovery, the blissful click as the cogs in my brain settled into place. Eureka. I had found it.

THE ROAD TO ČACHTICE CASTLE

Amid the dying embers of December 1610, a detachment of soldiers followed a snowy trail through the Hungarian countryside. Led by György Thurzó, Palantine of Hungary, they made for Čachtice Castle, a Gothic shadow on top of the hillside. The men had been sent by King Matthias II to investigate the rumours that were swirling around the castle and the widow who lived there – Erzsébet (Elizabeth) Báthory. There was talk of young girls going missing, terrible crimes taking place behind the castle walls. Thurzó would later describe the scene he found at Čachtice in a letter. He entered the castle only to stumble over the corpse of a girl lying in the hallway. The grounds were littered with dead young women, their bodies bearing scars and burn marks. Deep underground, the horrified soldiers discovered girls huddled together in cells, miserably awaiting their fate. It was a descent into Hell itself.

Elizabeth Báthory was a noblewoman, related by her mother to the King of Poland. Intelligent and forthright, she could read and write in five languages. She was also, however, prone to fits of rage and seizures. At fourteen she was married to Ferenc Nádasdy, a warrior-like noble who later became chief commander of the Hungarian forces during their war with the Ottomans. With her husband away, it fell to Báthory to run Čachtice – on the very edge of Christian Europe – and organize its defence against any possible attack from the Ottomans.

In 1604 Ferenc died, leaving his widow alone in the castle. Báthory and her husband had long held a reputation for harshness, cruelly punishing their servants' transgressions. At one time, the sound of her servants screaming as the countess chastised them in a Viennese townhouse roused monks cloistered on the opposite side of the street into protest. Yet in the wake of

Ferenc's death corporal discipline escalated into something more calculated and violent. Legend had it that Báthory had slapped a servant so hard that she had splattered her own skin with the girl's blood. Upon examining the spot where she had been splashed, Báthory had judged it to look younger than the rest of her skin. This supposedly triggered a spree of murderous narcissism, whereby the Countess lured the daughters of the local peasantry and minor gentry to Čachtice with the promise of work or education, only to set upon them with her four accomplices. There was torture, mutilation, sexual abuse; young flesh flayed and pierced with knives, needles and teeth, the most basic tools of sadism. The most infamous and enduring accusation was that the countess bathed in her victims' blood – although that was a charge not levelled until the 18th century, by which time Báthory's crimes had become indelibly entwined with the vampiric myths of the region. It was even suggested that she had been an inspiration for Bram Stoker when he penned *Dracula*.

Following Thurzó's grisly discoveries at Čachtice, it was Báthory's accomplices – three women and one man – who were placed on trial, not the noblewoman herself. The defendants were accused of the murder of 80 young women, although contemporary accounts suggested that they had killed as many as 650. Three of them were sentenced to death, and were tortured before their execution, whilst the fourth was imprisoned for life. Báthory herself was bricked up in a room in Čachtice Castle, condemned to a madness of four walls and the echoes of her victims' screams. She died three years later, in August 1614.

. . .

Night was falling by the time I reached Gill's complex of flats, and my euphoria had given way to a creeping sense of foreboding. I crossed through the shadows of the main square, aware of the solitary echo of my footsteps. Looking up, I saw that Gill's bedroom window was dark. It didn't matter – I was sure that *he* would be there. It was the only logical conclusion. Room 46 had been a distraction, a clever piece of misdirection. If I was right, there was only one place where Diana's kidnapper could be: the place where I returned to day and night, my haven and sanctuary. My bathroom.

Or, more accurately, Gill's bathroom. I had rung my sister on the walk back from the Underground, as I hurried through a line of commuters waiting by the bus stop.

"Edgar!" she said, the relief evident in her voice. "Are you OK? I've been trying to call you!"

"Don't worry about me, I'm fine. Listen, you're not at the flat, are you?"

"I should be so lucky," Gill said glumly. "I'm still at work. This could turn into an all-nighter."

"Good."

"Why?"

"It doesn't matter. Just stay where you are and whatever you do, don't go back to the flat."

I hung up before she could ask me any more questions. Gill had done her bit helping me to get inside Diana's flat, and had already risked the wrath of her boss once today. It was up to me to end this now.

I climbed the steps to Gill's flat and pressed my ear to the door. The only sound I could hear was my own heart pounding in my ears. Slipping the key in the lock, I turned it as quietly as possible. The door swung open with a conspiratorial silence. In the darkness of the hallway, I could make out two orange glows – one coming from the living room, the other shining out from beneath the bathroom door. I crept soundlessly through in the living room, where, at last, I found what I had been looking for.

Diana was lying facedown on the black leather sofa, her face obscured by her tumbling mass of red hair. She didn't move when I cried out. She showed no sign of life at all. I ran over and turned her on to her back, her limbs dead weights in my arms. Her face was unmarked, unblemished – a perfect alabaster statue. Pressing my ear against Diana's mouth, I was rewarded with the faint wisps of her breath.

Now, at last, it was time to call the police. But as I reached into my pocket for my mobile, I heard a floorboard creak behind me and a hand came down over my face, pressing a cloth over my mouth. I tried to knock it away, but my assailant had me in a firm grip. As I struggled to break free, all the while inhaling the soporific fumes soaked into the cloth, I wondered where he had been hiding. One glance down the hallway showed me that the door to Gill's bedroom was ajar. A final, futile deduction, as the strength drained from my limbs and a sweet fog descended over my vision like a curtain…

I awoke to find myself lying in a half-filled bath, my wrists shackled above my head, the handcuffs looped around the cold tap. Water sloshed around my head, stinging my eyes and flooding my throat and nostrils every time I moved. I stared helplessly up at the ceiling, noting that the lamp had been brought in from the living room and placed on the shelf above the bath. A new and ominous development.

Margery's son came into the bathroom soon afterwards, drawn by my cries for help. He pointed out the lamp's precarious position, propped up on a pair of ice cubes, and what would happen when the heat from the bath turned the cubes to water. He topped up the bath with a playful squirt of hot water, giggling at my frantic attempts to move my head out of the way. He showed me the key to the handcuffs and left it agonizingly in view by the sink, tapping my cheek before leaving me alone. A few minutes later I heard Sinatra start to sing 'My Way' from the living room, and I realized I was going to die.

. . .

Is there a sadder success story than a French pop star? Every hit a backwards step, every *encore* inviting derision beyond the homeland. Claude François dreamt otherwise. Known as Cloclo, he made his name in the 1960s with a series of Francophone adaptations of American jukebox staples, backed by a troupe of jiggling female dancers called the Clodettes. As he racked up the hits, Claude kept one eye across the Channel and the other over the Atlantic, weighing up which craze to copy next. His angelic public persona masked a complex, frequently unpleasant character – a perfectionist streak gone sour, a control freak who kept his first wife penned in their apartment for fear that she might stray, and hid the birth of his second child from his fans in case it diminished his sex appeal.

In 1967 François was shown a song entitled 'For Me', penned by a young songwriter called Jacques Revaux. Still smarting from his breakup with the singer France Gall, François tinkered with the lyrics and the melody, intro-ducing the theme of a dying relationship. The result – now called 'Comme d'habitude' ('As Usual') – was an unexpectedly glorious affair, bruised and defiant in equal measure, with swelling strings building to an emotional climax.

When 'Comme d'habitude' became a smash hit in François' native country, an aspiring English songwriter called David Bowie was approached to provide the song with a set of English lyrics. His version, entitled 'Even A Fool Learns To Love', was rejected and never released. A year later the Canadian singer Paul Anka was on holiday in the south of France when he saw Cloclo perform 'Comme d'habitude'. He snapped up the publishing rights to the song – for free – and came up with completely new lyrics, tailor-made for Frank Sinatra. Ol' Blue Eyes had expressed increasing disillusionment with his career, and in 'My Way' Anka felt he had provided him with the perfect *au revoir* – a farewell smirk, the last drunken, self-righteous conversation of the evening. It soon became Sinatra's signature tune, spending two years in the UK Top 40. Piqued by the astonishing success of 'My Way', David Bowie responded with his own four-minute melodrama, based around similar chord patterns – 'Life on Mars?'

If François was unhappy at the direction his song had taken, the deluge of royalties must have eased the pain. 'My Way' fuelled dreams that he could break America: Cloclo in the land of Coca-Cola. However, on the eve of an American tour in 1978, François was taking a bath in his apartment when he noticed a light bulb flickering above his head. Ever the perfectionist, he stood up and tried to adjust the light bulb, instantly electrocuting himself.

. . .

As the first ice cube plummeted down from the shelf into the bath, I glanced up to see the lamp teetering on its remaining support. Then the second ice cube shot out from beneath it, and the lamp came plummeting down through the steam.

The bathroom plunged into darkness.

"Ow!"

I yelled as a heavy weight cracked into my kneecap with a sickening impact upon the bone. Spluttering in agony, I thrashed about in the bath, water flooding in through my mouth and nostrils. By rights I should have been dead, but somehow I was still alive – albeit in a great deal of pain.

There was a crack of light as the door creaked open, and a familiar voice swam through the gloom:

"You all right, mate?"

"Ray!" I cried out, almost sobbing with relief. "Get me out of here!"

He ambled into the bathroom and flicked on the light switch, blinking with surprise at my predicament.

"Whoah," he said, scratching his head. "This is pretty out there."

"No shit, Ray!" I screamed, the lamp banging against my shins. "Do you want to give me a hand here?"

Gill's head poked round the bathroom door. Her look of curiosity turned into one of outright amazement.

"Edgar, what are you up to?"

"There's a key up there!" I said, nodding my head furiously in the direction of the sink.

Ray went over to the sink and picked up the tiny key. His moon face loomed over me as he leant over the bathtub and began fiddling with the lock on the handcuffs.

"Thank God you're here!" I babbled.

"Your call was so mysterious it got me worried," explained Gill. "I phoned Ray to see if he knew what was going on, and he suggested that we check out the flat together."

"You know, just in case," said Ray. "When we came in through the front door, I saw the extension cord leading from the hall socket into the bathroom. I thought it was asking for trouble, so I turned it off. Water and electricity, and all that."

I could have kissed him. My fastidious Scythian friend. A second later and I would have been fried. I wasn't sure that he was even aware what he'd done. Ray grunted with satisfaction, and I felt the handcuffs spring free, releasing my aching wrists.

"What on earth is going on here, Edgar?" asked Gill. "Why is there a lamp in the bath? And who handcuffed you to the tap?"

"He did!" I replied, sending water spilling across the linoleum as I scrambled out of the bath. "Margery's son. The workman. The guy who kidnapped Diana." I paused. "Look, Gill, there's something else I need to tell you—"

"It can wait," my sister replied firmly. "If there's some nutcase knocking around my flat I'd rather we got out of here, if that's all the same to you."

"I hate to interrupt," a voice interjected delicately. "But my ears were burning."

He was standing in the corridor waiting for us, dressed in a smart black suit and tie, his hair artfully tousled. I had encountered him in several guises, but his true self was the one I knew best and feared the most – the cracked genius against whom I had been pitting my wits for even longer than I had been aware.

The colour had drained from Gill's face, and a trembling hand flew to her mouth. At that moment, soaked and bruised as I was, with a sore knee and crashing headache and bleeding wrists, even I had the time to feel sorry for her.

"Richard?" she breathed.

A SHIFTY LYING FELLOW

Having finally been carried home on a Phaeacian ship, Odysseus woke up on a beach in Ithaca. As he sat up and brushed off the sand the weary traveller panicked, unsure of his surroundings. Not for the first time, the goddess Athene came to his rescue, disguising herself as a shepherd in order to deliver the glad tidings of his homecoming. Even though he had returned to his kingdom Odysseus remained wary, inventing a spurious cover story and a new identity.

> "He must be indeed a shifty lying fellow," the amused goddess noted, "who could surpass you in all manner of craft... Dare-devil that you are, full of guile, unwearying in deceit, can you not drop your tricks and your instinctive falsehood, even now that you are in your own country again?"[21]

In this regard, the king and the goddess were well suited. Without Athene's constant assistance, Odysseus would still have been mooning about on Calypso's island feeling sorry for himself. What Athene had achieved through magic, Odysseus attempted through lies and dissembling. But now, having reached home after two decades away, and with his wife Penelope overrun with avaricious suitors plotting the murder of their son Telemachus, the scene was set for the king's triumphant and vengeful return. And yet Odysseus seemed strangely cagey, almost reluctant to act. Instead of heading home or raising an army, he allowed Athene to transform him into an elderly beggar, and paid a visit to a loyal swineherd called Eumaeus. His disguise

---

21 Wikisource contributors, "The Odyssey (Butler)/Book XIII," *Wikisource,* <http://en.wikisource.org/w/index.php?title=The_Odyssey_(Butler)/Book_XIII&oldid=4016485> (accessed October 2, 2014).

gave Odysseus the opportunity to ask coy questions about himself and bask in the swineherd's praise, whilst talking admiringly about himself in the third person.

Why don't you go home, Odysseus? Your wife's been waiting twenty years – faithful Penelope, the bright sun to Clytemnestra's shadow – staunchly repelling the advances of her lustful suitors. Your loving son Telemachus has risked death travelling to the palace of Menelaus for news of his missing father. Why don't you just go home?

Because you're an arsehole, Odysseus, that's why. Too busy playing dress-up and pretending, using the false humility of disguise to show off. Just another self-obsessed, spotlight-seeking, ovation-chasing *actor*.

...

Richard sketched out a theatrical bow.

"Hello, Gill," he said. "I've missed you."

My sister looked disbelievingly from him back to me. "I don't understand," she said, her voice faltering. "What's going on here?"

"He was lying to you," I said gently. "This is Margery's son. I didn't put it together until the National Gallery. It was Richard who kidnapped Diana."

It had taken me far too long to put it all together. The painkillers were the key, not that I had realized it at the time. Gill had told me that Richard had been in hospital a couple of years back – but it hadn't been a car crash that had put him there, but The Finn's fists. Richard had been the persistent strip club customer Paavo had beaten up in a fit of jealous rage. There were so many crazed men erratically orbiting Diana, perhaps it wasn't surprising when they collided.

Not that my sister could have known any of this. She looked utterly bewildered.

"But we were going out," she said. "Why would he—?"

"I know."

"All this time?" she said to Richard. "All the time we were together, and you were just using me so you could stalk my friend?"

"Diana was in the States," he shrugged. "It was a perfect way to keep close to her. You were so proud of her, you mentioned her all the time. It was like we were never apart."

"You told me you loved me," Gill said faintly.

"You should be honoured," Richard replied. "It was my greatest performance."

"Your greatest performance?" Gill's gaze hardened. "You *bastard!*"

I caught her arm as she went for him, pulling her back.

Richard wagged his finger. "Now, now," he chided. "Play nice."

He sniffed, pinching his nose. Gill's eyes narrowed. "You're coked up, aren't you?" she said.

"That's really none of your concern any more," Richard replied archly.

"Is there *anything* you didn't lie about?"

"All acting is a lie, Gill. That's what makes it such art." Richard pulled a snub-nosed revolver from the waistband of his suit trousers and calmly trained it on my sister. "But this, I should warn you, isn't a prop. And I know how to use it."

I believed him. I had seen the bullet hole in The Finn's chest.

"Don't do anything silly, Richard," I said quickly. "We'll do what you say."

"How very accommodating of you!" he replied. "Why don't you come through to the living room with me, then? I believe that the star of the show is ready to take centre stage."

We trooped along the corridor under the shadow of a gun barrel. In the living room, Gill's hand flew to her mouth at the sight of Diana's prone body.

"Is she all right?"

"I haven't touched her, if that's what you mean," said Richard. "I've treated her like royalty."

"I'm sure she'll be grateful," Gill said icily.

"And so she should be! Before me Diana was just another dancer in the *corps*. Only I realized how special she was. Now, thanks to me, Diana has played all the great roles: Coppelia, the heartless doll. Odile, the white swan. Now she is Princess Aurora – Sleeping Beauty."

"You're out of your mind," said Gill, with a bitter laugh.

"I wouldn't expect *you* to understand," Richard said sharply. "What's more galling is the fact that after everything I've done for Diana, still she refuses to love me. Oh, she let me sleep with me if I paid her – but then she wouldn't even let me do that. She fucked other men just to taunt me. It was bad enough when Ivanov came along, and then there was Oscar Salazar. I knew that time was running out, so I had to make my move."

"So you kidnapped her," I said.

"All my life I've played extras," said Richard. "This time I got to play the arch-villain. It's so much more fun, believe me – you could get quite addicted to it."

"Margery must be so proud," I said sarcastically.

Richard smiled. "Mother told me you were getting closer. I think she may like you more than she likes me."

"The fact that I'm not a murderer may help."

"Ah," sniffed Richard. "I take it you're referring to The Finn. That was unfortunate. It appeared that he had been keeping a rather closer eye on Diana than I had realized. He barged into our hotel room and made a tremendous fuss. It was lucky I had my gun close to hand, or else I could have been in serious trouble. He was lucky, in a way. After what he did to me in the club I should have taken my revenge slowly, over a number of days. He should have spent as long in agony as I did in the hospital."

"And what about me?" I said. "Why did you drag me into it?"

"I knew that taking Diana would lead to awkward questions. I needed a scapegoat, a patsy – someone the police would naturally suspect. You fitted the bill perfectly. Gill used to go on about how you were obsessed with bathing, so I did a little research of my own. I knew you wouldn't be able to resist my little game. The plan was to leave you standing around in the National Gallery while I dealt with Diana here. The police are looking for you anyway – when they discovered a barbecued corpse in your bathtub, that would have been the end of it. Only you worked things out a little faster than I intended."

"Thanks," I said sourly. "Nothing like being underestimated by a psychopath."

"I don't think we're *quite* so different now, are we Edgar? A cursory inspection of your folders in the bathroom would suggest that we both understand the meaning of obsession."

"Leave him alone!" Gill said fiercely. "Edgar's nothing like you!"

"You really don't understand anything, do you?" sneered Richard.

Before Gill could reply there was a soft moan from the sofa. I glanced over to see Diana stir, her hand reaching up her temple.

"Sleeping Beauty awakes!" cried Richard.

"Diana?" I called out anxiously. "Are you all right?"

She groaned, pushing herself up into a sitting position. Her gaze was filmy, unfocused. She looked up and saw a room full of strangers.

"It may take a while for the prima ballerina to recover her former poise," said Richard. "She has been in a particularly deep sleep."

"So what now?" said Ray. "You can't kill us all."

Richard tapped the gun against his cheek. "The fact that we have company does pose some interesting new questions. I wonder whether the police will accept the idea that Edgar – deranged by Diana's rejection – could go on a violent killing spree before turning the gun upon himself. Let's find out, shall we?"

He pointed the gun at the centre of my forehead. I closed my eyes. No time for farewell speeches or last goodbyes.

When the bang came, there was no pain – no feeling at all, in fact. Realizing that the noise had not in fact been a gun's report, I opened my eyes and saw Sergei charge into the living room. Startled, Richard hesitated before training the revolver on him, giving the wiry skinhead time to grab him by the shirt and headbutt him smack in the face. There was a shocking crunch and Richard dropped to the floor, his nose a bloody fountain. Gill screamed.

"Jesus!" cried Ray. "Who the hell's this?"

Sergei ignored him, reaching down to snatch Richard's revolver from the floor. Tucking the weapon into his belt, he pointed at me.

"You come with me now. All of you."

My mouth ran dry. "Where?" I asked hoarsely.

"Where do you think? The bathhouse. Valery wants to talk to you. It is time to settle this."

. . .

There were fifty daughters of Danaus… Cleopatra and Asteria, Glauce and Hippodamia, Gorge and Iphimedusa, Rhode and Pirene, Cercestis and

Pharte... who were engaged to be married to their uncle Aegyptus's fifty sons. However, when an oracle warned him that one of his sons-in-law would bring about his downfall, Danaus ordered his daughters to murder their new husbands on their wedding night, and gave each of them a dagger with which to do the deed... to Mnestra and Euippe, Anaxibia and Nelo, Clite and Stenele, Actea and Podarce, Dioxippe and Adyte...

On the night of the marital massacre, one of the girls, Hypermnestra, spared her husband Lynceus in gratitude for his respecting her wish to remain a virgin. But that left forty-nine resolute assassins, determined to do their father's bidding. By sunrise forty-nine blades had been bloodied, and forty-nine severed male heads dutifully presented to Danaus... by Amymone and Automate, Agave and Scea, Hippodamia and Rhodia, Calyce and Gorgophone...

The Danaides may have pleased their father, but their killing spree invited the fury of the Gods. Upon their deaths the sisters were sentenced to an eternity in Tartarus, the dark pit of Hell... Chrysippe and Autonoe, Theano and Electra, Eurydice and Glaucippe, Autholea and Cleodora, Euippe and Erata, Stygne and Bryce... It was in Tartarus that Sisyphus struggled with his lonely burden, pushing a rock up a mountainside only to see it roll back down every time. Lustful Ixion was strapped to a spinning wheel of fire, whilst Tantalus stood in the shadow of a fruit tree, the branches arching their juicy burden just out of his despairing reach.

The Danaides were given their own hopeless task – trying to fill a leaking bathtub with water carried from River Lethe, the river of oblivion. Whilst merciful Hypermnestra indulged herself in the soft meadows of Elysian Fields, deep below the earth forty-nine sisters wearily carried their pails back and forth... Ocypete and Pilarge, Hippodice and Adiante, Callidia and Oeme, Celena and Hyperia, Hippomedusa... forty-nine pairs of eyes, blinking back the tears.

...

The black people carrier was waiting for us outside the complex of flats. As Sergei herded the five of us through the electronic gate, Walter unfolded himself from the driver's seat and opened the door. We climbed mutely inside, too shocked and frightened to resist. Gill and Ray sat in the first bank of seats, their hands nervously clasped in each other's. I sat next to Diana, who gazed out of the window at the night. Behind us Richard nursed his bloodied nose in the rearmost seat, beside a contemptuous Sergei. The unexpected appearance of the Russian had unarmed Richard in more ways than one – his coke-fuelled bubble had burst, leaving the actor looking hunted and forlorn.

As our journey continued I prayed for every traffic light to turn red, or that a tyre would blow or a police light burst into life in the rearview mirror, but instead the people carrier moved with agonizing ease down to the grimy environs of Old Street. Within minutes it was pulling up outside the Russian bathhouse and Sergei was gesturing at us to climb out. When Ray tried to help Gill out of the vehicle he shook his head.

"You stay here with Walter," he ordered. "The redhead and the other two come inside."

As I moved past them Gill grabbed me by the wrist.

"What's going to happen in there, Ed?"

"Nothing," I replied, hoping she hadn't heard the tremble in my voice. "We're going to sort this out once for and all, and then it'll all be over."

"I'm worried, little brother."

"Just stay here and do what they tell you," I said, with a reassuring smile. "We'll be back before you know it."

Sergei pulled me out and slammed the door shut before Gill could respond. Grabbing the reluctant Richard by the collar, he marched up to the bathhouse entrance and pressed the buzzer. As we waited for the door to open, Diana stared dreamily down the street. Following her gaze, I caught sight of a small figure in a hoodie hurriedly drawing back into the shadows.

There was no time to wonder who it was watching us. The bathhouse door opened with a loud click – with a final, helpless glance back at Gill and Ray, I let Sergei bundle me inside.

THE BANNIK'S WRATH

I kept tight hold of Diana's hand as we were manhandled through the foyer of the bathhouse, fearing that if I let go she would be lost forever, a vague spectre condemned to wander the bowels of this watery Hades. Richard whimpered as Sergei clipped him around the head and pushed him stumbling onwards. An icy draught whipped down the dark corridor; with every step, I expected to feel Death's cold tap upon my shoulder.

Valery was waiting for us in the changing rooms. He had traded in his towel and flip-flops for a dark blue tracksuit and trainers, a large gold cross dangling from his necklace. Yuri was still tied up naked in the shower, his pale skin lending him a ghostly aspect in the gloom. He raised his slumped head as we entered, and tried to scramble to his feet.

"Diana!" Yuri cried, straining at his bonds. "My love!"

She stared at him blankly.

"What's wrong with Diana?" demanded Yuri. "What have you done to her?"

"She's been drugged," I explained. "She doesn't recognize anyone."

Valery pointed at Richard. "This is him?" he barked. "The one who took the girl?"

"Looks that way, boss," said Sergei. "We followed Edgar to a flat and waited. When he didn't come out I decided to go take a look. The one in the suit had a gun on him, was going to use it too. I persuaded him otherwise."

"Where's the gun now?" Valery demanded.

Sergei produced the revolver from his waistband and handed it to the Russian, who examined the weapon with an expert eye.

"Put it with the others," he ordered, shoving Sergei towards the doorway. "I'll take it from here."

"I'm going to kill you, you bastard!" Yuri cried at Richard. "You hear me?"

"Shut your mouth," Valery said irritably. "Maybe I kill all of you. Nothing is worth this shit."

"Please don't hurt me!" Richard begged. "I don't even know who you are!"

"That does not matter. You have cost me time and money. Look at this man" – grabbing Richard by the scruff of his neck, Valery marched him over to Yuri – "he is meant to be my principal dancer. Look at him! This is because of you."

"I'm sorry!" stammered Richard. "All I cared about was Diana. If I'd have known you were involved I wouldn't have done a thing, I swear!"

He had melted from the all-powerful arch-villain to pitiful victim with such speed that I wasn't sure that I entirely believed it. Valery seemed disgusted by him, bundling Richard to the floor. The Russian looked over to Yuri.

"Are you satisfied now?" he asked. "I bring you the girl. She is safe and well. I will take care of the guy who kidnapped her. Now you and Lilia will come to Kiev as agreed and dance for me, yes?"

Yuri let out a harsh, disbelieving laugh. "Are you kidding me? You kidnap me, you beat me, you leave me tied up here for days... I would rather chop off my feet than dance a single step for you, pig!"

"That can be arranged," Valery said ominously.

I had kept purposefully quiet, hoping for an opportunity to slip away with Diana whilst the others talked. But now an urgent, acrid scent had reached my nostrils, apparently coming from the door through which Sergei had just disappeared.

"Excuse me?" I said tentatively.

"What?" snarled Valery.

"Can anyone smell burning?"

. . .

Beware, innocent bather, of the invisible danger that lurks within the *banya*! A wrathful spirit holds court on a throne of burning coals. Most commonly seen as an elderly man with long fingernails, the *bannik* is a shape-shifter that can assume any form it chooses. The *bannik* places a great demand on orderly, respectful behaviour – shouting, boasting or swearing are enough to rouse it to anger. Minor infractions could lead to boiling water and burning coals flying around the steam room, whilst serious offenders could be burned against the stove or even skinned alive. Wise bathers never forget to keep the *banya* clean, or to give thanks to the *bannik* by leaving it small tributes of soap and fir branches.

The *banya* is the great haunted house of Russian history, where evil spirits and witches roamed its smoky rooms and even mothers giving birth could not be safely left alone. Dark magic was woven into the bathhouse walls. If a *banya* burned down – hardly an unusual occurrence in medieval Russia, given the combination of rickety wooden structures and unreliable stoves – a sacrifice was needed to appease the *bannik*. A black hen was duly suffocated and buried, unplucked, beneath the *banya's* ashen remains.

. . .

"Burning?" said Valery, with a scowl. "What do you mean, burning?"

"You know – like something's been set on fire."

"I smell nothing," he snapped.

"*I* can smell it," Diana said dreamily.

Valery stopped and sniffed. The bitter odour had intensified, and I thought I could see a black tendril of smoke creeping beneath the door to the changing rooms. Suddenly the door flew open, and Sergei came running back in.

"Fire, boss!" he panted. "Out back."

"Then why the fuck are you here?" roared Valery. "Put it out!"

Sergei shook his head. "It's too fierce. We need to clear out the stuff and get out of here."

"Too fierce? We're in a bathhouse, idiot – fill up some buckets with water!"

"Buckets won't do anything, boss!" Sergei said helplessly. "This place is a firetrap. And what about the guns in the storeroom? As soon as the fire reaches them, the whole building will explode!"

Valery gestured angrily at the slumped forms of Yuri and Richard. "I am taking care of business here! This is no time to be running anywhere." His voice dropped menacingly. "Put out the fire, Sergei, or I'll put *you* out."

Sergei's eyes darted down to the wisps of black smoke around his feet, and then back to his boss. He nodded, and ran back in the direction of the fire. Valery shook his head, muttering something darkly under his breath.

It was at this moment that Richard appeared behind the Russian and brained him with a wooden bucket.

A shocking *thunk* reverberated around the bathhouse. Valery staggered forward, blood spurting from a deep gash in his skull. Richard lifted the bucket high above his head, preparing to strike the killer blow, only for Valery to drive his elbow deep into the actor's gut. The air exploded from Richard's lungs, the bucket hitting the tiles with a loud clatter.

With a roar Valery grabbed hold of Richard, half-stumbling, half-pulling him to the ground. The two men began to wrestle on a thickening mat of black smoke, punching and clawing at each other. Having lost the element of surprise, Richard was in serious trouble. Valery wrapped his hands around the actor's neck and began to squeeze. Richard's eyes bulged in his sockets, and he frantically tried to push his assailant away. I was ready to leave them to it and drag Diana out of the changing rooms, only to see – to my utter dismay – flames appearing in the doorway, cutting off our escape route. Sergei was right: the bathhouse was a firetrap. I guessed he had already made a run for it. And if we didn't do the same, we were all going to burn alive.

"Untie me!" shouted Yuri, lifting up his bound wrists. "Don't let me die here!"

I stayed rooted to the spot, frozen with indecision. Beside me Diana watched the fire creep into the room with an eerie, almost happy detachment. Then, through the smoke, I saw an adjoining door open at the far end of the lockers, and a small hooded figure crept inside the changing rooms. It was the same person who had been skulking in the shadows outside the bathhouse. When they glanced towards at me I caught a glimpse of a pale female face and piercing blue eyes, and suddenly everything became clear. After all, hadn't it been Lilia Kutznetsova who had told me about Valery's bathhouse in the first place? Pulling a knife from her pocket, she cut the rope above her husband's head. Yuri collapsed on the floor like a puppet with severed strings. Lilia slipped her arm underneath his shoulders and, with a great effort, lifted the fallen dancer to his feet.

. . .

If the history of bathing is a series of watermarks brushed across the page, here and there the edges of the parchment would be brown and gnawed, as though a careless reader had brushed them against the candle flame. Fire and water are the warring siblings of the elemental world, forever locked in a tug of war that threatens both violent confrontation and sudden, unexpected moments of empathy.

Princess Olga of Kiev was born in northwest Russia in the 10th century, a celebrated beauty who married Igor, ruler of the medieval state of Kievan Rus. In 945 Igor died at the hands of a belligerent tribe called the Drevlians, from whom he had rode forth to collect tribute. With their son Sviatoslav just three years old, and Olga now alone on the throne, the Drevlians sensed their opportunity. They offered the grieving widow the opportunity to marry their Prince Mal, and were invited to Kiev to discuss the issue. When the barbarians arrived the princess honoured them by throwing open the doors to her bathhouse, inviting them to wash off their journey before they came before her. Once the Drevlians were inside Olga had her men close the doors and set the building alight. The bathhouse burned to the ground, roasting the entire Drevlian party alive.

Had any of her subjects harboured doubts that a woman could rule Kievan Rus, the stench of charred human flesh on the wind should have been sufficient to silence them. A year after Olga's impromptu barbecue, she followed in her late husband's footsteps and went to the Drevlian lands to collect tribute, with her toddler son at her side. When the town of Iskorosten (now Korosten in Ukraine, near Chernobyl) refused to pay tribute, Olga's forces laid siege to it. As the previous sieges of Troy and Syracuse teach us, such stalemates only end one way – in chicanery – and Iskorosten was no exception. Suing for peace, Olga asked only for tributes of pigeons and sparrows to end the siege. When the grateful Drevlians offered up their household birds the princess had flammable wads of sulphur-soaked cloth attached to the creatures' legs, before freeing them to fly back to their coops and cotes. A great fire spread through Iskoroten, burning the city to the ground.

Once more the Black Widow had turned to fire as a tool of vengeance – once more, the smell of charred tinder and singed skin signalled her victory. Having folded the Drevlian territories into the Kievan Rus empire, the avenging of Igor's death was complete. But Olga was not finished. Even when Sviatoslav was old enough to rule, she continued to wield tremendous influence over Kievan Rus, ruling virtually side-by-side with her son. She converted to Christianity, and was formally received by Emperor Constantine VII in Constantinople. In the years following her death in c.969, Olga was declared a saint by the Orthodox Church, earning herself the honorary title of Isapóstolos – 'Equal to the Apostles'.

. . .

The fire stalked closer, heat rolling towards us in thick, billowing waves. Smoke stung my eyes. Valery and Richard were still rolling around on the tiles, but now it impossible to see who had the upper hand. I didn't care if either of them survived – Lilia and Yuri had stumbled out of the changing rooms through the adjoining door, and now Diana and I had to follow them. It surely wouldn't be long until the fire reached the weapons in the bathhouse storeroom.

"Diana!" I screamed. "We have to get out of here! Come on!"

There was a glimmer of comprehension in her eyes, and she reached out and put her hand in mine. Together we ran out of the changing rooms into a tiled antechamber with a plunge pool at its heart. The blue, rippling water appeared like a glorious vision, calling out to my bruised and battered body, whispering tender promises of safety.

Clutching on to Diana, I ran forward and leapt into the water.

As we sank below the surface the pool shuddered violently and I was aware of a deafening explosion. The fire had reached Valery's cache of weapons. But that was in another world, far above our heads. We were safe, cocooned in a watery haven.

I stayed underwater until my lungs were burning from the lack of oxygen, and then erupted back through the surface. As I gasped for air I saw Diana rise up beside me, her hair plastered to her forehead and her mouth open in an 'O' of shock. The antechamber had been swallowed up by a fearsome inferno, fire clawing at the walls.

Scrabbling the hair from her eyes, Diana suddenly let out a piercing scream. I turned to see a dark silhouette floating past us on the water – a burned corpse in a sodden suit, face down in the water. The last role Richard would ever play, and his most complete performance yet.

I dragged Diana away from the dead body and splashed over to the side of the pool, fastening her hand on the rim of the tiles. Summoning up my last reserves of strength, I dragged myself out of the water and helped Diana climb free. The heat was intense, thick smoke filling up my mouth and lungs. We stumbled out of the antechamber through burning corridors, uncertain of the direction, just desperate to get *away*.

Suddenly, through the flames, I spotted the hunched figure of Valery Limonov. Somehow the Russian had survived the explosion, and was staggering along the corridor. Shielding my eyes, I led Diana through the burning labyrinth after him. We fled through the fire, coughing and wheezing, until ahead of us I heard a door bang open and suddenly I saw the glorious promise of an alleyway outside.

We burst out into the night, bent double, coughing up smoke. I was aware of nothing but the soothing balm of fresh air and Diana beside me, her face streaked with tears.

"Are you OK?" I coughed.

Diana's face was flushed and streaked with black soot marks, steam still rising from her sodden clothes. As she stared at me incredulously, I saw that the druggy fog had lifted from her eyes. She had been reborn in the healing waters of the bathhouse. Diana started to reply and then burst out laughing, her chest shaking with hysterical amusement.

"I'm fine, Edgar," she replied, giggling helplessly. "Just dandy."

It was hysterical laughter of someone standing on the verge of a dizzying precipice who was defiantly refusing to let the wind blow them off the edge. As I watched Diana laugh I couldn't help joining in, and we dissolved on to the side of the pavement in helpless fits as the bathhouse crackled and blazed behind us.

In the distance, sirens began to wail. Across the road a door slammed and the black people carrier shot away with a squeal of tyres, leaving Gill and Ray standing dazed on the pavement. Further down the street, a naked man leant on a smaller, hooded figure as he hobbled away into the night. There was a loud crash and a roar from within the bathhouse – the *bannik's* final death wail? Diana and I laughed until we cried, the laughter only making my chest ache more, but there was no staunching the flow of tears spilling out from their salty taps – tears of shock, and relief, and the joy of survival.

THE DEATH OF MARAT

I ducked my head beneath the surface of the bath, water bubbling joyously in my ears, holding my breath for as long as possible before reemerging through a thick layer of bubble bath foam. I was a Hollywood bombshell, thrusting out my chest to a rapid applause of camera clicks. I was the Lizard King, slithering across the stage, drunk dizzy on the audience's rapturous screams. I was a streetwalker in a penthouse bathroom, strawberry sweet lips curving into a smile as I celebrated my new position.

A week had passed since our escape from the burning bathhouse. The police had been satisfied with my explanation for my involvement, Diana's testimony of her ordeal only confirming my innocence. They had even returned Curtis, who had happily reclaimed his spot near the soap dish. There had been some puzzled questions concerning the discovery of an unplucked chicken in the smoking ruins of the bathhouse, but I pleaded ignorance. That particular secret lay between Lilia and the *bannik*.

Throughout my interviews and in my police statement I endeavoured not to mention Oscar, mindful of his parting threat aboard the *Moira Shearer*. I could hardly avoid naming Valery, but thankfully the Russian had already fled Britain, boarding a private jet the day after the fire in order to avoid some awkward questions about the cache of firearms in his possession. I doubted that he would be returning any time soon. Later that week, I spotted an article in the arts section of the newspaper announcing that Yuri had decided to join the Chicago Ballet in order to be closer to his wife, first principal Lilia Kuznetsova. In the accompanying photographs I could still see the faint bruises on Yuri's face, and there was an unmistakably hunted look in his eyes. His wife was a picture of icy triumph. Yet somehow, after everything that had happened, I found it hard to begrudge Lilia her moment of victory.

If Diana had been disappointed by Yuri's decision, she refused to let it show. In the aftermath of her kidnapping she was quiet and withdrawn, still haunted by the grey blur of rooms that had been her time in captivity. At least Oscar had been true to his word, and there was an offer for her to join the *corps* of the Walker Ballet. It should have been cause for celebration, yet when Diana stopped by the flat with the news I detected a tension between her and Gill, the shadow of a secret shame. Diana thanked me profusely for saving her life, insisting on paying me a further month's wages for my efforts. But for all her kind words she was awkward and hesitant around me. I could hardly blame her. We had barely shared two conversations before her kidnap, yet my search for Diana had entailed learning the most intimate details of her life. She might not have known about the hours I had spent watching her bathe on her website, or the sex tape I had seen of her and Richard, but Diana seemed to sense that her privacy had been invaded. At some stage, I knew, we were going to have to talk.

But not tonight. Tonight I had other plans.

Reaching over to the hot tap, I carefully added a boost of scalding hot water to the bath. I was determined to make the most of this; it was going to be my last bath for a while. As the thick heat of August had given way to a mellow September, so my *Dermatitis Herpetiformis* rashes had calmed, my pimples deflating and my sandpaper skin softening. Freed from the hideous, infernal itching, I had come to a decision. The autumnal breeze carried with it the promise of new beginnings. Tomorrow I was going to pack up the volumes of the Ulpian Library, take down the ring-binder folders from the shelves, and move them all through into the bedroom. It was time to leave the bathroom. My book could wait, it was time to *live*.

This newfound optimism owed everything to one person in particular. Three days ago I had met Keiko for a coffee, and told her all about the blazing climax to the case. She had been suitably impressed, her eyes widening as I described our flight from the bathhouse. Tonight we were going to the Walker Theatre to watch the *Coppelia* production (tickets courtesy of Diana). To my astonishment, it appeared to be a genuine date. I couldn't quite believe my luck.

Next door, Gill's voice floated through from the living room wall as she sang along to the radio. I wasn't the only one going out tonight. My sister wouldn't tell me who she was seeing, but I had a feeling I knew. The last time I had spoken to Ray he had been in high spirits, with an infuriating grin that suggested he knew something I didn't. He also refused to roll a joint – a sure-fire sign that he was hoping to impress a certain someone. I was pleased for both of them. Gill had spent enough time impersonating Circe, surrounded by swine, and she deserved to go out with a nice guy. And as for Ray – well, he couldn't say I hadn't warned him.

As I scooped up a handful of foam and playfully blew it into the air Gill stopped singing and turned the radio down, plunging the flat into silence. I froze, suddenly and inexplicably disturbed. Then the doorbell let out a shrill yell.

. . .

She had come all the way from Caen to Paris to see him, clutching a copy of Plutarch's *Parallel Lives* to read on the long journey to the capital. The woman's name was Charlotte Corday, and she sought an audience with 'The People's Friend', Jean-Paul Marat. Since his days on the run in the sewers beneath Paris, Marat's star had risen, and he was now one of the most famous names of revolutionary France.

Upon arriving in the city, Corday sought Marat out at the National Convention, only to learn that he was sequestered at home. Marat's skin condition had returned with a vengeance and he was confined to his bathtub, a vinegar-soaked bandana plastered across his forehead. The following day – 13 July 1793 – Corday visited Marat at home. A servant turned her away, informing her that Marat was too ill to receive guests. Undeterred, Corday returned to her hotel and carefully composed a letter of introduction.

> "Citizen," she wrote, "I come from Caen; your love for your country makes me suppose you will like to know the unhappy events in that part of the Republic. I shall present myself at your house about seven o'clock; have the goodness to receive me and to accord me a moment's interview. I shall put you in a position to render a great service to the country."[22]

22 Ernest Belfort Bax, *Jean-Paul Marat: The People's Friend* (Grant Richards, 1901), p.300

It was a note calculated to prick up Marat's ears. Corday's home was a hotbed of Girondists – moderates who, although supportive of the abolition of the monarchy, felt that the French Revolution was gathering a dangerous, uncontrollable momentum. For Marat, ever the scourge of the establishment, the Girondists were little better than counter-revolutionaries. During the urban riots of early summer 1793, he had helped the Commandant-General of the Parisian National Guard, François Hanriot, purge the Convention of their deputies.

But the removal of the Girondists from power was not enough for Marat. He continued to attack them from his high-walled copper bathtub – where he worked on a board resting across the water, an inkstand on a table by his side – writing letters and newspaper articles, signing death warrants; haranguing, exhorting, accusing. When Corday returned to his house on the evening of 13 July, the sounds of her arguing with the household staff carried up to Marat in the bathroom. He ordered the woman's admittance, receiving her in his bathroom. When Corday recited a list of deputies in Caen with Girondist sympathies Marat scribbled down the names, murmuring: "It will not be long before they are guillotined."[23]

He was unaware it was his own death warrant he was signing. Earlier that morning, Charlotte Corday had visited a cutler's shop, where she had purchased an ebony-handled knife for forty sous. As Marat wrote she drew the knife from her corset and buried it into his chest. Marat cried out for help to his wife, Simonne Evrard, but the knife thrust had punctured his left lung and aorta. Drowning in his own blood, Marat slumped backwards in the tub, the voice of The People's Friend silenced forever.

...

Gill answered the door, and I struggled to make out the murmuring voices in the hallway. They spoke for a minute or so, and then I heard footsteps approach down the corridor. As the handle turned I realized that, in my bubble bath-scented fugue, I had forgotten to lock the bathroom door again.

"Wait!" I cried.

Keiko walked in anyway. In a graceful nod to the changing seasons, she was dressed in a chocolate brown overcoat, jeans, and a pair of knee-length

23 Belfort Bax, *Jean-Paul Marat: The People's Friend*, p.303

tan boots. I stared at her in a mixture of surprise, wonderment and helpless adoration.

"So this is the place," said Keiko, looking around the bathroom.

I nodded dumbly.

"I like what you've done with it," she said. "The books are a nice touch. Very homely."

"This is a surprise!" I said stupidly, aware that I had only a thin covering of bubbles protecting my modesty. "I thought we were meeting outside the theatre."

"Change of plans," Keiko said crisply.

"You're not having second thoughts, are you?"

She took out a piece of nicotine gum from her handbag and popped it in her mouth, chewing rapidly. Keiko had looked everywhere in the room but at me. If I didn't know better, I would have said she was nervous.

"I was thinking about all the stuff you told me the other day," she said finally. "The case. I couldn't see how Paavo fitted in. OK, so he's protective of Diana, but you were trying to help her. Why did he keep coming after you? Then, in Soaplands, he has the chance to kill you but he backs off. Why?"

"I don't know, Keiko. The guy was a psychopath!"

"And when I started thinking about that, something else started bothering me," Keiko continued. "Who told Oscar about the charity gala? The one where Diana danced?"

"I hadn't thought about it," I admitted. "Richard?"

"Why? The *last* thing he wanted was another competitor. This whole thing doesn't quite add up. The only way it makes sense is if there was someone else involved."

My skin prickled in warning.

"What do you mean, someone else?"

It was then that Keiko looked at me, a level gaze straight into my eyes.

"You," she said.

There was a long silence. Then the bathroom echoed to the sound of my astonished laughter.

"I'm not quite sure what you're saying," I told her. "That I was the one who told Oscar about Diana? And what – I was asking The Finn to try and kill me?"

"Yeah, that's pretty much it."

"He poured boiling water on my balls, Keiko! Boiling water! You think I wanted that?"

"I think you wanted to make sure you looked like the good guy."

It should have been funny, but Keiko's face was deadly serious. I couldn't believe what I was hearing.

"Seriously," I said, "this is crazy."

She nodded. "Yeah, I thought that at first." She glanced up at the row of ring-binder files, her jaws still moving furiously as she chewed on her gum. "What's in these?"

"My notes on bathing. Nothing interesting."

"D'you mind if I take a look?"

"I do, actually," I said quickly. "They're personal."

"Just a quick peek. I'll be extra careful."

"Please don't touch them!"

"It'll be fine."

"No!"

I stood up, water and foam dripping from my body, a despairing arm stretched towards her. Too late. Keiko reached up to the shelf and pulled down one of the files.

. . .

It was written that the Ulpian Library was moved into the Baths of Diocletian at some point during the 4th century AD. But the only record of this event lies in the *Life of Probus* in the *Historia Augusta*, one of the least reliable sources of classical history in existence. In all probability the Ulpian Library never found its way into a bathroom at all. The moral of this story: don't believe everything you read.

I slumped back down into the water, powerless to stop Keiko as she leafed through the file, her face hardening. My secrets came spilling treacherously forth — surreptitious photographs, carefully clipped newspaper articles, meticulous reports. A long-lens photograph through an apartment window of a redheaded woman putting on a T-shirt. Another shot of her reading the back of a paperback in a department store bookshop. A glowing review in *The Chicago Tribune* of a production of *Don Quixote*.

Keiko snapped open the ring binder and carefully tipped its contents on to the floor, carpeting the linoleum with stolen images of Diana – sharing a joke, jogging in a park, cooking dinner, sleeping in her bed at night.

"My God, Edgar," Keiko said quietly. "What have you been doing?"

Watching. Waiting. Feigning ignorance. Lying to my own soul.

Before I could say anything the bathroom door swung open at Gill's brisk knock, and my sister poked her head around the door.

"Is everything all right in here?" she asked. "I—"

She stopped and stared at the floor.

"Gill, could you give us a minute?" I tried. "I'm in the bath here!"

She ignored me. Kneeling down, Gill picked up a black-and-white photograph. In it Diana was sitting outside a café with Yuri, their hands clasped underneath the table, their noses brushing as they kissed.

"Edgar, what are these?"

"OK, so I paid someone to keep an eye on Diana in Chicago," I told her. "I had a feeling she was going to get herself into trouble, and I wasn't wrong, was I?"

"You had Diana followed?" said Gill, perplexed. "Why? I thought you didn't even remember her."

"That may have been an exaggeration," I admitted. "Things were getting serious with Oscar, Yuri and Richard, and I didn't want you thinking I was like them."

"Ed, this place looks like a stalker's darkroom!" shouted Gill, brandishing a wad of Diana photographs. "You *are* like them!"

"I was protecting her!"

Keiko laughed disbelievingly. Gill put her head in her hands. "Dear God," she murmured. "Not you too."

"Don't you see?" I told them desperately. "I had to break her and Yuri up but there was no way she would ever listen to me. I needed someone powerful to intervene, someone I knew wouldn't stick around afterwards."

"Someone with a well-known thing for redheads," Keiko added grimly.

"Everything was working perfectly," I told her, almost giddy. "I sent Oscar the message about the gala, he went and fell for her, and then Diana came to me for help. To *me*!"

She had said I was like Sherlock Holmes. How could she have known that all along I had been the Crooked Man?

"There's stuff here from *years* ago," said Gill, sifting through photographs. "How long have you been doing this?"

"I don't know – a while, I guess."

Even now, it was hard to admit the truth. But it had been a long time. Before the *Dermatitis Herpetiformis* had struck I had regularly shadowed Diana around London, following her from audition to audition, recording the minutiae of her existence with a tender precision. During that time I had come across The Finn, who was still trailing around after her like a wounded puppy. Upon Diana's return from America, I had cautiously approached him with an offer of work. For a small amount of money he had agreed to act as a *deus ex machina*, a violent spanner in the works. I submitted to Paavo's careful, inventive assaults knowing that every blow helped ensure that no one could question my innocence. Oh, I could teach Richard a thing or two about method acting. My burns and bruises were badges of honour, testaments to my love for Diana. Of course I had lied about her! How could I possibly have forgotten her? A day hadn't passed in the decade since our family holiday that she hadn't appeared in my thoughts.

"And what about me?" asked Keiko. "Where did I fit into your great master plan?"

"It wasn't like that!" I said, pleading. "You have to believe me. Everything changed when you appeared. I still wanted to find Diana but you showed me that I could be different. All of this stuff – the books, the folders, the photos… I was going to pack it all away tomorrow. If only you'd waited one more day!"

"Yeah," said Keiko. "Sorry about that."

Only minutes before I had been a Lizard King. Now I was a Friendly Floatee bath toy, frozen in Arctic ice. Gill tossed the incriminating photographs to one side and straightened up briskly.

"What are you going to do?" I asked weakly.

"What do you think I'm going to do?" said Gill. "I'm going to call Diana. Somehow I've got to tell her what you've been up to."

"No! Please!"

She paused in the doorway, and spoke without looking back at me. "It was bad enough that ex-boyfriend turned out to be a lying stalker. Now my little brother too?"

I had no reply. I had nothing. As my sister stormed out of the bathroom I looked up at Keiko and turned out my palms in a helpless, imploring gesture.

"You've been doing this for years," she murmured. "And you were worried whether or not *I* was sincere?"

Taking the chewing gum from her mouth, Keiko stuck it on to the bathroom mirror and followed Gill out of the bathroom. I stumbled after her, calling out her name, but she slammed the bathroom door in my face. Then her boots marched away down the hallway, striding out of the flat and out of my life.

Gasping for breath, I drew the bolt across the door with a trembling hand. The bathroom looked like a crime scene: the mouldy, dog-eared books, the strewn photographs streaked with bathwater and wet footprints. My head was spinning, and I had to fight back a violent urge to vomit. Like Seneca, weakly searching for an end to his suffering, I staggered blindly back towards the tub. I sank into the water, offering myself up to its warm, hungry embrace. As my lifeblood ebbed away into the water, the dark depths reached up to claim me.

. . .

Charlotte Corday remained eerily serene throughout her four-day trial. A Girondist sympathizer, she claimed that Marat had been driving France towards civil war, and that she had taken one life to save thousands more. A guilty verdict was inevitable; her death sentence a formality. On 17 July 1793, as thunderclouds darkened the sky, Corday was led through a rain of human spit to the guillotine. Following her execution a man named Legros, incensed by Marat's murder, picked up her freshly decapitated head and slapped it across the cheek.

In death Marat's reputation soared. He was lauded in poem and song; streets and squares were named in his honour. His death was commemorated in a painting by Jacques-Louis David – in *The Death of Marat*, David presented the writer slumped in the bathtub, his face airbrushed of its deformities, facing death with a beatific acceptance.

And what of Marat's bath, the high-walled copper tub that had served as study, court, and deathbed? In 1885 a dogged *Le Figaro* journalist tracked it down to a curé in Brittany, who duly realized that the bath was worth its weight in more than copper. A bidding war ensued – the American impresario P.T. Barnum had an offer turned down in favour of the Musée Grévin in Paris, where the bathtub still resides today.

STRANGE HORNS APPEARED
ON HIS FOREHEAD

"Edgar? Where are you?"

Mum's voice floats up through the attic floorboards. I know that I am supposed to reply but this is my special room and I don't want her up here. I am sitting with my back against the sloping roof under the skylight, my books arranged in a row beside me. Everywhere I look there are big cardboard boxes covered in white sheets. The air is hot and lazy, like warm bathwater. Dust glints in the sunlight.

I hear footsteps on the ladder, and then Mum's head pokes up through the hatch.

"There you are, Edgar!" she says, as if I have done something wrong. "What are you doing up here?"

"Reading," I tell her.

I hold up the cover of *The Hound of the Baskervilles* as proof. Before we went away on holiday I found some Sherlock Holmes books on Dad's bookshelf and asked if I could bring them to the house. I have already read *The Sign of the Four* and *The Adventures of Sherlock Holmes* and they are the best books I have ever read. Up here in the attic I can read without anyone bothering me. Also I am hiding from Gill and Diana, but I don't want to tell Mum that.

"It's lovely outside," she says. "Why don't you come and join us?"

Usually Mum likes it when I read books but sometimes she wants me to be in the same room as her. I think she can get quite lonely even when there are other people around, which is strange. I want to finish my book but I don't want to hurt her feelings so I put a bookmark in *The Hound of the Baskervilles* and put it back with the other Sherlock Holmes stories, careful to make sure they are lined up properly.

"My son the librarian," laughs Mum, but I don't get the joke.

We climb down from the attic to the landing, and through the window I can see out into the back garden. Gill and Diana are lying on sun loungers with the headrests down, blankly staring up at the sky through their sunglasses. I wish they weren't here. Most of the time they want me to go away but then sometimes they make me join in with their games. They are always laughing at me and I don't know why. They think they're so much older than me, but I bet I've read more books than them and that I do better at school. I don't know what Diana's doing here anyway – it's *our* holiday home. I said this to Gill before we left home and she got really mad at me. She said that Diana's family didn't have as much money as we did and that they didn't have a holiday home and I should just be grateful we did. Then Gill grabbed my arm and told me that if I told Diana what she'd said, I was DEAD.

When Mum and I go out into the garden everyone is smiling and being nice to each other for once. Mum watches us play a board game. I win but I try not to make a big deal out of it. Yesterday Diana found some water pistols in the shed and we had a water fight in the back garden. I was definitely winning but then Dad came out of nowhere with a hose and he soaked us all. I said he was cheating and it was unfair but he didn't care. Then Diana got him back by filling up a bucket of water from the outdoor tap and tipping it over his head. I had never seen anyone brave enough to do something like that to my Dad and it made me laugh really hard. For a minute Dad stood there with his arms out like a wet scarecrow, looking shocked, but then he picked up his hose again and chased Diana around the garden, spraying her with water. She screamed so loud that Mum came out to see if everything was OK but it looked like Diana was having fun even though she was screaming. That evening Mum was in a bad mood, banging the saucepans on the stove and slamming the dinner plates down on the table. I guess she felt left out.

As we were eating I told everyone that I'd been thinking about it and that I was going to become a private detective. Gill laughed at me the way she always does when I'm trying to be serious about something. I don't know what she wants to be when she grows up, but I hope she's really unhappy. Everyone else said they thought it was a really good idea, but I can tell that none of them believe me. I might be twelve but I'm not stupid. Diana grinned and said I'd have to watch out for something called 'fem fetals'. I didn't know what she meant but when she smiled at me I felt my face go red and I looked down at my plate. Even when she's trying to be nice to me Diana makes me feel uncomfortable.

That night, when I was going to sleep, Mum nearly caught me playing with my thing when she came in to say goodnight. I shouted at her that she was supposed to knock, and I was glad it was dark. Everyone seems to shout at each other these days. I asked Dad if this meant we didn't like each other any more but he told me it was just a phase and not to worry about it. I don't believe him.

I want to play another board game but Gill says she's bored. Diana pulls out a camera from her little bag and says "How about a family photo?" Everyone thinks this is a good idea apart from me. Mum makes us scrunch together around the table whilst Diana pushes her sunglasses on top of her head and adjusts the zoom.

"How are we looking?" Dad calls out to her. "Edgar hasn't broken the lens, has he?"

Everybody else laughs. The camera clicks. Diana checks the picture, giggling.

"What is it?" asks Gill.

"It's Ed," says Diana. "He's scowling like a dragon!"

I wish she wouldn't call me Ed. It's bad enough my family doing it. Gill says that because Diana is pretty she thinks she can get away with any-thing but I don't see that Diana is *that* pretty and maybe Gill is just jealous. Everyone apart from me is now crowding around the camera, laughing at the photograph.

"Dragon!" laughs Dad. "That's a good one!"

"Look at the sulky baby!" Gill joins in.

"I'm not a baby!" I shout. "I didn't want to be in your stupid photograph anyway!"

"Edgar!" my Mum says, but I'm not listening to her any more.

I run off out of the garden and into the woods, where it is dark and quiet. No one is laughing and all I can hear are the thoughts in my head. Even though I am still mad part of me wishes I hadn't run off like that. That's what little children do, and I am not a little child. High above my head the trees hold hands, blocking out the sunlight. I follow a path deeper into the wood, hopping over gnarled roots. I know the trails here as well as the streets around our home. Better, maybe. I bet I could find my way to the lake or the quarry with my eyes closed. One time I followed a path all the way to the fields at the far edge of the wood, although I got shouted at when I got home for being late and worrying Mum and Dad. Last year another family stayed in the cottage next door and there was a boy my age. I showed him the wood and we went there every day. This year the cottage is empty. Mum and Dad said I could invite a friend like Gill had but the other boys at school think I am weird and would laugh at me if I asked them to come on holiday with me. They are childish and stupid, and I would rather be on my own.

I wish that I'd run back to the attic instead of the wood, or at least brought *The Hound of the Baskervilles* with me. I pretend I am a hunter, checking the ground for clawed footprints but the ground is too dry and hard. There are no mysteries to solve here. I keep looking for an hour or so before deciding to go back. I don't want anyone to get properly worried, not really, and anyway it must be nearly time for tea.

As I follow the path back towards the house I hear voices coming from the lake. It sounds like two people arguing. I creep as quietly as I can towards them, catching a glimpse of shining blue water through the bushes.

"Come on!"

"Diana, I don't want to." I can hear that Gill is mad. She speaks to me like that a lot too.

"It's fun!" says Diana. "Don't be such a spoilsport!"

"Just because I don't want to do what you want to do, it doesn't make me a spoilsport."

"No, but it does make you boring."

I have to put my hand over my mouth to stop myself from laughing. When my sister speaks again, her voice is very cold.

"I'd rather be boring than a show-off tart," she says. "I saw you flirting with Dad yesterday. What do you think you were playing at?"

"*He* started it. I was just being polite!"

"You can't help yourself, can you?"

"It's not my fault men like me."

"Go to hell!"

I duck down behind a large fern as Gill runs past me. She is wrapped in a large swimming towel and water is dripping from her hair. I wonder if I should go and see if she is all right but Gill would probably just shout at me too. Hearing a splash from the lake, I stand up from behind the fern and creep closer to the water's edge. Holding my breath, I peer around the tree.

The sun is low in the sky, turning the lake a creamy golden colour. Diana is swimming in the shallows, her bare shoulders glistening as she cuts through the water. As I stare at her I spot her swimming costume lying in a damp bundle by the side of the lake. My mouth runs dry.

Diana stops and begins to treads water with her back to me, looking out towards the sun. Then, without warning, she stands up. Her skin is ghostly pale, covered in tiny droplets of water that run down to the bottom of her spine, and her red hair melts into the sunset. She leans back, running her hands through its wet strands. Even though she is the one in the water, I am the one shivering. Diana doesn't look like a human any more. She looks more than that – like some kind of goddess.

A twig snaps beneath my foot, and Diana glances over her shoulder. At first she looks startled, but when she sees me she smiles. I know I should run away but my feet feel glued to the spot. Diana could duck back into the water to cover herself up but instead she stays standing upright like a beautiful statue. I am desperate for her to turn around so I can see more of her, but also a bit scared that she might actually do so. I begin to back away from lake. She laughs – a lovely, hurtful noise. She is impossible.

As I turn to flee, my foot catches on a tree root and I stumble to the ground. Suddenly my palms and my bare legs are itching and stinging. I have fallen into a nettle patch. My skin feels as though someone has lit it with a match. Crying out, I scramble to my feet.

"Edgar?" I hear Diana call out. "Are you all right?"

I run away through the trees with my skin on fire, excited, terrified, doomed.

13726445R00122

Printed in Great Britain
by Amazon.co.uk, Ltd.,
Marston Gate.